5 Reasons We Think You'll Love This Book

 Join the Melkerson family on an unforgettable summer holiday.

 Seacrow Island is home to a fantastic host of eccentric and entertaining characters.

 A heart-warming read, with family and friendship at its core.

 Perfect for fans of classic stories such as *Little Women* and *Anne of Green Gables*.

 By much-loved author Astrid Lindgren, winner of the Hans Christian Andersen Award.

Here's a taste of what's to come . . .

Tjorven was standing on the jetty when Westerman came back from the island that morning and she shouted with excitement when he put down a complaining little baby seal, with black, damp eyes, in front of her. It was the sweetest thing she had ever seen. 'Oh, how sweet he is,' exclaimed Tjorven. 'Can I pat him?'

'Certainly,' said Westerman, and then he said something quite unbelievable. 'You can have him if you like.'

Tjorven stared at him. 'What did you say?'

'You can have him—if your father and mother will let you, of course. I'll be only too glad to be rid of him. You can feed him until he's big enough to be of some use.'

Tjorven caught her breath. As a matter of fact Westerman was not one of her favourite people, but just now she felt that she adored him. 'Oh,' she said, and wondered how you could say thank you for anything so marvellous.

'I'll make you a cross-stitch pot-holder. Would you like that?'

Westerman did not realize that Tjorven meant to give him the greatest gift that she could possibly make and he said, 'Well, I can't exactly say that I'd like one, but you take the seal anyway, because I just don't dare go home to the wife with a baby seal.'

Then Westerman went away and Tjorven stood absolutely overwhelmed. 'Bosun, it's crazy! We've got a seal,' she said.

Bosun nosed the seal. He had never seen anything like it before, but if Tjorven wanted to have it, he would make friends with this strange little creature which lay growling at him.

'Now don't frighten him,' said Tjorven and pushed Bosun aside. Then she shouted as loudly as she could, 'Come here, come here, everybody! It's absolutely crazy! I've been given a seal!'

OXFORD
UNIVERSITY PRESS

Great Clarendon Street, Oxford OX2 6DP
Oxford University Press is a department of the University of Oxford.
It furthers the University's objective of excellence in research, scholarship,
and education by publishing worldwide. Oxford is a registered trade mark of
Oxford University Press in the UK and in certain other countries

First published in Sweden as Vi på Saltkråkan by Rabén & Sjögren, 1964

This translation first published 1968

This edition first published 2016

ISBN: 978-0-19-274557-6

3 5 7 9 10 8 6 4

Printed in Great Britain
Paper used in the production of this book is a natural,
recyclable product made from wood grown in sustainable forests.
The manufacturing process conforms to the environmental
regulations of the country of origin.

Translation © Oliver & Boyd Ltd, 1968

Translation by Evelyn Ramsden

Astrid Lindgren

SEACROW ISLAND

OXFORD
UNIVERSITY PRESS

Also by
Astrid Lindgren

Contents

A Day in June

If you go down to the quay in Stockholm on a summer morning and see a little white boat called *Seacrow I* lying there, that is the right boat to take and all you have to do is to go on board. For at ten o'clock precisely she will ring her bell for departure and back out from the quay. She is now setting out on her usual trip, which ends at the island that lies the farthest out in the sea of all the islands in the Stockholm archipelago. *Seacrow I* is a purposeful, energetic little steamer and she has made this journey three times a week in summer and once a week in winter for more than thirty years, although she is probably quite unconscious of the fact that she ploughs through waters different from any others on the face of the earth. She crosses wide expanses of open water and steams through narrow channels, past hundreds of green islands and thousands of grey, bare rocks. She does not go fast and the sun is low when at last she reaches the quay at Seacrow Island, the island which has given her its name. She has no need to go any farther, for there is only the open sea beyond with its bare rocks and its islands where nobody lives except eider ducks, gulls, and other sea birds.

But there are people on Seacrow Island. Not many, at most twenty—that is, in the winter. But in the summer there are the summer visitors as well.

Just such a family of summer visitors was aboard *Seacrow I* one day in June a few years ago. It consisted of a father and his four children, and their name was Melkerson. They lived in Stockholm and none of them had been to Seacrow Island before. And so they were very excited, especially Melker, the father.

'Seacrow Island,' he said. 'I like the name. That was why I took the house.'

Malin, his nineteen-year-old daughter, looked at him and shook her head. What a scatterbrained father she had! He was almost fifty, but he was as impulsive as a child and more irresponsible than his own sons. Now he was standing there as excited as any child on Christmas Eve, expecting them all to be wildly enthusiastic about his idea of taking a summer cottage on Seacrow Island.

'It's like you, Daddy,' said Malin, 'it's exactly like you to take a cottage on an island which you have never even seen, just because you like the name.'

'That's what I would have thought everybody did,' Melker replied. He thought for a moment and then said, 'Or perhaps one has to be an author and be more or less crazy to do a thing like that. Only a name—Seacrow Island! Perhaps other people would have gone and looked at the place before taking it.'

'Lots would have—but not you.'

'Well, never mind, I'm on my way there *now,*' said Melker cheerfully.

And he gazed around him with his gay, blue eyes. He saw all the things he loved most: the pale waters, the islands and reefs, the old grey rocks, the shore with its old houses and jetties and boathouses—he felt as if he wanted to stretch out his hand and caress them. Instead, he grasped Johan and Niklas by the nape of the neck.

'Do you realize how beautiful it all is? Do you realize how lucky you are to live in the midst of all this for a whole summer?'

Johan and Niklas said that they did realize it and Pelle said he realized it too.

'Well, why don't you shout for joy then?' said Melker. 'Would you mind my asking for a spot of jubilation?'

'How do you do it?' Pelle asked. He was only seven years old and could not show joy to order.

'You yodel,' said Melker, and laughed. Then he tried to yodel a little himself and all his children giggled obediently.

'You sound like a cow mooing,' said Johan, and Malin remarked, 'Wouldn't it be better, just to be on the safe side, to wait until we've seen the cottage before you start crowing?'

Melker did not think so. 'The agent said the cottage was wonderful, and one has to believe what people say. He assured me that it was an old, homely, delightful cottage.'

'If only we could get there soon,' said Pelle. 'I want to see the cottage now.'

Melker looked at his watch. 'In an hour's time, my boy! By that time we shall all be very hungry, and guess what we shall be doing then?'

'Eating,' suggested Niklas.

'Exactly. We'll sit outside the house in the sunshine and eat the wonderful meal that Malin will have cooked for us. We shall be having it on the green grass, of course—and we will just sit there and feel that summer has come!'

'Oh!' said Pelle. 'I'll soon be shouting for joy.'

But then he decided to do something else. His father had said there was an hour to go, and there must still be things he could do aboard this boat. He had done most of the exploring. He had climbed up all the companionways and looked in all the exciting corners and cupboards. He had put his nose into the pilot's room and been chased away. He had tried to get up to the captain on the bridge and had been sternly ordered off. He had stood looking down into the engine room, watching all the machinery as it went around and around. He had drunk lemonade and eaten rolls and had thrown bits of his rolls to the hungry gulls. He had chatted with almost everybody on board. He had tried to see how fast he could run from one end of the boat to the other, and he had got in everybody's way at every stopping place as the crew threw baggage ashore. Now he began to look around for something new, and it was then that he discovered a couple of passengers he had not noticed before.

Far astern he saw an old man sitting with a little girl, and on the seat beside the girl was a cage with a raven in it. A live raven! That made Pelle hurry, for he loved all living creatures, everything that moved, flew, or crawled beneath the sky, every bird, fish, and four-footed animal. 'Dear little animals,' he called them all and he included frogs, wasps, grasshoppers, beetles, and other small insects. But now here was a raven, a real live raven.

The little girl smiled at him, a sweet, toothless smile, as he stopped in front of the cage.

'Is this your raven?' he asked, and poked a finger between the bars to try to stroke the bird. But this was a mistake, for the raven immediately pecked at his finger and he hurriedly drew it back.

'Be careful!' said the little girl. 'Yes, he *is* my raven, isn't he, Grandpa?'

The old man beside her nodded. 'Yes, of course, it's Stina's raven,' he explained to Pelle. 'At any rate, while she's with me on Seacrow Island.'

'Do you live on Seacrow Island?' said Pelle, delighted. 'I'm going to live there too this summer. I mean, Father and I are going to live on Seacrow Island.'

The old man looked at him in an interested way. 'Are you, indeed? Then I suppose it's you who have taken the old Carpenter's Cottage?'

Pelle nodded eagerly. 'Yes, it's us. Is it nice there?'

The old man put his head on one side and looked as if he were thinking. Then he broke into a funny little laugh. 'Yes, it's nice, but of course it depends on what you like.'

'What do you mean?' asked Pelle.

The old man laughed again. 'Well, either you like it when it rains in through the roof or you don't.'

'Or you *don't*,' came as a sort of echo from the little girl. 'I *don't*.'

Pelle grew rather thoughtful. He must tell Daddy that, but not just now. Now he wanted to look at the raven. It must be fun to have a raven, because everyone would want to come and look at it, especially a big boy like him. Of course, Stina was only a little girl, at most five years old, but Pelle was willing to put up with her as a friend for the sake of the raven, at any rate until he had found something better.

'I'll come to see you one day,' he said kindly. 'Which house do you live in?'

'In a red one,' said Stina, which was a lead, but not much more.

'You can ask where old man Söderman lives,' said her grandfather. 'Everyone knows it.'

The raven blustered about in its cage and seemed very restless. Pelle had another try at poking in his finger, but the bird pecked him again.

'He's very wise,' said Stina. 'The wisest bird in all the world, Grandpa says.'

Pelle thought this was boasting, as neither Stina nor her grandfather could possibly know which bird was the wisest in the world.

'My grandma has a parrot,' said Pelle, 'and she can say "Go to blazes"!'

'There's nothing difficult in that,' said Stina. 'My grandmother can say that too.'

Pelle laughed loudly. 'It isn't my grandma who says it! It's the parrot!'

Stina did not like being laughed at. She was offended. 'You should say what you mean then,' she said crossly. She turned her head away and looked out over the rail. She did not want to talk to Pelle any more.

'Goodbye,' said Pelle and went off to find his scattered family. He found Johan and Niklas on the upper deck, and as soon as he saw them he knew that something was wrong. Both of them looked so gloomy that Pelle felt anxious. Had he done something he shouldn't have done? 'What is it?' he asked.

'Look over there,' said Niklas, and pointed with his thumb. Leaning against the rail a little farther away stood Malin and beside her a tall young man in a light-blue polo-necked sweater. They were chatting and laughing together and the boy in the sweater was looking at Malin, *their* Malin, as if he had just found a beautiful little nugget of gold where he least expected it.

'Here we go again,' said Niklas. 'I thought it would be better when we got away from town.'

Johan shook his head. 'Don't you believe it! If you put Malin on a rock in the middle of the Baltic, there'd be some boy or other swimming out to the rock within five minutes.'

Niklas glared at the polo-necked sweater. 'We ought to put up a notice beside her, *Anchorage Forbidden!*'

Then he looked at Johan and they both laughed. They did not really mind when anyone began to pay attention to Malin, which, according to Johan, happened about once every quarter of an hour. They were not really serious, but in spite of it all they were secretly a little anxious. What if Malin fell in love one fine day and it all ended in an engagement and marriage and that sort of thing?

'How would we get on without Malin?' Pelle would say, and that was what they all thought and felt. For Malin was the family's anchor and support. Ever since the day their mother had died, when Pelle was born, Malin had been like a mother to all the boys, including Melker, a childish and very unhappy little mother for the first few years, but by degrees more and more capable of 'wiping their noses, washing, scolding, and baking' as she herself described it.

'But you only scold when you really have to,' Pelle always maintained. 'Usually you are as soft and kind and good as a rabbit.'

Until recently Pelle had not understood why Johan and Niklas had been so against Malin's admirers. He had felt absolutely sure that Malin would go on belonging to the family forever, no matter how many polo-necks circled around her. It was Malin herself who had disturbed his peace of mind. It happened when Pelle was in bed one night, trying to go to sleep. Malin was in the bathroom next door and was singing a song, which finished, 'She left school, got married, and had a family.'

'Left school.' Yes, that was just what Malin had done, and

then . . . then he supposed you just waited for the rest. Now he understood what would happen! Malin would marry and they would be left all alone with Mrs. Nilsson, who came for four hours a day and then went. It was an unbearable thought, and Pelle rushed in despair to his father. 'Daddy, when will Malin get married and have a family?' he asked in a trembling voice.

Melker looked surprised. He had not heard that Malin had any plans of that sort, and he did not realize that it was a question of life and death to Pelle.

'When is it going to happen?' Pelle insisted.

'That day and hour must remain hidden from us,' joked Melker. 'There's no need for you to worry about it, son.'

But Pelle *had* worried about it ever since, not all the time, of course, or even every day, but now and then on special occasions, like now, for instance. Pelle stared towards Malin and the polo-necked sweater. As a matter of fact they were just saying goodbye, because the young man was getting off at the next stop.

'Goodbye, Krister,' shouted Malin.

And the sweater shouted back, 'I'll come over with my motorboat one day and look you up!'

'You'd better not,' muttered Pelle angrily. And he decided to ask his father to put up one of those notices Niklas had talked about—*Anchorage Forbidden*—on the jetty at Seacrow Island. Obviously it would have been easier to have Malin to themselves in peace if she had not been so pretty. Pelle realized that. Not that he had looked at her particularly, but he knew she was pretty. Everybody said so. They thought that fair hair and green eyes like Malin's were very pretty. No doubt the polo-necked sweater thought so too.

'Who was that?' asked Johan, when Malin came over to the boys.

'No one in particular. Just someone I met at a party the other day. Quite nice.'

'You be careful,' said Johan. 'Write those words in your diary in capital letters.'

For Malin was not the daughter of an author for nothing. She wrote too, but only in her secret diary. In it she gave free rein to all her secret thoughts and dreams and described all the exploits of the Melkerson boys, including Melker's.

'You wait until I publish my secret diary, then you'll all be laughing on the other side of your faces.'

'Ha, ha! You'll come out the worst of anyone,' Johan assured her. 'I'm sure you're careful to mention *all* your sheiks in the right order.'

'Keep a list, so you'll never forget any of them,' suggested Niklas. 'Olaf the Fourteenth, Karl the Fifteenth, Lennart the Sixteenth, Johan the Seventeenth. It'll be a lovely little list.'

And Johan and Niklas were convinced that the polo-necked sweater would be Krister the Eighteenth.

'I would like to know how she describes him in her diary,' said Niklas.

'A boy with very short hair,' suggested Johan. 'Generally foul and sloppy.'

'That's only what *you* think,' said Niklas.

But Malin did not write a word about Krister the Eighteenth in her diary. He got off at his stop and left no lasting impression, for only a quarter of an hour later Malin had a much more important meeting, which made her forget everything else. It was when the boat arrived at the next jetty and she saw Seacrow Island for the first time. Of this meeting she wrote:

'Malin, Malin, where have you been so long? This island has been lying here waiting for you, calmly and quietly, for such a long time, with its little boathouses, its old village street, its jetties and fishing boats and all its beauty, and you have not even known of its existence. Isn't that dreadful? I wonder what God thought when He made this island. "I will have a little bit of everything," I expect He thought. "I will have bare, grey rocks, green trees, oaks and birch trees, meadows with flowers, yes, the whole island will be adrift with red roses and white hawthorn on the June day one thousand million years ahead when Malin Melkerson arrives." Yes, dear Johan and Niklas, I know what you would think if you ever read this. "*Must* you be so conceited!" But I am not being conceited. I am only glad that God made Seacrow Island just as it is and not in any other way, and that He then thought of placing it, like a jewel, farthest out in the sea, where it has remained in peace just as He first created it, and that He has allowed me to come here.'

Melker had said, 'You'll see—all the islanders will come down to the quay to welcome us. We'll be a sensation.'

But it was not quite like that. It was pouring rain when the steamer arrived, and on the quay stood one solitary little person and a dog. This person was female and about seven years old. She stood absolutely still as if she had grown up out of the quay. The rain poured down on her but she did not move. It seemed almost as if God had made her as part of the island, thought Malin, and had put her there to be the ruler and guardian of the island to all eternity.

I've never felt as small, wrote Malin in her journal, *as I did when I walked down the gangplank in the streaming rain under that child's gaze, carrying all my luggage. Her eyes seemed to take in everything. I thought she must be the Spirit of Seacrow Island, and as if we should not be accepted by the island if we were not accepted by that child. And so I said as sweetly as I could, as one does to little children, What's your name?*

'Tjorven,' she said. Just that!

'And your dog?' I said.

She looked me straight in the eye and asked calmly, 'Do you want to know if he's my dog or what his name is?'

'Both,' I said.

'He is my dog and his name is Bosun,' she said, and it was as if a queen had deigned to present her favourite animal. And what an animal! He was a St. Bernard, the biggest one I've ever seen in my life. He was just as majestic as his owner and I began to wonder whether all the creatures on this island were of the same breed and very superior to us humble beings from the city. But then a friendly soul arrived, who turned out to be the island's shopkeeper. He seemed

12

to be a normal human being, for he welcomed us to Seacrow Island and told us that his name was Nisse Grankvist. But then he said rather surprisingly, 'Go home, Tjorven,' to the majestic child. Just imagine, he dared command her and he was actually her father! But his command did not have much effect.

'Who said so?' asked the child sternly. 'Did Mummy?'

'No, I say so,' said her father.

'Then I won't go home,' said the child. 'I'm here to meet the boat.'

As the shopkeeper was busy checking his goods from the boat, he had no time to deal with his obstreperous daughter, so she stood there watching while we collected our belongings. We must have been a sorry sight just then, and nothing escaped her, for I felt her eyes on us as we set off towards Carpenter's Cottage.

There were other eyes watching us besides Tjorven's. Behind the curtains of the windows all along the street, eyes were looking out at us as we trailed along. It was pouring rain and even Father began to look rather thoughtful.

When it was coming down at its very hardest, Pelle said, 'Daddy, did you know that it rains in through the roof of Carpenter's Cottage?'

Daddy stopped dead in the middle of a puddle and asked, 'Who says?'

'Old man Söderman,' said Pelle, and it sounded as if he were speaking of an intimate friend.

Daddy pretended to be quite indifferent. 'Oh, I see! Old man Söderman, whoever this prophet of woe may be, says so! And of course old man Söderman _knows_, although the agent said nothing of the sort to me.'

'Didn't he know?' I said. 'Didn't he say it was a pleasant old summer residence, particularly when it rained, because then there was a delightful little swimming pool in the middle of the living room?'

Daddy gave me a long look but did not answer. And then we arrived.

'Hello, Carpenter's Cottage,' said Daddy. 'Allow me to introduce the Melkerson family—Melker and his poor little children.'

It was a red one-storey house, and the moment I saw it I had no doubt at all that it did rain in through the roof. But I liked it. I liked it from the very start. Daddy, on the other hand, was horrified. I don't know anyone who goes from one extreme to the other as quickly as he does. He stood quite still and stared despondently at the summer cottage he had rented for himself and his children.

'What are you waiting for?' I said. 'Nothing's going to change it.' So he took heart and we all went in.'

Carpenter's Cottage

No one in the family ever forgot that first evening in Carpenter's Cottage.

'Ask me whenever you want,' said Melker afterwards, 'and I will tell you exactly what it was like. A mouldy smell, icy cold bed linen, Malin with that little frown between her eyes, which she thinks I never notice, and me with a lump of anxiety in my chest. Had I done something absolutely crazy? But the boys were as happy as squirrels and rushed in and out, I remember that. And I remember the blackbird singing in the whitebeam tree outside the cottage, and the waves lapping against the jetty, and how quiet it was. And I was suddenly filled with wild excitement and thought, "No, Melker, you haven't done anything crazy this time. This is something good, something really wonderful, something tremendously good!" But, of course, there *was* that old, musty smell and . . .'

'And then you lit the kitchen stove,' said Malin. 'Do you remember that?'

But Melker did not remember . . . he said.

'That stove doesn't look to me as if it were meant for cooking,' said Malin, letting all her parcels and bags slide onto the kitchen floor. The stove was the first thing she had seen on coming in. It was rusty and looked as if it had not been used since the turn of the century. But Melker was encouraging.

'Those old stoves are fantastically good. It only needs a little handling and I'll fix it. But let's look at the rest of the house first.'

There was something of the turn of the century about the whole of Carpenter's Cottage, a very dilapidated old cottage. The tenants of many summers had not treated it well, but long ago it must have been a cherished and well-cared-for craftsman's home, for even in decay it had something wonderfully homely about it, which everyone felt.

'It'll be fun living in this old dump,' said Pelle, and giving Malin a hasty hug he rushed after Johan and Niklas to see what they were finding in the attic.

'Carpenter's Cottage,' said Malin. 'What sort of carpenter lived here, Daddy?'

'A young, happy carpenter who married in 1908 and moved in here with his sweet, young wife and made cupboards, tables and chairs and sofas for her exactly as she wanted them, and kissed her madly and said, "It shall be called Carpenter's Cottage and it shall be our home on earth!" '

Malin stared at him. 'Do you know all that or are you just making it up?'

Melker smiled a little shyly. 'Um . . . yes . . . it's something I made up, although I shouldn't wonder if it isn't true.'

'Well,' said Malin, 'at any rate, there must have been someone once long ago who was happy with this furniture and polished and dusted it and spring-cleaned it. Who does the house belong to?'

Melker thought for a moment. 'Someone called Mrs. Sjöberg or Mrs. Sjöblom or something like that. An old lady . . .'

'Perhaps she's your carpenter's wife,' said Malin, laughing.

'She lives in Norrtälje at present,' said Melker. 'A man called Mattsson acts as her agent and rents the place during the summer. It looks to me as if it has been rented mostly to vandals with very destructive little children.'

He looked around at what had once, no doubt, been a very pleasant living room. It was not very beautiful now, but Melker was quite content.

'This,' he said, 'this is going to be our sitting room.' And he patted the whitewashed stove. 'We'll sit here in the evenings in front of the wood fire, listening to the storm outside.'

'While our ears flap in the draught,' said Malin and pointed to the window, where one of the panes was broken.

She still had her little anxiety frown between her eyes, but Melker, who had already taken Carpenter's Cottage to his heart, was not worried about a cracked window.

'Don't fuss, my dear. Your clever father will put in a new pane of glass tomorrow, don't you worry!'

Malin did not stop worrying altogether, for she knew

Melker and she thought with a mixture of impatience and tenderness: He thinks he will be able to do it, he really does, but he forgets what usually happens. If he tries to put in a new pane of glass it means three more will be broken. I must ask that man Nisse Grankvist if there is anyone who can help me.

Aloud she said, 'Now I think it's time we got down to it. Did you say you were going to light the kitchen stove, Daddy?'

Melker rubbed his hands together, full of business. 'Just that! You can't leave that sort of thing to women and children!'

'Well, then,' said Malin, 'the women and children will go to look for the well. I hope there is such a thing!'

She heard the boys tramping around upstairs and shouted to them, 'Come on, boys! We must fetch some water!'

The rain had stopped, for the moment at any rate. The evening sun was making brave but futile attempts to break through the clouds, eagerly encouraged by the blackbird in the old whitebeam tree. He went on singing regardless, until he saw the Melkerson children come out into the wet grass with their water pails. Then he stopped.

'Isn't it wonderful that Carpenter's Cottage has its own guardian tree!' said Malin and touched the whitebeam with loving tenderness as she passed it.

'What are guardian trees for?' asked Pelle.

'To be loved,' said Malin.

'To climb, can't you see?' said Johan.

'And that will be the first thing we do tomorrow morning,' Niklas declared. 'I wonder if Daddy had to pay extra because there's a fabulous climbing tree.'

Malin laughed at that, but the boys continued to think of things they thought Melker should pay extra for: the jetty and the rowboat which was moored to it, the attic, which they had already investigated and which was full of exciting things.

'And the well, if it's fairly good water,' suggested Malin. But that Johan and Niklas did not think could be considered worth paying extra for.

Johan pulled up the first pailful and Pelle gave a shriek of delight. 'Look, there's a tiny frog at the bottom!'

A little groan of anguish came from Malin.

Pelle looked at her in surprise. 'What's the matter? Don't you like frogs?'

'Not in drinking water,' said Malin.

But Pelle jumped about in excitement. 'Oh, can I have it?' he said. Then he turned to Johan. 'Do you think Daddy had to pay extra for frogs in the well?'

'Depends on how many there are,' said Johan. 'If there are lots, I expect he's been let off cheap.' He looked at Malin to see how much frog she could stand, but it did not look as if she had heard.

Malin's thoughts had wandered off in another direction. She was thinking about the gay carpenter and his wife. Had they lived happily in their Carpenter's Cottage? Had they had lots of children, who one by one had begun to climb in the whitebeam and perhaps had fallen into the sea now and then? Were there just as many wild rose bushes in the garden in June then as now? And was the path to the well white with fallen apple blossoms then as now?

Then she suddenly remembered that the gay carpenter and his wife had been dreamed up by Melker. But she decided to believe in them all the same. She decided one more thing: However many frogs there were in the well, however many broken windowpanes, however dilapidated Carpenter's Cottage was, nothing would stop her from being happy here and now. For now it was summer. It should always be a June evening, she thought, dreamy and still, like this one. And quiet. Beyond the jetty the seagulls circled and now and then one of them uttered a wild shriek or two, but otherwise this unbelievable silence, which seemed to tingle in the ears. A thin mist of rain lay over the sea and it was lovely in a melancholy way. Drops of water fell from the bushes and trees and there was the feel of more rain in the air and of earth and salt water and wet grass.

'Sit out in the garden in the sunshine and eat our supper and feel that summer has come'—that was what Melker had imagined doing on their first evening at Carpenter's Cottage. This was something quite different, but it was still summer. Malin felt that so strongly that tears came to her eyes. But she felt hungry too and she wondered how far Melker had got with the kitchen stove.

He had not got very far.

'Malin, where are you?' he yelled as he always did as soon as anything went wrong. But Malin was out of hearing and he realized reluctantly that he was alone and would have to manage by himself.

'Alone with my God and an iron stove, which is shortly to be heaved out of the window,' he murmured bitterly. But then he had to cough and could not say more. He glared at the stove, which did nothing but angrily billow out smoke at him, although he had done it no harm, apart from lighting a fire in it with great tenderness and care. He raked the fire with the poker and a fresh cloud of smoke billowed out over him. Coughing wildly, he rushed to open all the windows, and just as he had done that the door opened and someone came in. It was the majestic child who had been standing on the jetty when they arrived, the child with the strange name—Korven, or Tjorven, or whatever it was. She looked like a well-fed sausage, thought Melker, round and wholesome. The face which was visible under the raincoat was, as far as he could see through the smoke, a particularly clear, charming child's face, broad and good-humoured with a pair of bright, inquiring eyes. She had the enormous dog with her, which seemed even more colossal indoors than out. He seemed to fill the whole kitchen.

Tjorven had stopped on the threshold. 'It's smoking,' she said.

'You don't say,' replied Melker bitterly. 'I hadn't noticed.' Then he coughed until tears came into his eyes.

'Yes, it is,' Tjorven assured him. 'Do you know what? Perhaps there's a dead owl in the chimney. We had one once.' Then she looked curiously at Melker and smiled broadly. 'Your face is black all over.'

Melker coughed. 'I'm a kipper, a freshly smoked herring. You can call me Uncle Melker.'

'Oh, is that your name?' said Tjorven.

Melker did not have to answer for luckily Malin and the boys came back at that moment.

'Daddy, we found a frog in the well,' said Pelle eagerly, but then he forgot all about frogs because of the fantastic dog which he had seen on the jetty a short while ago and which was now standing in his own kitchen.

Melker looked hurt. 'A frog in the well? Really? That agent said this was a homely little summer residence. But he forgot to tell me that it was a zoo with owls in the chimney and frogs in the well and giant dogs in the kitchen. Johan, go and see if there's an elk in the bedroom!'

His children laughed as they were expected to—Melker would have been hurt otherwise—but Malin said, 'Oh dear, it's smoking!'

'Are you surprised?' said Melker. He pointed accusingly at the iron stove. 'I am going to write to the Ankarsrum Foundry to complain about the stove. I am going to say, "You delivered an iron stove in April 1908 which is a disgrace to you. What do you mean by it?" '

No one was listening, except Malin. The others had crowded round Tjorven and her dog and were plying her with questions.

Tjorven told them kindly that she lived in the next house to Carpenter's Cottage. Her father had a shop there, but the house was so large that there was room for them all. 'Me and Bosun and Mummy and Daddy and Teddy and Freddy—'

'How old are Teddy and Freddy?' asked Johan eagerly.

'Teddy is thirteen and Freddy is twelve and I am six and Bosun is two. I can't remember how old Mummy and Daddy are, but I can go home and ask,' she said obligingly.

Johan assured her that this was not necessary. He and Niklas looked at each other happily. Two boys, exactly their own age in the house next door! It was almost too good to be true.

'What in the world are we going to do if we can't get this stove to work?' wondered Malin.

Melker tore his hair. 'I suppose I had better get up on the roof to see if there really is a dead owl in the chimney as that child suggested.'

'Oh dear,' said Malin. 'Be careful! Remember, we've only got *one* father.'

But Melker was already outside the door. He had seen that there was a ladder against the wall so that it ought not to be too difficult for him to get up onto the roof. His boys followed him, even Pelle. Not even the world's largest dog could keep him in the kitchen when Daddy was going to get owls out of the chimney, and Tjorven, who had already selected Pelle as her friend and follower although Pelle did not know it, strolled out after them in a leisurely way to see if anything amusing was going to happen.

It looks as if it might be fun, she thought. Uncle Melker had taken the poker with him to try to get the owl out and he was having to hold it between his teeth while he climbed up the ladder. Exactly like Bosun when he fetches a bone, thought Tjorven. She could not imagine anything more amusing than that, and she laughed quietly to herself under the apple tree where she stood. Then one of the rungs gave way and Uncle Melker slid down a couple of feet. Pelle was frightened, but Tjorven laughed again, silently and heartily.

Then she stopped laughing, for now Uncle Melker was up on the roof and she thought it looked dangerous. Melker thought so too.

'This is a nice house,' he murmured, 'but rather high.'

He began to wonder if it were not a little too high to balance on for someone who would soon be fifty.

'If I ever live to be that old,' he muttered, and wobbled along the ridge of the roof with his eyes glued to the chimney. Then he cast a glance downward and almost fell when he saw his sons' upturned, anxious faces so far below him.

'Hold on, Daddy,' shrieked Johan.

Melker staggered and almost lost his temper. Above him was nothing but the open sky. What was he to hold on to? Then from down below he heard Tjorven's penetrating voice.

'Tell you what, Uncle Melker, hold on with the crook of the poker!'

But now Melker had happily reached safety next to the chimney. He looked down into it. There was nothing there but murky darkness.

'Hey, Tjorven, you said something about owls—dead ones,' he yelled. 'There aren't any owls up here.'

'Not even an old shriek owl?' called Niklas.

Then Melker shouted angrily, 'There aren't any owls up

here! I've already said so!' And again he heard Tjorven's penetrating voice.

'Do you want one? I know where there is one—but he isn't dead.'

Afterwards the atmosphere in the kitchen was a little strained.

'We'll have to live out of cans for the time being,' said Malin.

They all gazed sadly at the stove which would not behave itself. Just now there seemed nothing they would rather have had than a little warm food.

'It's a hard life,' said Pelle, because his father used to say that sometimes.

Then there was a knock on the door and in came a strange woman in a red raincoat. She hastily put down an enamel saucepan on the stove and smiled a great big smile at them all.

'Good evening! Oh, there you are, Tjorven! I thought so! How badly it's smoking,' she said, and before anyone could do anything she went on. 'I'd better tell you who I am. My name is Marta Grankvist. We are next-door neighbours. Welcome!' She spoke quickly and smiled the whole time and, before anyone in the family noticed, she had crossed to the stove and was looking up into the chimney. 'Have you opened the damper? It would be better if you had!'

Malin burst out laughing, but Melker looked hurt.

'Yes, of course I opened the damper. It was the first thing I did,' he assured them.

'Well, it's closed now,' said Marta Grankvist. 'And now it's open,' she said as she turned it around. 'Probably it was open when you came and Mr. Melkerson shut it.'

'He's always so careful,' said Malin.

They all laughed, even Melker and most of all Tjorven.

'I know this stove,' said Marta Grankvist, 'and it's first-rate.'

Malin looked at her thankfully. Everything seemed so much better since this wonderful person had come into the kitchen. She was so gay and spread a feeling of security around her. What luck to have her as neighbour, thought Malin.

'I made a little stew to welcome you,' said Marta Grankvist, and pointed to the saucepan.

The tears came to Melker's eyes. That often happened when people were nice to him and his children.

'To think that there are such kind people!' he stammered.

'Yes, we're all kind here on Seacrow Island,' laughed Marta Grankvist. 'Come on, Tjorven. We must go home now. If there's anything more you need, just tell me.'

'Well, there is a cracked windowpane in there,' said Malin shyly, 'but we can't ask too much.'

'I'll send Nisse over later when you have eaten,' said Marta Grankvist.

'Yes, because it's him who puts in all the windowpanes on Seacrow Island,' said Tjorven, 'and it's me and Stina who break them.'

'What did you say?' said her mother sternly.

'But never on purpose, of course,' Tjorven hastened to explain. 'It just happens like that.'

'Stina—I know her,' said Pelle.

'Do you?' said Tjorven, and for some reason she did not seem very pleased.

Pelle had been strangely quiet for a long time. Why bother to talk to people when there was a dog like Bosun in the room? Pelle was hanging around his neck and he whispered in his ear, 'I like you.'

And Bosun let himself be hugged. He just looked at Pelle with friendly, rather sad eyes, with a gaze that bared the whole of his steadfast dog's soul for anyone who cared to see.

But now Tjorven was going home, and where Tjorven went Bosun went too.

'Come on, Bosun,' she said, and then they were gone.

But the kitchen window was open and they all heard Tjorven's voice as she went past outside.

'Mummy, do you know what? When he walked on the roof, Uncle Melker held on with the poker.'

They heard Marta Grankvist's reply too. 'They come from the town, you see, Tjorven, and I suppose they have to hold on with pokers.'

The Melkersons all looked at one another.

'She's sorry for us,' said Johan. 'She needn't be.'

But as far as the stove was concerned Marta was quite right. It was splendid and burned so briskly that it soon became glowingly red and spread wonderful warmth through the whole kitchen.

'The blessed fire of the home,' said Melker. 'Humans had no home until they discovered fire.'

'And found out about stews,' said Niklas, and began to eat so that he could say no more.

They sat around the kitchen table and ate, and it was a time of deep, comfortable homeliness. The fire roared in the stove and the rain roared outside.

It was raining harder than ever when Johan and Niklas went to bed. Unwillingly they left the warm kitchen and went up to their attic, which was cold and damp and very unpleasant in spite of the fire in the stove. But Pelle was already asleep there, wrapped in blankets and with a warm cap on his head, pulled well down.

Johan stood shivering at the window and tried to see over to the Grankvists, their neighbours, but the rain was so heavy that it was like looking through a dense curtain of streaming water. *Shop*—he could make out the sign. And the house—that was red, just like their own cottage, and the garden sloped down towards the sea and there was a boat jetty just like their own.

'Tomorrow we may be able to make friends with those boys who . . . ' said Johan. But then he suddenly stopped, for something was happening over at their neighbours' house. A door opened and someone came running out into the rain. It was a girl in a bathing suit, and her fair hair streamed behind her as she galloped down towards the jetty.

'Come here, Niklas. Something interesting for you to see . . .' said Johan. Then he stopped again, for now the door was opening again and another girl came out. She was in a swimsuit too, and she galloped down towards the jetty after the other one. The first girl was already there. She dived in and as soon as her nose was above water again she shrieked, 'Freddy, did you bring the soap?'

Johan and Niklas looked silently at each other.

'Those are the "boys" we were going to see tomorrow,' said Niklas at last.

'Oh dear,' said Johan.

They lay awake for a long time that evening.

'You can't possibly get to sleep until your feet have thawed at least a little bit,' said Niklas.

Johan agreed. Then they were silent for a long time.

'Well, at any rate it's stopped raining now,' said Johan finally.

'No, it hasn't,' said Niklas. 'It's only just begun over here in my bed.'

Either you like it when it rains in through the ceiling or you don't . . .

Niklas did not exactly like it dripping down on his bed but it didn't bother him too much, for he was only twelve years old and rather easygoing by nature. On the other hand both he and Johan realized that Malin would have a sleepless night if they reported this misery to her just now. So they moved Niklas's bed very quietly to one side and put a pail to catch the drips from the ceiling.

'That noise makes you sleepy,' mumbled Johan when he had got back to bed again. 'Plop, plop!'

Downstairs Malin sat blissfully ignorant of the plopping and wrote in her diary, for she wanted to remember the first day on Seacrow Island.

I am sitting here alone, she finally wrote, *but it feels as if someone is watching me. Not a person. Just the house—Carpenter's Cottage! Carpenter's Cottage, do please like us. You'd better make up your mind to it, because you are going to have to put up with us. You don't know who we are yet, you say? I'll tell you. That tall, gangling fellow who is lying in bed in the little room by the kitchen and spouting poetry aloud to send himself to sleep is Melker. You must guard against him, particularly if you see him with a hammer or a saw or some other tool in his hand. Otherwise he is very nice and quite harmless. As for the three scruffy little boys in one of the attics, I hope you are fond of children and are used to all sorts of goings-on. I suppose the carpenter's children could not always have been so very good. The person who is going to clean your windows and scrub your floors with love, but with more and more roughened hands, is yours truly, Malin. Although I'll make the others help too, you can be sure of that. We'll all try to make everything look its best here. Good night, Carpenter's Cottage, we'd better go to sleep now. A cold attic is waiting for me too—but you can be sure of my staying down here a little longer in this nice warm kitchen with its glowing range, for here I feel in touch with your warmly beating heart.*

Then Malin suddenly noticed how late it was. A new day had already begun, a day in which the rain had stopped so that it would be bright and clear, as she saw when she went to the window. She stood there for a long time.

'What a wonderful kitchen window,' she murmured. And she knew that she had never seen anything she liked better than what she saw outside. The still water in the light of dawn, the jetty, the grey stones on the shore, everything. She opened the window and heard the bird song which jubilantly wafted in over her. It issued from a host of small throats, but above them all she could hear the blackbird in the whitebeam.

He had just wakened and was full of the joy of life. And poor Melker in the little room by the kitchen was still not asleep, but he yawned, Malin could hear that. He was still reciting poetry in a loud voice. She felt that he was happy.

Row, Row to Fish Island

It feels as if we have lived on Seacrow Island all our lives, wrote Malin a week later. *I already know all the people who live here. First of all there are Nisse and Marta, who keep the shop. I know that they are the world's kindest (especially him) and the world's most capable (especially her) people.*

He looks after the shop. She looks after the shop, too, but she also deals with the telephone exchange, the post office, her children, Bosun, and the household in general, and in addition whenever anyone on the island needs help she goes and helps them. It was typical of Marta to come to us with a hot stew on our first evening—Just because you all looked so lost, as she said.

What else do I know? That old man Söderman's stomach rumbles terribly—he told me so himself—and he is going to the doctor to get something for it.

And I know that Westerman does not look after his land properly, and spends his time fishing and hunting. Mrs. Westerman told me all about it.

Marta and Nisse, old man Söderman, the Westermans—are there any others? Yes, the Janssons, of course. They have a farm and we get our milk from them. It is one of our country pleasures to walk through the cow field in the evening to get milk from the farm.

The island also has a schoolmaster, a young man called Björn Sjöblom. I met him when I went for the milk on Wednesday evening, and he seemed to be a nice, honest young man, absolutely straightforward and frank.

And the children here, thank God for them! Pelle plays with Tjorven and Stina, especially with Tjorven. I think there is a little rivalry about him going on between them. Something on the lines of 'I saw him first.' But Tjorven has taken him over completely, I expect. Anything else would be impossible. She is a remarkable child, everyone's darling, although no one really knows why. The atmosphere brightens wherever her good-natured, funny face appears. Daddy insists that she has something of the eternal child about her, confident and warm and sunny. She is the whole of Seacrow Island's Tjorven, wandering about all the paths and into all the cottages. Wherever she goes she is greeted with 'Why, there's our Tjorven!' just as if she were the nicest thing that could happen at that moment. When she is angry—and that happens sometimes, for she's no angel—it is as if some natural force has been let loose, and then there's thunder and lightning, no mistake! But it soon passes.

Stina is a quite different type. A funny, cute little child, with a remarkable toothless charm. I can't think how she managed it, but she has knocked out all her front teeth at the same time, and it gives her a wild, picturesque look when she laughs. She is the island's greatest storyteller, fantastically persistent. Even Daddy, who is fond of all children and likes to talk to them, has already become a little wary of Stina, and often makes a slight detour when he sees her coming, although he denies it.

'On the contrary,' he said the other day, 'it's one of the best things I know when Stina comes and tells me stories— because it's such a relief when she finishes!'

Johan and Niklas lead a happy and contented existence with Teddy and Freddy, who are a pair of little Amazons, although they are very charming. I don't see much of my brothers nowadays, especially when it comes to washing up. I just hear in passing that 'We're going out fishing,' 'We're going swimming,' 'We're going to build a hut,' 'We're going to make a raft,' or 'We're going to the island to lay nets.' This last is what they are doing this evening. Tomorrow they will be going out to take them up, they tell me. At five o'clock. If they ever manage to wake up that early.

They did. They woke at five o'clock, dressed quickly and ran down to the Grankvist jetty, where Teddy and Freddy were waiting with their boat. Bosun had woken up early too. He stood there on the jetty, looking reproachfully at Teddy and Freddy. Were they really going out to sea without taking him with them?

'Oh, well, come on,' said Freddy. 'Where should a bosun be if not in a boat? But you know Tjorven will be furious when she wakes up.'

It seemed as if Bosun hesitated for a moment when he heard Tjorven's name, but only for a moment. Then he jumped softly down into the boat, which shuddered under his great weight.

Freddy patted him. 'Perhaps you think you'll get home before Tjorven wakes up, but you're wrong there, little Bosun.' Then she took the oars and began to row.

'Dogs can't reason like that,' said Johan. 'Bosun doesn't think anything at all. He just jumped into the boat because he saw you and Teddy in it.'

Both Teddy and Freddy declared that Bosun could think and feel like a human being.

'But better,' said Teddy. 'I bet there's never been an unkind thought in that dog's skull,' she said, and caressed the giant head.

'What about this skull then?' asked Johan and gave Teddy's blond head a tap.

'It's chock-full of terrible thoughts sometimes,' Teddy confessed. 'Freddy's kinder. She's much more like Bosun.'

They had to row for almost an hour to reach Fish Island, and they passed the time talking about the thoughts inside their various skulls.

'Now, Niklas, what do you think about when you see something like this, for example?' asked Teddy and made a sweeping gesture which took in the whole beautiful newly awakened morning with the white summer clouds in the sky and the glint of the sun on the sea.

'I think about food,' said Niklas.

Teddy and Freddy stared at him. 'About food? Why?'

'Well, that's what I think about most of the time,' said

Niklas with a grin, and Johan agreed with him.

'Yes, there are only two other thoughts at most slopping around in there,' he said, tapping Niklas's forehead.

'But thoughts are as thick as a shoal of minnows inside Johan's head,' said Niklas. 'Sometimes they come tumbling out of his ears when it gets too crowded. It's because he reads too many books.'

'I do too,' said Freddy. 'Thoughts may suddenly come bursting out of my head as well. I wonder how it will feel!'

'I think different thoughts when I am Teodora from when I am Teddy,' said Teddy.

Johan looked at her in surprise. 'Teodora?'

'Why, didn't you know? My real name's Teodora, and Freddy's is Frederika.'

'That was Daddy's idiotic suggestion,' declared Freddy. 'Mummy turned it into Teddy and Freddy.'

'My Teodora thoughts are like a dream, they are so lovely,' said Teddy. 'When they come to me I write poems and decide to go to Africa to work among the lepers, or perhaps to be an astronaut or the first woman on the moon or something like that.'

Niklas looked at Freddy, who was working hard at the oars. 'And what are your Frederika thoughts then?'

'Don't have any,' said Freddy. 'I'm Freddy all the time, but my Freddy thoughts are fairly sound. Would you like to hear the latest?'

Johan and Niklas were curious. Of course they wanted to hear the latest Freddy thought.

'It's this,' said Freddy. 'Can't either of those lazy boys row for a bit?'

Johan quickly relieved her of the oars, but he was a little anxious as to how he would get along. He and Niklas had rowed in the evenings in the old boat belonging to Carpenter's Cottage. They had practised in complete secrecy so that they wouldn't feel too awkward when they were in a boat with Teddy and Freddy.

'We do know something about boats, even though we aren't island dwellers,' Johan had assured the two girls when they had first met, and Freddy had said a little scornfully, 'You've carved bark boats, have you?'

Freddy and Teddy had both been born on Seacrow Island so they were islanders through and through. They knew almost everything about boats and weather and wind, and how to fish with every kind of net and line. They could clean herrings and skin perch. They could splice ropes and tie knots and row the boat with one oar just as well as they could with two. They knew where the perch grounds were and the reed beds where you could find a pike if you were lucky. They could recognize all the sea birds' eggs and calls, and they knew their way around the confusing world of island reefs and creeks which made up the archipelago around Seacrow Island better than they knew their mother's kitchen.

They did not boast about their knowledge. Apparently they thought it was something you were born with if you were an island girl, just as a duck is born with webbed feet.

'Aren't you afraid of growing fins?' their mother used to ask them, when she needed help with the telephone exchange or in the shop, and as usual had to fetch her daughters out of the sea. They were there in all weathers, and they moved in the water just as easily as they jumped about on the jetties or climbed up the masts of the old shipwrecked trawlers in the creek.

Johan had blisters on his hands when at last they reached the island. They smarted, but he was happy, for he had rowed well. It was quite enough to make him happy and excited, almost too much so.

'Poor boy, he'll be just like his father,' Melker used to say. 'Up and down all the time.'

Just now Johan was very 'up.' All four were. If Bosun was, he hid it very well. He wore the same melancholy look as always, but perhaps he was happy somewhere deep down in his dog's soul, as he lay comfortably on the warm rock with his back against the grey, sun-warmed wall of an old boathouse. From where he lay he could see the children in the boat, taking up the nets. They shrieked and shouted so much that Bosun became anxious. Were they in danger and needing help? It sounded as if they were, and Bosun could not possibly know that they were simply shrieking with delight over their catch.

'Eight perch!' said Niklas. 'Malin won't like this. She said that she wanted to have perch with mustard sauce for supper tonight, but not for a whole week!'

Johan grew more and more excited. 'Oh, wonderful!' he

shrieked. 'Who can possibly say that fishing for perch isn't fun?'

'Only the perch,' said Freddy quietly.

For a short moment Johan was sorry for the perch, and he knew someone who would have been even sorrier for them if he had been there. 'It's lucky we haven't got Pelle with us,' said Johan. 'He wouldn't have liked all this.'

Bosun up on his rock cast one last anxious look towards the boat and the children, but he realized that they did not need his help, so he yawned and let his head sink down between his paws. Now he could sleep.

And if it was true, as Teddy and Freddy insisted, that Bosun could think and feel like a human being, perhaps he wondered before he fell asleep what Tjorven was doing at home and whether she was awake yet.

She was. Very much awake. When she discovered that Bosun was not beside her bed as usual she began to wonder. And when she had wondered for a while she realized what had happened, and then she was extremely angry, exactly as Freddy had foreseen she would be.

She climbed crossly out of bed. Bosun was *her* dog. No one had the right to take him out to sea. But Teddy and Freddy were always doing it—and without even asking her. It couldn't go on like this.

Tjorven marched straight to her parents' bedroom to complain. Her parents were asleep, but Tjorven burst in anyway, went straight to her father and began to shake him.

'Daddy, do you know what?' she said furiously. 'Teddy and Freddy have taken Bosun out to the island with them.'

Nisse opened an unwilling eye and looked at the alarm clock. 'Must you come at six o'clock in the morning to tell me that?'

'Yes, I couldn't come before,' said Tjorven. 'I've only just found out about it.'

Her mother moved sleepily. 'Don't make such a fuss, Tjorven,' she murmured. It would soon be time for Marta to get up and begin a new day of hard work. This last half-hour before the alarm clock rang was as precious to her as gold, but Tjorven did not understand that.

'I'm not making a fuss. I'm just angry,' she said.

No one, unless they were stone deaf, could go on sleeping in a room where Tjorven was being angry. Marta felt herself becoming grimly wide awake and she said impatiently, 'What in the world are you making this fuss about? I suppose Bosun's not allowed to have a little fun now and again!'

Then it burst out. 'But what about me!' shrieked Tjorven. 'Aren't I ever going to have a little fun? It's not fair!'

Nisse groaned and buried his head in the pillow. 'Go away, Tjorven. Go somewhere else if you're going to be angry— somewhere where we can't hear it.'

Tjorven stood in silence. She was quiet for a few seconds and her parents began to hope that the silence would continue. They didn't understand that Tjorven had only just begun.

'Well, all right then!' she shouted at last. 'I *will* go away.

I'll go and never come back again! But you'll be sorry when you start to moan about not having your Tjorven any more.'

Then Marta understood that this was a serious matter and she stretched out her hand towards Tjorven in an attempt to calm her down. 'Surely you won't disappear altogether, little Bumble?'

'Yes, I will. That'll be the best thing,' said Tjorven. 'Then you can sleep and sleep all you want.'

Marta explained to her that they wanted their own little Tjorven always—but perhaps not at six o'clock in the morning in their bedroom. But Tjorven would not listen. She stormed out, slamming the door behind her.

She went out into the garden in her nightgown. 'Go on, sleep, then!' she muttered, and there were tears of bitterness in her eyes.

But then it began to dawn on her that she had woken up too early. The day seemed very new. She could feel it in the air and in the dewy grass that chilled her bare feet and she could see that the sun was not yet where it ought to be. Only the seagulls were awake and screaming as usual. One of them sat at the top of the flagpole and looked as if he owned the whole of Seacrow Island.

Tjorven did not feel quite so furious now. She stood there thoughtfully, pulling up little bits of grass with her toes. It annoyed her when she had behaved so childishly. Run away from home—only babies did that sort of thing, and Daddy and Mummy knew it as well as she did. But it would be impossible to turn back now, not just like that. There must be some honourable way of getting out of the difficulty. She thought hard and pulled up a great many tufts of grass before she finally realized what she must do. Then she ran to her parents' open bedroom window and poked in her head. Her parents were dressing and were as wide awake as she could wish.

'I'm going to be Söderman's maid,' announced Tjorven. She thought it was a very good suggestion. Now Mummy and Daddy would understand that this was what she had meant all the time and nothing as childish as running away.

Söderman lived alone in his cottage down by the sea. And he often complained that he had no help in the house.

'Can't you be my maid, Tjorven?' he had said to her once. But Tjorven had not had time then. What a good thing that she had remembered it now. You wouldn't need to remain a maid for very long. Then you could come home to Mummy and Daddy again and be their own Tjorven as if nothing had ever happened.

Nisse stretched out a fatherly hand through the window and stroked Tjorven's cheek. 'So you're not angry any longer, little Bumble?'

Tjorven shook her head shyly. 'No.'

'Well, that's good,' said Nisse. 'It's no good losing your temper, you know, Tjorven. It doesn't get you anywhere.'

Tjorven agreed.

'Do you think that Söderman really wants a maid?' asked Marta. 'He's got Stina.'

Tjorven had not thought of this. It was last winter when Söderman had asked her and then there had been no Stina, for then she had been living in town with her mother. Tjorven thought, but not for long. 'A maid has to be strong,' she said, 'and I'm that.'

And then she set off at a run to tell Söderman about his luck as soon as possible. But her mother called her back.

'Maids can't go to work in their nightgowns,' she said, and Tjorven understood that.

Söderman was behind his cottage sorting his nets when Tjorven at last appeared.

'They have to be strong, tra-la-la,' she sang. 'Fantastically strong, tra-la-la.' She interrupted herself when she saw Söderman. 'Söderman, do you know what?' said Tjorven. 'Guess who's going to wash up for you today?'

Before he had had time to guess a head popped out of the open window behind him. 'I am,' said Stina.

'No,' Tjorven answered her, 'you're not strong enough.'

It took quite a long time to convince Stina of this, but at last she had to give in.

Tjorven had a very hazy idea of the duties of a maid. Such a being had never set foot on Seacrow Island as yet, but she believed that they must be strong, iron-hard people, something like the icebreakers which came when the ice had to be broken up for the boat in winter. She began to wash up with just about the same sort of strength in Söderman's kitchen.

'You have to break something,' she assured Stina, as Stina exclaimed when a couple of plates fell to the ground.

Tjorven emptied a liberal supply of soap into the basin so that everything became one glorious mass of froth. She washed up energetically and sang so loudly that her voice travelled as far as Söderman, while Stina with a sour face sat on a chair, watching. She was the lady of the house, Tjorven had declared.

'They do not need to be so strong. Not so fantastically strong at any rate,' sang Tjorven. Then she suddenly announced, 'I'm going to make pancakes too.'

'How do you do that?' Stina wondered.

'You just stir and stir,' said Tjorven. She had finished the washing up and she quickly emptied the basin out of the window. But underneath the window Matilda, Söderman's cat, lay sunning herself. She jumped up with a terrified yowl and rushed through the kitchen door, enveloped in a cloud of froth.

'You shouldn't wash cats,' said Stina sternly.

'It was an accident,' said Tjorven. 'But if you do wash them you have to dry them too.'

She took the dish towel and they both began to dry Matilda and calm her. It was clear that Matilda thought she was being shamefully treated because she yowled angrily now and again and afterwards she went off to sleep.

'Where's the flour?' asked Tjorven when she finally got around to thinking about her pancakes again. 'Get it out!'

Stina obediently climbed up on a chair and pulled out the flour tin from the cupboard. It was difficult because she had to stretch to reach it and it was heavy. And really Tjorven was right; Stina was not strong enough.

'Help! I'm dropping it!' she shrieked. The flour tin tipped in her weak hands so that most of the flour showered on Matilda, who had just fallen asleep on the floor below.

'Looks like a different cat,' said Tjorven, amazed.

Normally Matilda was black, but the animal that now flew shrieking out of the door was as white as a ghost and its eyes were wild.

'She'll frighten the life out of every cat on the whole of Seacrow Island,' said Tjorven. 'Poor Matilda, she's really having a bad day.'

The raven, Hop-ashore Charlie, was shrieking in his cage; it sounded as if he was laughing at Matilda's misfortunes. Stina opened the cage and let the raven out.

'I'm teaching him to speak,' she said to Tjorven. 'I'm going to teach him to say "Go to blazes." '

'Why?' asked Tjorven.

'Because Pelle's grandmother can say it,' said Stina. 'And her parrot can too.'

Then they saw someone standing in the doorway, and it was none other than Pelle himself.

'What are you doing?' he asked.

'Making pancakes,' said Tjorven. 'But Matilda has run away with almost all the flour, so I don't think we can do much.'

Pelle came in. He felt at home in Söderman's cottage as all children did. It was the smallest cottage on the island, only a kitchen and a little bedroom, but there were so many things to look at, not only Hop-ashore Charlie, although for Pelle he was the most important, but a stuffed eider duck and a couple of bundles of old comics and a strange picture of people in black clothes driving coffins on sleighs over the ice. *Cholera is raging,* said the caption underneath. And then Söderman had a bottle with a whole sailing ship inside it. Pelle never tired of looking at it, and Stina never tired of showing it to him.

'How did they get the boat into the bottle?' Pelle wondered.

'There, you see!' said Stina. 'Your grandma can't do that!'

'No, because it's one of the most difficult things to do,' said Tjorven. 'Look at me,' she added.

And then they forgot the ship in the bottle as they looked at Tjorven. She was standing in the middle of the floor and on her head sat the raven. It was a wonderful fairy-tale sight which struck them quite dumb.

Tjorven felt the bird's claws in her thick hair and she smiled happily. 'Just think if he lays an egg in my hair!'

But Pelle soon dashed her hopes. 'He can't. It has to be a female for that, you know.'

'But,' said Tjorven, 'if he can learn to say "Go to blazes" then he can learn to lay an egg.'

Pelle looked longingly at the raven and said with a sigh, 'How I wish I had an animal. I've only got some wasps.'

'Where are they?' asked Stina.

'At home at Carpenter's Cottage there's a wasps' nest right under the eaves. Daddy's been stung already.'

Stina smiled a contented, toothless smile. 'I've got lots of animals—a raven and a cat and two little lambs.'

'But they aren't yours,' said Tjorven. 'They belong to your grandfather.'

'I have them as mine when I'm here with him,' said Stina. 'So there.'

Tjorven's face clouded over and she said gloomily, 'I've got a dog. If only those beasts would bring him home.'

Her Bosun! At that moment he was wandering around the island entirely on his own. And those so-called beasts had not even noticed he was gone.

They were having a wonderful morning. 'Let's swim first,' Teddy had said and so they did. The water was as it always is in the month of June. Only lunatics of twelve and thirteen would throw themselves voluntarily into anything so bitterly cold. But they were lunatics and they did not die of it. On the contrary they thrived on it. They threw themselves into the water from the rocks and dived and swam and played and raced in the water until they were quite blue with cold. Then they lit their campfire in a sheltered spot and sat around it and felt in their blood all the Indians, settlers, head-hunters, and Stone Age men that have ever sat around campfires as long as the human race has lived on the earth. They were fishers and hunters now, living the free life of the wild country, and they grilled their prey over the glowing ashes while seamews and seagulls shrieked above them and tried to tell them that all fish on the island were really theirs.

But the trespassers stayed there regardless, eating their delicious fish and making the most appalling noise. 'Craak,

craak, craak,' they croaked like cormorants, for they had just formed a secret club, the secret name of which was to be the Four Seacrows, and it was to remain a secret forever. But their war cries were not secret. All the seamews and seagulls heard it and did not like it. 'Craak, craak, craak!' echoed over the islets, islands, and creeks, but no one heard anything else for the rest was secret.

The glow from their fire turned into ashes. Then Freddy caught sight of a drifting boat out in the bay. It was so far away that they could scarcely see it, but it was empty, they could make out that much.

'How some people tie up their boats!' said Johan.

Then Teddy stood up as a grim thought occurred to her. 'You can say that again,' she said when she had taken a look. In the little creek into which they had dragged their boat there was no boat to be seen. Teddy looked sternly at Johan. 'Yes, you can say that again. How do *you* tie up a boat actually?'

It was Johan who had said that he would see to mooring the boat—and he had added that it would be done properly.

'Isn't it odd how a boy can be so exactly like his father?' Malin used to say of Johan. And it certainly was odd.

They could still see the boat far out in the sunshine. Freddy stood up on a stone and waved to it with both hands. 'Goodbye, goodbye, little boat. Give our love to Finland!'

Johan had become very red in the face. He looked shamefacedly at the others. 'It's all my fault. Are you very angry with me?'

'No,' said Teddy. 'That sort of thing can happen to anyone.'

'But how are we going to get away from here?' wondered Niklas, trying not to sound as anxious as he felt.

Teddy shrugged her shoulders. 'I suppose we will have to wait until someone passes. Although that may be a couple of weeks,' she said. It was a temptation to frighten everyone just a little.

'Bosun will starve to death by then,' said Johan. He knew the vast amount Tjorven's dog could eat.

That made them think of Bosun. Where was he? They had not seen him for a long time, it suddenly occurred to them.

Freddy shouted for him but he did not come. They all shouted so that the seagulls flew away terrified, but no dog appeared.

'No dog and no boat. Tell me what else we haven't got,' said Teddy.

'No food,' said Niklas.

But then Freddy pointed triumphantly to her knapsack, which she had put in a cleft in the rock.

'We've got that, though! A whole knapsack full of sandwiches! And seven fish!'

'Eight,' said Johan.

'No,' Freddy reminded him, 'we've eaten one.'

'No, there *are* eight,' said Johan. 'You can count me in. The biggest silly fish in the whole archipelago.'

They all stood there not knowing what to do next. Something of the glamour of the day began to fade and now they began to long to get home.

'Besides,' said Teddy, and she suddenly looked anxious, 'besides, I think there's a mist coming up out there.'

But at that very moment they heard the friendly *dunk, dunk, dunk* of a motorboat out on the sea, very faint at first but getting stronger and stronger.

'Look, it's Björn's boat,' said Freddy, and both she and Teddy began to jump and shriek like wild things. 'And, look, he's towing our boat!'

'Who's Björn?' asked Niklas while they waited, watching the motorboat coming nearer and nearer.

Teddy waved to the man in the boat. He was a sunburned young man with a pleasant rugged appearance. He looked like a fisherman, because the boat he had was the type that real fishermen used.

'Hi, Björn,' shrieked Teddy, 'you've come at just the right time! He's our schoolmaster,' she explained to Niklas.

'Do you call him Björn?' said Johan in surprise.

'That's his name,' Teddy assured him. 'We're friends with him, of course.'

The boat slowed and came in towards the rock on which the children stood.

'Here's your old boat,' yelled Björn and threw the line to Teddy. 'Just how do you tie up these days?'

Teddy laughed. 'In lots of different ways.'

'Oh, is that so?' said Björn. 'Well, I don't think you should use this last way again. You can't be sure I'll always come along to pick up all your lost things.' Then he added, 'Get off home immediately! There's a fog coming up and you'll have to hurry if you want to get home before it.'

'And what about you?' asked Freddy.

'I'm going to Har Island,' said Björn, 'otherwise I could tow you.'

And then he left them and they heard the *dunk, dunk, dunk*, of the motorboat disappearing in the distance.

If Bosun had been there they would have set off immediately, and then Melker would not have needed the tranquillizers that evening. But life consists of great and small events and they hang together as closely as peas in a pod. And one single little fish can cause a great deal of bother, forcing grown men like Melker to take tranquillizers.

It was not so small, that little fish. It was a tough old fish weighing about two pounds with which Bosun on his wanderings round the island had become acquainted. The acquaintanceship consisted of glaring at each other for just over an hour, Bosun on a rock on the shore, the fish in shallow water close by. Bosun had never before met such a glance as he now got from those cold fish eyes, and he could not drag himself away from it. And the fish looked as if it was thinking, Don't go on staring, you big idiot. You'll never frighten me. I'll stay here as long as I like!

But many precious moments were wasted with that fish. It was a long time before dog and children and fish and nets and bathing suits and knapsacks were at last collected into the boat. Meanwhile, the fog rolled closer and closer. Huge, formless banks of fog came in from the sea and the children were not far from their island before they sat wrapped in fog as if in a damp, grey, woolly blanket.

'It's like a dream,' said Johan.

'Not the sort of dream I like,' said Niklas.

Somewhere, far away, they heard the tooting of a foghorn. Otherwise, all was silent. Whether Niklas liked it or not, it was as silent as a dream.

Lost in the Fog

At home on Seacrow Island the sun was still shining and Melker was painting garden furniture. The furniture had once been white but now the paint was peeling and grey. 'How unfair!' he complained to Malin. 'It ought to be fixed up immediately.' And, after all, nowadays painting was so easy. No need to mess with brushes and paint. You only needed a handy little spray—and besides it was so quick, he added.

'You think so?' said Malin.

On their arrival she had asked Nisse Grankvist at the shop to refuse to sell Melker various things he might ask for, but which he ought not to be allowed to have.

'No scythe, no axe, no crowbar,' she had said.

'Crowbar?' said Nisse, laughing. 'Surely he can't do himself any harm with a crowbar?'

'You wouldn't say that if you had lived with him for almost nineteen years,' Malin replied. 'Oh, well—give him a crowbar if he wants it, but be sure you have plenty of first-aid kits in the shop, that's all.'

However, she had forgotten to say anything about paint sprays so Melker stood there now, happily spraying a garden chair.

Tjorven had given up her job as Söderman's maid after two hours of long and faithful service. Now she, Pelle and Stina were crowding around Melker. Painting in that way looked like fun. All three would have loved to help him with it.

'No,' said Melker, 'this is my toy. It's my turn to enjoy myself for once.'

'Are you a spray painter, Uncle Melker?' asked Tjorven. Melker let a cascade of white flow over the chair.

'No, I'm not, but a handyman must be able to deal with anything.'

'Are you a handyman, then?' asked Tjorven.

'Yes, he is,' Pelle assured her.

'Yes, I am,' said Melker. 'A really handy handyman, even if I say it myself.'

At that very moment, one of Pelle's wasps arrived, and as Melker had already been stung once, he swished at it with the spray to fend it off. No one ever knew exactly how it happened. Melker's misfortunes almost always remained mysteries, but Malin in the kitchen heard shrieks and rushed to the window. She saw Melker standing with his eyes shut and his face completely covered with paint. Handyman that he was, he had spray-painted himself, and his face was white all over. Like Matilda, thought Tjorven, and had a good laugh to herself, but Pelle cried.

In fact, there was not much the matter with Melker, as

he had had enough foresight to protect his eyes by quickly shutting them, and he kept them shut as he staggered towards the kitchen door to get Malin to help. He felt around with his hands and stuck out his face as far as he could, partly so that the colour would not drip down on to his shirt and partly so that Malin could see immediately which part of him needed attention this time.

Then he bumped against a tree, an apple tree which the gay carpenter had apparently planted there just for the love of it. Melker loved apple trees too, but his cries of pain were now the angriest and wildest that Malin had ever heard.

Pelle cried harder than ever and Stina had begun to cry too, but when Tjorven saw Uncle Melker's creamy white face, now garnished with small pieces of moss, she was sensible enough to run behind the house, for she felt a great burst of laughter welling up in her throat and she did not want to make Melker more upset than he was already.

When Malin had cleaned Melker up and given him some ointment for his eyes, he wanted to cut down the apple tree.

'There are too many trees around here,' he shouted. 'I'll go to Nisse's and buy an axe.'

'No, thank you,' said Malin. 'I want to have a little peace and quiet now.'

Alas, she did not know how little peace and quiet she was going to have that day.

It began when Melker suddenly missed Johan and Niklas.

'Where are the boys?' he asked Malin.

'Out on the island, as you well know,' said Malin. 'But I think they ought to have been home by now.'

Tjorven heard this and pursed her lips angrily. 'I think so too. Stupid Teddy and Freddy. They ought to have been home with Bosun before now, but I suppose it's difficult for them because of the fog.'

Melker had decided to wait a few days before going on with his painting. Now he stood on the steps of Carpenter's Cottage, blinking in the sun. In spite of the ointment, he felt as if his eyes were full of gravel.

'What nonsense is that about fog?' he said to Tjorven. 'The sun is shining so brilliantly it's making my eyes smart.'

'Here, yes,' said Tjorven, 'but beyond Little Ash Island there's a fog as thick as porridge.'

'Yes, Grandpa says so too,' Stina informed them. 'And Grandpa and I know everything because we listen to the radio.'

It took about two hours before what Malin called 'Melker's great quake' broke out. It happened exactly as it always did.

Malin knew that her father was a courageous person, how courageous only she really knew, for she had seen him in various crises in his life. Others perhaps thought of him only as the weak, sometimes absurdly childish Melker, but beneath his outward personality there was another, one that was strong and entirely unafraid, that is to say in everything concerning himself.

'But as soon as it has anything to do with your children, you are absolutely absurd,' said Malin.

That was when he stood and wept over Johan and Niklas.

But before he had got to that stage he had been to Nisse and Marta in the shop three times.

'It's not that I'm worried,' he had assured them with his shy smile when he went in the first time. 'Your children are used to the sea, so I'm not worried about them,' he stated the second time, 'but—Johan and Niklas out in this thick porridge!' he said, for now the fog had reached Seacrow Island and it frightened him.

'My children are out in exactly the same porridge,' said Nisse.

The third time Melker came over to the shop, Nisse laughed, and said, 'What do you want me to do?'

Melker smiled his shy smile. 'As I said . . . it's not that I'm worried, but don't you think it's about time to warn the Coast Guard?'

'Why?' asked Nisse.

'I'm so terribly worried,' said Melker.

'There's no reason to be,' said Nisse. 'The Coast Guard can't see in this fog either. And anyhow what can have happened to the children? The fog will lift by degrees and the sea is absolutely calm.'

'Yes,' said Melker. 'I only wish I were.'

He went down to the jetty full of misgivings and when he saw the grey, formless fog rolling towards him in waves, he was seized with panic and shouted at the top of his voice, 'Johan! Niklas! Where are you? Come home!'

But Nisse, who had followed him, slapped him kindly on the shoulder. 'Now, look here, Melker, you shouldn't come to live out here among the islands if you're going to take it like that. And it doesn't improve matters to stand here thundering like a foghorn. Come on, we'll go home to Marta and get some coffee and cake. What do you say to that?'

But Melker was as far away from coffee and cake as anyone could be. He looked at Nisse with desperate eyes. 'Perhaps they're still out there on the island. Perhaps they're sitting in one of the boathouses, all warm and comfortable. Do you think that's possible?' he asked.

Nisse said it could well be. But just then a motorboat glided alongside the jetty. It was Björn and he dispelled the hope that the children were on the island. There were no children on the island, he said, for he had just passed it a few minutes ago and had looked to see.

Then Melker went off, muttering to himself. He did not dare to speak because he was afraid they would hear the tears in his voice. He said nothing when he went in to Malin either. She was in the sitting room with Pelle, and Pelle was drawing. Malin was knitting and the old clock on the wall was ticking softly. The glow from the stove lit up the room, which was one large pool of absolute peace.

How calm, how quiet, how peaceful, and how wonderful life could be, thought Melker, as long as one did not have two children in peril on the sea. He sank down on the sofa with a heavy sigh. Malin looked at him curiously. She knew exactly what was happening and in due time the great quake would arrive. He would need her then, but until then she kept quiet and went on knitting.

Melker no longer noticed her. Neither her, nor Pelle. They were neither of them anything to him. Just now he had only two children and they were fighting for their lives far out at sea. He saw them in his mind's eye much more clearly than he saw Malin and Pelle, and they behaved in different ways all the time. Sometimes they were lying half dead of hunger and cold in the bottom of the boat, crying for their father with feeble voices. Sometimes they were in the sea and were trying with their last strength to crawl up onto a little rock. They hung on with their fingers and shouted wildly for their father. And then came an enormous wave—where it came from he couldn't say for the sea was dead calm, but come it did—and tore the children from the rock. Then they sank, their hair floating like seaweed below the water. Oh, why can't children stay three years old all their lives, and sit quietly in their playpens so that there is no need for all this worry!

He heaved one heavy sigh after another. Then at last he became aware of Malin and Pelle and realized that he would have to pull himself together.

He looked at Pelle's drawing and saw that it was a horse, but a horse that looked exactly like old Söderman. In ordinary circumstances Melker would have laughed, but now all he said was, 'You draw very well, Pelle. And you, Malin? What are you knitting?'

'A pullover for Niklas,' said Malin.

'He'll be very glad to have it,' said Melker, but he swallowed quickly, for he knew, of course, that Niklas was at the bottom of the sea and would not need a pullover ever again. Niklas, his own son. He remembered the time when Niklas was two years old and had fallen out of the window. Even then Melker had realized that such a lovely child could not live long! But no, it was Pelle who had fallen, he suddenly remembered, and he looked almost angrily at poor Pelle, whose only fault at that moment was that he was not at the bottom of the sea.

Now Pelle was an intelligent child and understood more than Melker or even Malin realized. When he had sat for a good while, listening to the sighs his father heaved at regular intervals, he put away his drawing. He knew that sometimes grown-up people needed comfort and so without a word he went to Melker and flung his arms around his neck.

Then Melker began to cry. He clasped Pelle violently to him and wept silently and desolately with his face turned away so that Pelle could not see.

'Everything will be all right,' said Pelle soothingly. 'I'm going out now to see whether the fog has lifted a bit.'

It had not—rather the opposite. But Pelle found a stone down on the shore, a little brown stone which was absolutely round and smooth. He showed it to Tjorven, who was out in the fog too. It was thrilling, magical weather which she liked, though less so when she had no Bosun at her side, since he was somewhere out in that thick grey porridge.

'Perhaps it's a wishing stone,' said Pelle. 'Just hold it in your hand and wish, and then your wishes will come true.'

'If you believe in it,' said Tjorven. 'Wish that we had two pounds of candy and then you'll see.'

Pelle giggled. 'You must wish for something proper if you

wish at all.' And he held the stone in his outstretched hands and wished as solemnly and properly as he could. 'I wish that my brothers will come home soon from the wild ocean!'

'And Bosun too,' said Tjorven. 'And Teddy and Freddy, but as they're all in the same boat there's no need to wish specially about them.'

It was evening now, but not like the usual June evenings. Everything was dull and unnatural from the dense fog over all the rocks and islands, all the channels, and all the boats, which were creeping along slowly, sounding their foghorns. And there was fog over the children's little boat, which ought to have been back at its own jetty by now, but which was not.

'There came three ships a-sailing,' sang Freddy.

'I can't see a single one,' said Teddy, resting on her oars. 'I've never seen so few boats about. How long have we been rowing, do you think?'

'Oh, about a week,' said Johan. 'That's what it feels like anyhow.'

'But it will be fun to get to Russia,' said Niklas. 'We'll soon be there, I should think.'

'I should think so too,' said Teddy, 'considering how we've rowed. If only we had kept a straight course we would have passed our jetty by two o'clock and been right up in Jansson's cow meadow by now.'

All four laughed loudly. They had laughed a great deal during the last five hours. They had rowed and rowed and shivered, argued a little, eaten their sandwiches, sung, shouted for help, rowed and rowed, and hated the fog and longed to get home, but still they had laughed quite a lot. It was Melker who was being shipwrecked at this moment—not the children.

But now evening had come and it was becoming more difficult to laugh. They shivered more than ever and grew hungrier and hungrier and saw no end to their misery. This fog was unnatural. An ordinary June mist ought to have cleared long ago, but this one was lasting, holding them in a grey, ghostlike grip as if it could never let them go. They had taken turns at the oars to keep themselves warm, but it no longer helped and it seemed useless to row when they didn't know where they were going. Perhaps they were going farther and farther out into the open sea with each stroke of the oars, and the thought frightened them. The sea was certainly calm, but if this fog, which they hated so much that they would have liked to tear it to pieces with their bare hands, were ever to lift, it would need wind. And if a strong wind blew up and they were far out to sea in a little boat, there would certainly be nothing to laugh at.

'The whole of this archipelago is absolutely littered with islands,' said Freddy, 'but do we bump into one of them? Don't you believe it!'

They longed to feel firm ground under their feet. One little island was all they wanted. There was no need for it to be particularly large or beautiful or at all wonderful, said Teddy. They would not mind if it were an ugly, scrubby little island as long as they could go ashore and make a fire and perhaps find out where they were, and get some sort of roof over their head. And perhaps someone quite extraordinarily kind would even come to meet them, bringing hot chocolate and cake.

'She's going crazy!' said Johan.

But they enjoyed going crazy about food. They all began to imagine plates piled with steak and pork chops.

'And perhaps a little mushroom omelette,' suggested Freddy. They were all enthusiastic about the mushroom omelette, even Bosun, it seemed, for he gave a little bark. He had said nothing the whole time and probably disapproved of this adventure, as any wise dog would, but he lay in the bottom of the boat, silent and patient.

'Poor Bosun!' said Freddy. 'He's hungrier than all of us because he has a much bigger tummy to be hungry with.'

They had shared their sandwiches with him, and when their sandwiches were finished they had offered him raw fish, but he had refused it.

'I'm not surprised at that,' said Johan. 'I'd rather starve than eat raw fish.'

'Is there absolutely nothing left in the knapsack?' asked Teddy.

'A bottle of water,' said Freddy.

A bottle of water! After all their wonderful dreams of hot chocolate and steak, it seemed an incredible letdown to have nothing but a bottle of water. They sat silent and miserable for a long time. Niklas wondered which would be worse, to freeze to death or to starve to death. Just at that moment he was finding the cold almost too much to bear. His thick jacket did not help, and he was shivering right to the marrow of his bones when he suddenly remembered their campfire out on the island. It must have been a campfire in another life, it felt so far away now. But it reminded him of the box of matches he had in his pocket and he fished it out. With stiff fingers he lit a match. The clear, comforting little flame flared for a moment and he held his hand around it to feel the warmth. Then he suddenly saw something in the boat.

'What's that over there? Is it a primus stove?'

'Yes,' said Teddy. 'Who in the world left it there?'

'Probably Daddy,' said Freddy, 'when he and Mummy were out fishing the day before yesterday. He persuaded Mummy to go with him by promising to make her some coffee in the boat, don't you remember?'

'We haven't any coffee,' said Freddy. 'Only water.'

Niklas pondered. Warm water would warm them at any rate, and just now they needed warmth more than anything else. He looked around for the scoop they used to bail the water out of the boat. It was an ordinary scoop and it could be used as a saucepan. He told the others what he thought of doing and they looked on with interest as he lit the primus stove and filled the scoop with water from Freddy's bottle.

Johan had an idea. 'We can cook our fish in this,' he said.

Teddy looked at him with real admiration. 'Johan, you're a genius,' she said.

Then they got busy. They cleaned and rinsed the fish in a frantic hurry, cut them into fillets and spent an almost happy hour cooking them in the scoop. It was a lengthy process, for there was only room enough for four fillets at a time, but eventually all the fish was cooked—and eaten with great approval. Bosun had most of it, but they all had plenty.

'Can you understand,' said Freddy, 'how it's possible to eat four bits of fish without any salt, and think it's the best thing you've ever tasted?'

'Why not?' said Johan. 'If you can even drink old fish water and think it's delicious!'

But the life seemed to return to them as they drank the musty, hot, smoky fish soup. It warmed them right down to their toes. Suddenly they began to hope again that something would turn up, that the fog would lift or that they would wake up at home and find that it was all a bad dream.

But the hours had passed and the fog did not lift. No boat came and it was not a dream, for you can't shiver so much in a dream. The fish soup only helped for a short time and the primus stove had gone out for good. Now the cold came creeping back and with it the weariness and despair. It was no good trying to hope any more. They would have to stay there as prisoners in the fog right through the night and perhaps forever.

Suddenly Freddy started and jumped up. 'Listen!' she cried. 'Listen!'

And they heard! Somewhere far away in the mist they heard the *dunk, dunk, dunk* of a motorboat. They listened as if their lives depended upon it and then they began to shout. It might be Björn's boat or it might be someone else's, but whoever it belonged to, they *must* get it to come nearer.

65

And it did. It drew closer and closer and they shouted themselves hoarse, in frantic joy at first—then in despair and fury. Full of bitterness they sat there and heard the *dunk, dunk, dunk* of the motorboat grow fainter again and slowly die away until at length there was nothing—nothing but the fog. Then they gave up and silently settled down in the bottom of the boat beside Bosun so that he would give them a little of his warmth.

Nisse Grankvist's shop on Seacrow Island was one of the most peaceful spots on earth. Not that it was quiet and dead—on the contrary. Everybody collected there from Seacrow Island and the other islands around. They came to shop and to gossip and to hear the news and to pick up their mail and to telephone. The shop was the centre of Seacrow Island. People liked Nisse and Marta, for they were gay and helpful and it was very homely in their little shop, filled with the good smell of coffee and dried fruit and fish and various other things. There was chatter and laughter all through the day, but despite that the shop was a very peaceful place.

But not on this foggy evening. Instead it was filled with sorrow and fear and despair. For Melker Melkerson's 'great quake' was creating more noise than all the inhabitants of the island put together.

'Something must be done *now*,' he shouted. 'I want all the Coast Guard, all the helicopters and all the rescue planes there are to come and search *now*!' He glared at Nisse as if it was his business to deal with it all.

Malin took hold of her father's arm. 'Daddy dear, calm down!'

'How can I calm down when I am just about to become fatherless!' shouted Melker. 'I mean . . . oh, what do I mean! Anyhow it's too late now. I don't think they are still alive— any of them.'

The others stood there silent and depressed, listening. Nisse and Marta and Malin and Björn. Even Nisse and Marta were anxious by now. This thick fog in the month of June was strange. Nothing of the kind had ever happened before within living memory.

'What an idiot I was! Why didn't I take the children with me when I took them their boat?' said Björn. He had a guilty conscience, which was keeping him here in the shop on Seacrow Island although he ought to have been on his way home long ago.

But it was not only his conscience and the poor parents that made him stay, for there was Malin too, who was so serious now and so unlike the gay, happy girl he had met the other evening. He found it hard to take his eyes off her. Silent and helpless, she stood there listening to her father's outbursts. With a tired movement she pushed her light hair from her forehead and he saw her eyes, dark and anguished. He was so sorry for her. Why couldn't her father control himself a little if she could?

Nisse had warned the Coast Guard at the nearest station, not because he thought there was any immediate danger, but it would be a bad thing if the children had to spend the night in the fog.

'Just one Coast Guard station! What's the good of that?' burst out Melker, who wanted all the lifesaving apparatus of the entire Baltic to come to Seacrow Island this foggy June evening. But after he had shouted and carried on for a long time it seemed as if all his strength suddenly gave out. He sank down on a sack of potatoes and sat there so pale and distressed that Marta was sorry for him.

'Would you like a tranquillizer?' she asked kindly.

'Yes, please,' said Melker. 'A whole jarful.'

He found it very difficult to take pills even at the best of times and he had no faith in them, but just at this moment he was ready to try anything, if it could give him a moment's peace and quiet.

Marta gave him a little white pill and a glass of water. As always, he put the pill on his tongue, took a mouthful of water and swallowed violently. As always, the water ran down his throat but the pill remained on his tongue. This did not surprise him, as his pills had a habit of doing this. He tried once more but the pill still remained on his tongue. Bitter—horrible.

'Take an enormous gulp,' said Malin. Melker did so. He took an enormous gulp and everything went down the wrong way, the pill too, for this time it went with the water.

'Oh,' said Melker, coughing, and then the pill came up and lodged somewhere behind his nose, where it stayed for the rest of the evening. And as far as could be seen it did not make Melker any calmer.

Up till now Malin had controlled herself, but now she

suddenly felt that she was going to cry—not just because the tranquillizer had stuck behind Melker's nose but because everything was so miserable. As she did not want her father to see her tears, she ran outside. She let them flow, leaning her head against the wall and crying quietly.

It was there that Björn found her. 'Is there anything I can do?' he asked sympathetically.

'Yes . . . don't be kind to me,' mumbled Malin, without looking up. 'Because if you are I shall cry until there's an absolute flood.'

'Then I won't say anything,' said Björn, 'except that you're sweeter than ever when you cry.'

He was on his way home to Norrsund to the school where he taught the children from all the islands. At the top of the schoolhouse was his bachelor flat. It did not take him more than ten minutes to get from Seacrow Island to his home and Malin saw him disappear towards the jetty.

'It will be all right tomorrow,' he shouted. 'I promise!'

Immediately afterwards she heard the *dunk, dunk, dunk* of his motorboat out at sea.

It was the very chugging sound that the children heard in their boat a few minutes later and which disappeared so annoyingly.

'Now I'm really fed up,' said Johan, and crawled up from the bottom of the boat where he had been sitting pressed close to Bosun for the past half hour.

'Are you going to jump into the sea?' asked Niklas, his teeth chattering so that he could hardly speak.

'No, I'm just going to row to the nearest jetty and put you all ashore,' said Johan glumly.

Freddy looked up with a face blue with cold. 'Thank you, that would be fine—and just where *is* the nearest little jetty?'

Johan clenched his teeth together. 'I don't know, but I'm either going to find it or die in the attempt. I'm not going to let any old fog decide how long I've got to sit here in the middle of the sea.'

He began to row. The fog was still as thick as cotton wool. Oh, how he hated it. Why didn't it drift off to the North Sea, or wherever it belonged?

'But I'll show you,' he mumbled bitterly to the fog. He felt as if the fog were his personal enemy. He rowed five powerful strokes and then the boat struck a stone.

'Bang,' said Teddy. 'Here's the jetty!'

It was not a jetty, but it was land. They had been sitting for a couple of hours just five strokes away from land.

'That's the sort of thing that's enough to drive you crazy,' said Teddy, and like mad creatures they tumbled out on the shore. They shrieked and jumped about and Bosun barked. They all went absolutely wild. How wonderful to have firm ground beneath their feet again!

But what sort of firm ground was it? Was it one of those islands where people came to meet you with hot drinks, or just a deserted island where they would have to sleep under a fir tree? Teddy had said she didn't mind if it was an ugly little scrubby island, and that seemed to be exactly what this was.

Johan walked up the shore in front of the others and began

70

to feel that he really was the leader. This was an expedition through unexplored territory with unknown dangers at every turn.

He rounded a corner before the others and then he saw something which made him stop in his tracks. It was a roof sticking up above some trees, just in front of him.

The others had caught up with him and he pointed proudly to his discovery.

'There's your house! Probably full of warm drinks!'

Then Teddy and Freddy began to laugh—wild, relieved laughter. It seemed to put an end to their horrible adventure in the fog and Johan and Niklas laughed too, although they did not know what they were laughing at.

'I wonder what kind of a house it is?' said Niklas when they had stopped laughing at last.

'Just you listen carefully and I'll tell you,' said Teddy. 'It's our school!'

None of the Grankvists and none of the Melkersons got to bed before twelve that night. Pelle and Tjorven had gone to sleep at the usual time, but they were dragged from their beds to join the party which took place in the Grankvists' kitchen to celebrate the happy ending of this disturbing day.

It had been disturbing to the very end. When Björn landed his boat at the Grankvists' jetty and Melker saw his lost sons sitting there safe and sound and wrapped in blankets, the tears ran down his cheeks and he took a leap to join them on board and hold them in his loving arms. But he took off rather too violently so that, having touched down on the stern, he plunged straight on into the water on the other side of the boat—and the tranquillizer behind his nose was not the slightest use to him.

'This is the last straw!' he bellowed.

Malin sighed when she saw him splashing in towards the jetty in a fury. *Nobody* but Melker could have suffered so many misfortunes in a single day.

Tjorven stood watching, not quite awake. 'Why are you swimming with your clothes on, Uncle Melker?' she mumbled. But then she saw Bosun and forgot everything else. 'Bosun!'

He jumped ashore and raced towards her and she threw her arms around him as if she would never let go.

'You see! My wishing stone *did* help,' said Pelle, when they were all sitting around the big table in the Grankvists' kitchen. Pelle was radiant. Oh, what a night! What a good idea to pull people out of bed in the middle of the night to eat pork chops! And Johan and Niklas were home after all.

'Isn't it strange, how you can get quite dizzy with food?' said Teddy with her mouth full.

Freddy sat with a pork chop in each hand. She bit first one and then the other. 'I think it's wonderful,' she said. 'I *want* to be dizzy in the head with food.'

'Real food,' said Johan. 'Not something that you imagine when you're out at sea.'

'But I thought that was good, too,' said Niklas.

They ate and enjoyed themselves and began to think more and more that after all it had been rather a good day.

'The chief thing is to take it all calmly,' said Melker, helping himself to another chop. He had changed his clothes and was dry and so happy that the air seemed to shine around him.

'Is that what you say?' said Malin.

Melker nodded importantly. 'Yes, it's impossible to live out in the islands otherwise. I admit that I was rather worried at one point, but, thanks to your tranquillizer, Marta—'

'You calmed down—behind your nose, anyhow,' said Nisse. 'But apart from that—'

'Apart from that—I'm thankful,' said Melker. And he really was. The noise around the table increased, for the children were dizzy with food and warmth and joy at being home, away from nightmares and fog. Melker listened to his children's voices and was thankful. He had them all here with him. Not one of them was floating under the water with hair like swaying seaweed.

'They've all got lungs, they can all speak, and no one is missing,' he said quietly to himself. Malin looked at him across the table.

'What are you sitting there murmuring about, Daddy?'

'Nothing,' said Melker.

And Then Came Midsummer

It was midsummer, a clear, shining midsummer day, but what was the matter with Malin?

The whole morning she had been sitting in the grass behind the lilac hedge, writing in her diary, and when Johan tried to approach her she snapped, without even looking up, 'Go away!'

Thereupon Johan, snubbed, went back to his brother and reported, 'She's still angry.'

'She ought to be thankful,' said Niklas. 'Now she's got something to write about. She wouldn't have a diary at all if it weren't for us.'

Pelle looked worried. 'Perhaps she'd have more amusing things to put down then—things that she thinks are more fun, I mean.'

They looked anxiously across at Malin, and Johan said, 'This time she's bound to write quite terrible things.'

It was Midsummer's Eve yesterday, wrote Malin, *and a Midsummer's Eve I will never forget, but for safety's sake I will write down a few lines to remind me about it. Then I can pass it on to my daughter if I ever happen to have one, and perhaps she will come home to me some Midsummer's Eve and, bursting with happiness, will ask me, 'Did you have such a wonderful time when you were young, Mummy?'*

Then I will point sourly to a couple of yellowing pages in my diary and say, 'Just read for yourself what your poor mother suffered from your small, horrible uncles!'

But actually even the world's most frightful little uncles cannot spoil the beauty of a Midsummer on Seacrow Island. The colours of the summer which is blooming around us now, nothing can destroy that. We go around in a cloud of perfumes of saxifrage and clover; marguerites nod in every ditch, and buttercups shine in the grass; the pink froth of wild roses covers our poor, bare, grey rocks, and violets grow in the crevices. Everything smells sweetly, everything is in full bloom, everything is summer and the cuckoo cuckoos and all the birds chirp and sing. The earth is full of joy and so am I. High above my head the swallows dart while I sit here and write. They are nesting under the eaves of Carpenter's Cottage and are close neighbours to Pelle's wasps, although I don't think they have much to do with each other. I like the company of the swallows and the wasps and butterflies but I would be grateful if you, Johan, would stop sticking your nose out from behind the corner of the cottage, because I am furious with you all and shall continue to be for a little longer—if I can. At any rate, until I have written this reminder of my first Midsummer's Eve on Seacrow Island.

75

I was woken by singing. Dad was up early and was putting the last touches to the garden furniture—with an ordinary paintbrush this time. He was standing right below my window and singing quite beautifully. I jumped up and into my clothes, and saw that the bay was lying out there, blue and shining, and that my beloved brothers were up with nothing to do. So I made them come with me to Jansson's cow meadow. We returned home with our arms full of flowers and green leaves and turned the whole of Carpenter's Cottage into a leafy bower with summer perfume in every corner.

And when the _Seacrow I_ came steaming up the bay she was like a floating leafy hut, decorated with young birches from stem to stern. Someone aboard was playing an accordion and people in summer clothes were singing, just like Daddy, but not so beautifully.

The whole of Seacrow Island was on the jetty, of course, for most people go down to meet the boat anyhow, and today it was Midsummer. We were all there—all except Björn.

I was looking elegant—most elegant—in my light-blue dress with the full skirt. Both Johan and Niklas whistled when they saw me, and that must be the greatest compliment one can have. If one's brothers whistle when they see one, it shows there are some grounds for being pleased with oneself. So I felt very happy, and full of expectation.

Pelle was not so happy. 'Must we wear these horrible clothes, just because it's Midsummer's Day?' he asked. I suppose it isn't right to torture small children with 'Sunday clothes', but one gets tired of all those dirty jeans and longs to see something else now and then.

'Yes, you must,' said Daddy, 'and after all it's not that bad. And if you're just a little careful not to get dirty and wet, you'll be on the safe side.'

'Tell me to be careful not to do anything that's fun and then you and Malin will be on the safe side,' said Pelle.

Then he suddenly saw Tjorven—Tjorven, who up till now had been seen dressed in nothing but jeans and a ragged little sweater. Here she was in a white embroidered dress and her bearing was quite indescribable. One could see from a long way off that she thought, Now you're really seeing something!

Even Bosun seemed subdued by this entirely new foster mother. Pelle drew back shyly. Then Tjorven climbed down from the heights of her triumph and said, 'Pelle, what about it? Shall we throw sticks for Bosun? It's about the only thing we can do while we're dressed up like this!'

Perhaps she said this to keep Pelle away from Stina. Stina and old man Söderman were also on the jetty. Söderman told us that his stomach was better, which pleased us all, for here on Seacrow Island we all share each other's joys and sorrows.

'Ha, ha! Now some of the summer visitors will be arriving, ha, ha!' said Söderman, and when Daddy asked him if he didn't like summer visitors, he looked quite surprised. Evidently that was quite a new thought to him.

'Like them? Pah!' he said. 'Most of them are only from Stockholm and the rest are just rubbish too.'

Daddy laughed and did not seem in the least offended. He already considered himself a native, as he always does wherever he may be, and I think this is the reason why he has so many friends everywhere. Besides, people feel that with all his childishness, vagueness, and helplessness he needs warmth and protection. Well, I don't know how he does it, but everybody likes him. I heard old man

Söderman say in the shop once when he had not noticed that I was there, 'That man Melkerson isn't quite all there, but that's the only thing I have against him.'

However, be that as it may, back to the jetty! The Grankvist Amazons—that's what Daddy calls Teddy and Freddy—were there in new jeans and red polo-necked sweaters. They and Johan and Niklas were sitting on empty oil drums and croaking like cormorants now and then. They have some sort of secret club, those four, and go around being 'secret' for days on end, which annoys the little ones beyond endurance as they are not allowed to belong. Pelle avenges himself by calling his brothers 'secret Johan' and 'secret Niklas,' smiling scornfully when he says it, while Tjorven simply declares that it's a crazy club. After the behaviour of the club last night I agree with her wholeheartedly.

As we stood there waiting for the boat to dock, Johan and Niklas suddenly rushed forward and each took one of my arms.

'Come on, Malin, we're going home now,' said Johan.

I struggled, of course, and wondered what they wanted to do at home.

'We can read an instructive book or something,' said Niklas.

'You know you like being read to,' said Johan.

'Of course I do, but not in the middle of a lovely Midsummer's evening,' I told them.

I found the explanation for it almost at once. The explanation came down the gangplank in all his glory and it was none other than Krister, the boy who was on the boat the day we came here. I am accustomed to my brothers hating anyone who 'comes and hangs about Malin'—their words, not mine!—but apparently right from the very beginning poor Krister has been more unpopular than anyone else. I don't think there's anything particularly wrong with him. He is rather inclined to be too sure of himself, but I would soon cure him of that. He is handsome enough and wears what Daddy calls good clothes.

As soon as he got off the boat he came straight up to me. When he smiled I thought he looked very nice, for he has lovely teeth, but Johan and Niklas glared at him as if he had a wolf's grin—and no wolf's allowed to come here and eat up our sister, no, thank you!

'Poor little Malin,' said Krister, 'all alone on Midsummer's Eve. Come along, and we'll turn Seacrow Island upside down.'

This remark did not make him any more popular with Johan and Niklas.

'She's not alone,' said Johan crossly. 'She's with us!'

Krister patted him on the shoulder. 'Yes, yes. Now off you go to the sandpit with your buckets and spades. I'll take care of Malin.'

I think it was at that very moment that they declared serious war on Krister. I could see them gnashing their teeth. They went back to Teddy and Freddy and immediately a frightful squawking arose from their direction, which sounded full of hate and revenge.

'Malin, this evening you and I are going to dance. I've already decided,' said Krister. And when I explained to him that I was used to deciding for myself with whom I wanted to dance, he said, 'Decide for me, then we needn't have any arguments about it.'

There was no sign of Björn. Anyhow, I didn't know whether he danced. And I wanted to dance in my light-blue dress, it being Midsummer and everything, so I said to Krister, 'Well, we'll see!'

However, it can be Midsummer as much as it likes, but the higher powers have decreed that I have to be a mother to my three brothers and I should certainly not have allowed the smallest one to leave me and go with Tjorven, at least, not when he was in his Sunday best. Suddenly I heard everybody laughing, and I said to Krister, Come and see what's amusing them all!

And then I saw! What I saw was Pelle—who was not to get wet. There he was, standing in the sea up to his waist, Tjorven too, and they were splashing water at each other as hard as they could. They were absolutely wild—there is no other word for it—and Tjorven shrieked, 'Now we might just as well go swimming!' And they did. They threw themselves in the water and came up shouting and splashing each other even more. They were absolutely sea-wild and so absorbed in their own enjoyment that they had entirely forgotten the rest of the world around them. But they woke from their wildness when Marta and I came rushing towards them, woke, and saw they were wet—in the same sort of way as Adam and Eve saw that they were naked. But Pelle and Tjorven unfortunately were not naked. They were dressed in their very best clothes, and I have never seen a well-starched party dress look more like a wet rag.

'We couldn't help it,' said Tjorven. 'It just happened.'

She tried to explain to Marta how it 'just happened' and as far as I remember, this is what she said.

'We were just going to paddle and we were ever so careful, because we were both looking so elegant, but Pelle said we should at least go out as far as to the knees and so we did, but then Pelle went out a little farther. I dare you to go as far as this, he said. And so I went farther and said, I dare you to go as far as this, then! But then I saw that the bottom of my dress was a bit wet and I said to Pelle, I'm not wet! And then he splashed a little water on me so that I would be wet, and then I splashed a little on him, and then he splashed a little on me, and then we splashed more and more, and more and more, and then we just went swimming. That's how it happened.'

'Well, anyhow, no more swimming today,' said Marta sternly.

We had to go home, each of us with our sopping wet child. Behind Carpenter's Cottage I have a clothesline strung between two apple trees. I hung up Pelle's clothes on it and there they danced their Midsummer's dance, the only one they would have, with the South wind.

But next Midsummer, I'll have a clothesline twice as long, for it is obvious that it will be needed. More about that later!

Marta and I both returned with our usual, everyday children, and Marta said, It will be a long time before I put Tjorven into a party dress again.

'Can I be sure of that?' said Tjorven.

Marta herself looked sweet in her national costume, with its pleated woollen skirt and big white scarf. Oh, that Marta! Who arranged the Midsummer Pole and the Midsummer Games on Seacrow Island? Marta! Who is the president of the Housewives Union? Marta! Who is the leader of the choir? Marta! And who got the whole of Seacrow Island, every single person, to dance around the Midsummer Pole? Marta! And no one else but Marta!

The Midsummer Pole had been raised in the meadow behind Söderman's cottage and when we got there it had begun to rain, for even Marta cannot regulate the weather. But her housewives collected bravely beneath their umbrellas and sang at the top of their voices, and I did too, and the earth was lovely and the sky beautiful, in spite of the rain. But, dear God, hear the prayer of the birds and let it clear up before evening, for there is one little female bird here who is longing to dance on the jetty!

And so I did. But before that point was reached, a great deal had happened, and the clothesline between the apple trees was beginning to sag. For on it hung not only Pelle's shirt, jacket, and shorts, but a shirt belonging to Krister, as well as Daddy's shirt and trousers and Johan's shirt and trousers. I do not know what Niklas's trousers had done not to be allowed to go swimming the whole day. All the other trousers were allowed to, but, of course, life is very unfair.

Actually Krister's shirt had not been swimming; I had washed it for him because he fell down during the egg-and-spoon race at the exact spot where Daddy had dropped his egg a minute before. Kind man that he is, Daddy went home and gave one of his own shirts to Krister.

'Thanks,' said Krister. 'I'll go and have a swim while I'm waiting.'

Johan and Niklas and the Grankvist Amazons stood there giggling. No one could say that they seemed particularly sorry for Krister's misfortune with the egg. I heard Krister ask them where one could swim and Teddy pointed.

'Is it shallow there?' asked Krister.

'Yes, it's so shallow you can walk right over to Finland,' said Johan with a giggle.

'And that's what I think you'd better do,' said Niklas, but by then Krister had already gone, so he did not hear.

The children's sack race was about to begin and I went over to watch it, but suddenly Johan rushed up to me, very pale, and grabbed me by the arm. 'Do you know if Krister can swim?' he said. 'What happens if he can't? It's deep where he's gone in!'

I knew that it was deep too, but I, like Johan, had never imagined that there were people who could not swim, and I had no idea whether Krister was one of those.

'Come on,' I said. And we ran for all we were worth, Johan and Niklas and Teddy and Freddy and I. We arrived just in time to see Krister wading into the sea.

'Stop' shrieked Johan.

Obviously Krister did not hear. He waded out quickly as if he really did think he could walk over to Finland, but after a couple of steps he was already in deep water and then he disappeared. He just disappeared! And I have not yet recovered from the shock.

Johan kicked off his shoes and dived straight in and I shouted to the others, 'Run and get help!'

Niklas and Freddy ran. Teddy and I stood trembling, in a cold sweat. Johan was under water for a long time and each second was agony. I was just about to go in myself, when at last he came up—but without Krister. He shook his head in despair. 'I can't find him!'

'You'd better hunt a little more in that direction,' said Teddy. 'That's where he went under.'

Then someone behind me raised a finger and pointed and said, 'No, that's where he went under. And over there by that stone is where he came up again.'

I turned—and there stood Krister, dripping wet and very pleased with his stupid joke.

But Teddy went on pointing and repeated, 'No, that was where he went under. I saw him myself!'

'Yes, I did too,' said Krister.

And then, at last Teddy realized who it was she was talking to. She was furious. You should never do that kind of thing! she said, and I agreed with her.

'I agree,' said Krister. 'And you shouldn't lure people out into deep water before you know if they can swim or not, either.'

Johan had been down hunting again. Now he came up and saw Krister. One could see how relieved he was and at the same time how put out. Imagine trying to save a person who was already on dry land! Johan did what he always does with anyone he thinks is rather unpleasant—turned it into a sort of joke. He gave a shout and sank slowly back under the water again, exactly as if he had fainted with pleasure at seeing Krister.

He should not have done that, for just at that moment everybody on Seacrow Island arrived with Daddy at their head. They obviously thought someone was drowning, and Daddy caught a glimpse of Johan before he disappeared.

'Johan!' shouted Daddy, and threw himself in the water before I could stop him. It was like watching a film. First Johan's head came up and then Daddy's. They stared at each other in silence.

'What do you want?' said Johan at last.

'I want to go ashore,' said Daddy angrily, and he did so.

'Uncle Melker, why do you always go swimming with your clothes on?' asked Tjorven. No one can keep her away when anything is happening.

'It just happens that way,' said Daddy, and Tjorven was silenced. Then Daddy took hold of Freddy's ear. 'Didn't you say that someone was drowning?'

Teddy came to her rescue. 'The whole thing was a mistake!'

Krister attempted to explain, but everyone was very angry with him and I heard what Niklas said to Freddy. 'That young man's a pain in the neck, whatever anyone says.'

I think that Björn thought so too. He had realized the position by degrees, but he just went about looking miserable and never came near me.

In any case, it was a wonderful, beautiful Midsummer's evening and there was dancing on the jetty exactly as I had hoped. Old man Söderman played his concertina and we danced, all of us danced, oh, how we danced, while the sun sank in the bay and the mosquitoes buzzed around us. Björn did not dance. Perhaps he couldn't. But Krister could. Goodness, how my light-blue dress swirled around as we flew backward and forward, and how I enjoyed it!

'Malin,' said Söderman during one of his little drink pauses, 'promise me one thing! Never grow old!'

If only he knew how old I am <u>sometimes</u>! Secret Johan and his secret followers stood there guarding me. Every time Krister and I danced past, Johan shouted, 'Take care, Malin!'

Finally I got tired of him and hissed, 'What of?'

'Yourself,' he said. And the other three giggled. Krister did not care. It did not matter to him how much they laughed, and I must say that boy knows a thing or two! Quite uninhibited, and without paying any attention to the little brothers who were listening, he recited to me during one of Söderman's beer pauses:

A pale pink rose gleamed on her brow
Among the yellow, flaxen hair.
A sweet, old-fashioned Swedish maid.

For I had a pink wild rose in my hair and I stood there, feeling just like the old-fashioned Swedish maid, until Johan broke my dream.

'Well, actually in some cases it's different,' he said. 'Some people have hair like an old Swedish pig.'

Then all four of them looked at Krister's crew cut and giggled. Where does all that giggling in thirteen-year-olds come from, I wonder?

But I still was not really angry with them. I did not become angry until they disturbed my Midsummer Night's Dream down by Jansson's Creek. I wanted to dream it alone, without Krister, and quite positively without any little brothers, but I was not allowed to.

Jansson's Creek is a solitary, strange place. Krister and I went there when the dancing had finished. There is an old boathouse with a couple of old punts, but otherwise nothing to show that there are people in the world. Everything is mystical and beautiful and silent. Now, at night, a couple of swans were floating on the dark water. They shone whitely as if they were fairy-tale birds. Perhaps they were, for everything was unreal and fairylike, and in some way, ancient, and one felt that at any moment these swans might shed their plumage and become heathen gods, dancing and playing on flutes. The water lay black under the high cliffs on the other side of the creek, but out to sea the water was pale and the night was not night, but only a pale little dusk which was trying to become night.

Krister and I sat on a rock. I wanted to be absolutely quiet, but he did not understand that. He thought that everything must go the way he wanted, and so he began to look into my eyes and to wonder whether they were green or grey—my eyes, that is. Then we heard a voice just behind us, followed by giggles.

'Actually they're purple.'

That was the last straw. I was furious and I shouted, 'What are you doing there? Explain at once!'

'Certainly,' said Niklas, popping up his head. 'We're sitting here, flirting, like other people.'

At that, Teddy and Freddy giggled for several minutes and I grew angrier still. I'm tired of all this, I said.

And then Johan piped up. Well, why don't you go home then? Surely you don't have to sit and flirt until you're tired!

The beasts! Daddy had told them that they might stay up as long as they liked as it was Midsummer's Eve.

'It seems to me that it's a little too thick with brothers around here,' said Krister. 'Isn't there anywhere we can get away from them?'

'At home perhaps,' I said. 'I don't suppose they'd want to go there.'

So we went back to Carpenter's Cottage and I made a sandwich for Krister in the sitting room, which smelled of lilies of the valley and birch leaves.

Daddy was asleep. Pelle was asleep. All was quiet and peaceful. We sat on the sofa with the window behind us open to the night, which would soon begin to lighten.

'How can you bear to have those brats hanging around you all the time?' asked Krister. And I said, truthfully, that I could bear it very well because I loved them, stupid though they were.

'Right now I love them too—fantastically!' said Krister. 'Simply because they're not here.'

Or so he thought—so I thought too. Until I heard those giggles again, outside the window this time. In the summer dusk a little procession of giggling children went by, with the most hideous hats in the world on their heads. There are some strange things in our attic!

Every time they passed the window they lifted their hats politely and giggled so much at each other's jokes that they had to lean against the trees to keep their balance.

'Good evening! Have you heard that butter has gone up several pennies a pound?' they said, and, 'Excuse me, but is this the way to Stockholm?' and, 'Do you happen to know if there's any snuff left for Grandpa?'

When Johan said this last sentence, Niklas giggled so much that he really did fall over and lay on his back in the grass like a beetle and just screeched with laughter.

Luckily, just at that point Nisse came to fetch his daughters and it seemed as if Johan and Niklas had grown tired of the game too and they went up to bed. I heard them clumping up the attic stairs to their room and I gave a sigh of relief.

Krister had begun to be annoyed and I was not surprised. I offered him another sandwich and some more tea and tried to make up for my brothers' awful behaviour.

'A fine lot of brothers you have!' said Krister. 'Have you chloroformed your youngest brother to keep him so quiet?'

'Thank goodness, he's one of those angelic children who go to sleep at night,' I said.

Then I suddenly heard Pelle's voice. 'That's what _you_ think!' Daddy has fixed a rope from the boys' attic in case of fire. On this rope the 'angelic child who goes to sleep at night' was now dangling outside the window, and from the attic window above I could hear wild giggles. I could have cried.

'Pelle,' I said in a miserable voice. 'What are you hanging there for?'

'To see that no funny business is going on down there. Johan told me to have a look!'

Then Krister got up and made for the door. 'When brothers begin to hang from ropes outside windows, that's the end,' he said, giving up. "Bye, Malin,' he said and disappeared into the dawn, and that was the end of my Midsummer's Eve.

Still, it was quite a good Midsummer's Eve even so, I thought.

'All right, Johan, I know you're lying behind the hedge,' said Malin, and put her diary down in the grass. 'Come here, and we'll settle all this here and now. If you will carry in all the wood and water for the whole of today I may just possibly forgive you.'

Live for the Day

The summer ran its course. The sun shone and the rain fell at regular intervals. Sometimes there was a storm, and the bay was white and all the windows of the house shook and rattled. At times like this Tjorven had to go very carefully when she walked down to the quay to meet the Stockholm boat and little Stina was once almost blown into the sea. Söderman's cat refused to go out. Söderman himself spent three days mending his herring nets.

Sometimes it thundered. The Melkersons sat for one whole night in their kitchen, watching the lightning streaking down into the sea, lighting up the water as if it were day. The thunder rolled over the island and out over the sea, sounding almost like the day of doom. Who would dare to sleep in that noise?

'I'm beginning to get tired of this night life,' said Pelle at last.

There was no real order at all in the nights here on Seacrow Island, he thought. Though it had been quite easy to stay awake on Midsummer's Eve because there was a party. Nisse

Grankvist had explained to him that every kind of weather was lovely and Pelle believed blindly all that Uncle Nisse told him. It was only when it rained through the roof that he wondered a little. But even that came to an end, for one fine day his father climbed up on the roof and put tarred paper and slates over the worst places. Malin had said that the whole of the Melkerson family was to observe a two-minute silence while Dad was on the roof. It certainly worked, because he finished the job without anything going wrong. But things did not go so well the next day when he had to climb up again, because then he fell down. His children anxiously hurried to help him, but Melker assured them that he was perfectly all right. He had simply come to the sudden conclusion that this was not the day for doing the repairs.

'But surely you need not have come to a conclusion so suddenly that you had to fall down and hurt yourself,' said Malin.

But for the most part everything was fine and the whole summer was one long delight. Pelle had already begun to dread the awful day when they would all have to go back to town. He had an old comb with as many teeth as the summer had days. Every morning he broke off a tooth and noticed anxiously how the comb grew thinner and thinner.

Melker saw the comb one morning and threw it away. To worry about the future was the wrong attitude towards life, he said. One should enjoy each day as it came. On a sunny morning like the present one, life was nothing but happiness. How wonderful it was to go straight out into the garden in pyjamas, feeling the dew-wet grass under one's feet, and then take a dip from the jetty and afterwards sit down at the painted garden table to read a book or the paper while drinking delicious coffee, with the children milling around! He could ask nothing better from life. And so Pelle was not to bother with any old comb. Pelle allowed him to throw it away without protest and when that was done, his father returned to his book and Johan and Niklas began to grumble about whose turn it was to wash the dishes.

Both of them were convinced that their washing-up days came too often, but Malin was just as certain that when the time for washing up came around it would be difficult to find boys who could do such a complete vanishing trick as Johan and Niklas.

'I'm sure you're wrong,' said Niklas.

'Who washed up yesterday,' retorted Malin, 'if not yours truly, Malin?'

Niklas could not understand this. 'That's queer, I thought it was me.'

'Didn't you notice?' said Pelle, spreading his marmalade on his bread and butter. 'Didn't you notice it was Malin washing up—not you?'

One of his wasps arrived at that moment and wanted to have some marmalade too. Pelle held out his bread and butter in a friendly way, for one has to feed one's pets. Pelle was certain that the wasps knew who was their master. He would sit in his attic window and whistle to them and talk to them, and had promised them that they might stay at Carpenter's Cottage for as long as they liked.

He now looked with interest at the little wasp, which had begun to eat the few grains of sugar that had been spilled, and he wondered how it felt to be a wasp. Were wasps sad or frightened like people—not grown-up people, of course, but little boys about seven years old? How much did wasps actually know?

'Daddy, do you think wasps know it's the 18th of July today?' asked Pelle. But his father was deep in his own thoughts.

'Live for the day,' murmured Melker. 'Yes, excellent idea.'

'What's so excellent about it?' asked Johan.

'That's what it says in this book,' said Melker enthusiastically. 'Live for the day. That's the reason why I've thrown Pelle's comb away.'

'How can a book tell you to throw my comb away?' wondered Pelle.

'It says live for the day—that means that one should live every day as if one had only today and no more. One should be aware of every moment.'

'And you think that I ought to stay here and wash up!' said Niklas reproachfully to Malin.

'Why not?' asked Melker. 'The feeling that you are really doing something with your hands makes you feel you are alive.'

'Then perhaps you'd like to wash up?' suggested Niklas.

But Melker said he had a lot of other things to do, enough to make him realize that he was alive for the whole day.

'What does life feel like, anyhow?' asked Pelle. 'Is it something you feel with your hands?'

Malin looked tenderly at her little brother. 'As far as you're concerned, I think it's in your legs. When you say that you feel as if you had springs in your legs, that's the feeling of life.'

'Is it?' said Pelle, amazed.

How much there was that one did not know, even though one was a person and not a wasp. Perhaps wasps did not realize that today was the 18th of July, but they realized perfectly well that there was marmalade in a bowl on a table in a garden, and they came in such swarms that Malin grew annoyed and shooshed them away. Then one of them decided on vengeance, but instead of going for Malin it went quite unfairly to poor, innocent Melker and gave him a jab in the neck.

Melker jumped up with a roar and was just about to kill an innocent little wasp which was creeping around the table, having done nothing wrong, when Pelle stopped him.

'Stop it!' he shouted. 'Don't touch my wasps! They want to live, just the way you said.'

'What did I say?' asked Melker. He could not remember that he had said anything about wasps.

'Live for the day, or whatever it was,' said Pelle.

Melker lowered his book, the book with which he had been about to slay the wasp. 'Oh yes, of course. But I don't think they should begin the day by stinging my neck.' Then he stroked Pelle's hair lovingly. 'You're the kindest little boy in the world to animals,' he said. 'It's a pity you haven't a pet of your own.'

He rubbed his neck. It was painful, but he did not mean to let such a little thing spoil his morning. He rose energetically from the table. Live for the day—that was it! And he knew just what he was going to do!

The next moment a large motorboat came chugging in towards the jetty. When Johan and Niklas spied who was in the boat, they looked at each other darkly.

'I thought we finished him off at Midsummer.'

Krister had obviously forgotten everything except that Malin was the sweetest, loveliest creature within reach here among the islands. If there had been anything sweeter or lovelier on any of the other islands he might have gone there, but now he could think of no better place than the Melkerson's jetty.

'Hello, Malin! Want to come out in the boat with me?'

Her three brothers held their breath. Was she really going off in a motorboat? If so, they could not guard her.

Malin looked delighted. It was obvious she had nothing against a little trip out to sea.

'How long are you going to be away?' she shouted.

'The whole day,' yelled Krister. 'Bring your bathing suit in case we find a good place to swim.'

Johan shook his head warningly. 'Just you be careful. Live for the day. Do you really want to spend a whole day in that boat?'

Malin laughed. 'Of course! It's much more fun staying at home, washing up and cooking, but I mustn't be selfish. I must see to it that you have a little fun too sometimes!'

'You'll be sorry,' said Niklas.

Malin looked questioningly at her father. 'Do you think you'll get on all right without me?'

'Of course,' said Melker. 'Leave everything to your father.'

Melker sometimes had a guilty conscience about Malin. Perhaps she had more work and more responsibility than was right for a nineteen-year-old. He was anxious for her to have any fun she could. Besides, it suited him for her to be away today when he wished to be alone.

'Off you go, my dear,' he said. 'Leave the housekeeping to me. I shall enjoy it.'

But before Malin had collected her various belongings, Pelle was down on the jetty. He was buttoning up his windcheater, eyeing Krister sourly.

'Hello,' said Krister. 'Why are you putting that on?'

'You always have to wear a windcheater when you go to sea,' said Pelle coldly.

'Oh, so you're going to sea too! Who with?'

'With you and Malin,' said Pelle, 'to see that there's no funny business.'

At that moment Malin appeared and she looked at Krister pleadingly. 'Oh, he can come with us, can't he?'

It was obvious that Krister was not anxious to have a troublesome little brother in the boat, and Malin said to him crossly, 'You don't seem to like children particularly!'

Krister took hold of Pelle and dropped him roughly into the boat. 'Oh yes, I do,' he assured her. 'I'm very fond of children, but only if they're girls and about nineteen years old, otherwise I don't much care for them!' He held out his hand and helped her aboard. 'But I suppose I must be thankful that you're not bringing *all* your brothers with you.'

The two who remained behind stood looking after the boat until she looked like a tiny speck out in the bay; then they began to do what had to be done. They cleared the table and carried the breakfast things out into the kitchen, heated the water, washed up and put away the china. They did it quickly and well, for they were used to doing these things when they were forced to—and, besides, Teddy and Freddy were waiting for them on a raft at the Grankvist jetty.

And Melker was waiting just as eagerly for them to go. He wanted to be alone, for now he was going to try out his invention, his secret water pipe that would free him from all drudgery.

There were certain things that had to be done every day, which did not make life all that pleasant. Melker considered that the continual carrying of water was one of these. Goodness knows what Malin did with all the water that had to be carried in for her, but the water pails always looked empty and reproachful when anyone came into the kitchen. It went without saying that Malin, with four men in the house, should not have to carry water. Johan and Niklas did it if they happened to be in the neighbourhood just when it was needed and if they were told to do so. But all too often there was no one but Melker on hand to fill the empty pails. But it was going to be an altogether different matter in the future. Melker Melkerson had found a water pipe in the boathouse, that glorious old boathouse which housed so much rubbish. He had secretly been rubbing the pipe with sand to clean it. Now he had only to set it up.

'It's as simple as that,' Melker assured himself, as he planned what to do. 'First—fix up an apparatus at the well with the pipe at the correct angle. Second—fasten this apparatus securely to two of the lower boughs of the tree. Third—attach the pipe to the apparatus with wire so that it is quite steady and pass it through the kitchen window after you have carefully measured and made sure it's long enough. Fourth—place a large trough under the pipe in the kitchen. Fifth and sixth, the water will run into the kitchen and you can stay outside without doing a thing. Of course, the water will still have to be drawn up from the well by hand, but that's a minor problem. We will still have to draw up fifteen to twenty buckets of water every morning, but once that's done we'll be free for the rest of the day, and Malin will have all the water she wants.'

Melker began with a light heart. The work was harder than he had expected, but he talked gently and encouragingly to himself all the while. 'That's two things going splendidly,' he said when he had manoeuvred the pipe into the right position. 'No . . . three! This beautiful wooden pipe, the water flowing straight into the kitchen, and of course Melker Melkerson's cleverness in fixing it all.'

Everything went well—just as he had expected—and he knew that it would all work out exactly right. He had no time to get the trough, which was a pity. He would have to try it out with just a pail, so he needed someone in the kitchen to tell him when the pail was full.

As if sent from heaven, Tjorven arrived at that very moment and Melker laughed. 'Tjorven, you've come at just the right time!'

'Have I?' said Tjorven, delighted. 'Have you been longing for me to come?'

A friendship had grown up between Melker and Tjorven of a special kind that sometimes exists between a child and an adult: a friendship of two equals who are absolutely honest towards each other, each having an equal right to say exactly what he thinks. Melker had enough of the child in him and Tjorven enough of something else, not exactly maturity, but a strange inner strength, to make it possible for them to talk together as equals—or, at any rate, almost as equals.

Tjorven faced Melker with more bitter truths than anyone else, and he sometimes gasped and was just about to scold her when he realized that it would be entirely useless. She was what she was and said what she thought. As a matter of fact, she was genuinely friendly and devoted and she liked Uncle Melker very much indeed.

He explained to her what a fine invention this was. In the future Malin would have the water brought straight into the kitchen for her.

'Like Mother,' said Tjorven. 'She has water brought straight into the kitchen, too.'

'Oh no, she hasn't,' said Melker.

'Yes, she has!' said Tjorven. 'Daddy brings it in.'

Melker laughed in a superior way. *This* was something quite different and a nice little surprise for Malin, he said.

Tjorven looked at him seriously. 'And so that you won't have to work so hard yourself.'

Melker made no comment on that remark. 'Now you stand here by the pail,' he explained to Tjorven, 'and give me a shout when the water starts coming. And when the pail is full, you shout again. Understand?'

'Yes. I'm not as stupid as all that,' said Tjorven.

Melker ran out to the well, as excited as a child. He pulled up a pailful of water and poured it into the pipe. He laughed with joy when he saw it on its way towards the kitchen and heard Tjorven shout from inside. The whole thing was functioning just as he had intended.

But not quite . . . unfortunately, not quite! The pipe leaked and most of the water ran out on to the ground. He saw this with annoyance, but, still, that could be mended. Wooden vats that leaked were put into the sea so that they would swell and tighten up. He could do the same with his wooden pipe, that is, if he had the strength to take it apart again. All that wire—yards and yards of it—which he had wound around the pipe would not be easy to dismantle. Wouldn't it have the same effect if a lot of water were poured through the pipe where it stood? It would gradually tighten up that way.

He went ahead with all the zeal and enthusiasm he always brought to everything he did, and when he had poured about ten pails of water through the pipe, he thought the pipe really had tightened a little—or was it only his imagination?

He stood there scratching his neck and watching the water as it poured out onto the ground, and then he suddenly became aware that Tjorven was shouting to him from the kitchen. He had a feeling that she had been doing so for a long time without his noticing it, and he shouted eagerly, 'Is it full now?'

Tjorven stuck a grim face through the window. 'No,' she said, 'only the whole kitchen, right up to the door!' And then she said, 'Are you deaf, Uncle Melker?'

It was clear that the pipe had functioned better than Melker had supposed. Even though most of the water had leaked out onto the ground in transit, there had still been enough left over to fill both the pail and the entire kitchen floor!

Johan and Niklas burst in a little later and found their father on the floor with a cloth in his hands and they asked in surprise, 'Are you scrubbing the floor?'

'No,' said Tjorven, who was sitting on the top of the woodbin, looking on. 'He's just been making a nice little surprise for Malin. Guess what he's done? He's fixed up a way to get water from the well straight into the kitchen.'

'Out you go!' roared Melker. 'Out! All of you!'

But far away from Melker's delightful surprise, Malin was enjoying her day very much. Live for the day—she had most of the necessary ingredients, certainly—sun, water, soft summer breezes, a warm, hard rock to lie on, the sweet smell of flowers mingling with the smells of the sea. All these wonderful little green islands with their bare, grey rocks, their flowers and their sea birds. Where could one spend a better day than on one of them? Of course, it would have been better without Krister, because his chatter drowned out the faint lapping of the water. His chatter began to irritate her so much that she wished he would keep quiet, but she knew that would never happen.

On Midsummer's Eve she had told him she liked to be absolutely quiet and absolutely alone. Not always, of course, just now and then, she had hastened to assure him. But, anyhow, sometimes she felt that she *must* be alone.

'I like being alone too,' Krister had assured her. 'But it depends who with. With you I could be alone as long as you like!'

Poor Krister, he was not allowed to be alone with Malin. Pelle did not like his chatter either but, nevertheless, he had settled down near the two of them so he would not miss a single word. He was collecting stones on the shore and watching tiny fish in the water, but he kept his ears open all the time.

'I'm going over to Åland for a week with the motorboat. Want to come too?' said Krister.

Pelle looked up. 'Do you mean me?'

Krister quite truthfully assured him that he did not mean Pelle, but the person he did mean only smiled and did not answer.

'Malin, will you come?' asked Krister eagerly.

'No—I don't think I want to,' said Malin.

'For goodness' sake,' said Pelle, and picked up a little white stone.

'It's a fine thing, to have brothers listening to everything you say!' said Krister.

He suggested that Pelle should take himself off a little farther down the shore. He thought there were much better stones down there, but Pelle shook his head. 'No, then I wouldn't be able to hear what you're saying.'

'Why do you have to hear everything I say?' asked Krister. 'Is it all that interesting?'

Pelle shook his head. 'No, I think it's stupid.'

Krister was used to people liking him—not children, of course, because he couldn't be bothered with them—but it irritated him that this little half-pint did not seem to like him at all and he wanted to know why.

'So you think I'm stupid,' he said in a friendlier tone of voice than he had so far used to Pelle. 'But there must have been stupider men than me who've gone out with Malin!'

Pelle looked at him silently and did not answer.

'Or perhaps there haven't,' said Krister.

'I'm just trying to think,' said Pelle.

Malin laughed and so did Krister, but not as heartily as she did.

After a moment's thought Pelle agreed that perhaps there had been one or two who were more stupid than Krister.

'How many have there been altogether?' asked Krister curiously. 'Can you count them?'

'Of course,' said Malin. She got up quickly and dived into the sea. 'But it's none of your business,' she said when her head bobbed up from the water again.

But Pelle had no objection to explaining. 'A couple of dozen at least,' he said. 'They call and call and call all day when we're at home—in town, of course. When Daddy answers the telephone he says, "This is the Melkersons" automatic answer phone. Malin is not at home." '

Malin shouted to Pelle, 'Shut up, can't you!'

Then she lay on her back in the water and floated, and as she looked up into the blue sky, she tried to work out which two had been stupider than Krister, but she could not reach any conclusion. Then she suddenly felt how much nicer this day would have been without him—this day and every day, and she decided then and there that this was the last time she would go out with Krister. Then she thought of Björn and sighed a little. She had been seeing a good deal of him lately. He was like one of the family in the Grankvist house, and Carpenter's Cottage was just a stone's throw from there. So he came almost every day on various pretexts and sometimes with no excuse at all. He brought fish he had just caught, or fresh mushrooms, which he put quietly on the kitchen table; he helped Johan and Niklas arrange their fishing tackle; he sat on the steps of Carpenter's Cottage talking to Melker —but Malin knew perfectly well who he came to see. He was so sweet, so polite and so absolutely nice and so much in love with her. She tried to see whether she was a little in love with him—she would like to be so much, but she could never feel her heart beating any faster when she thought of him. She wondered whether she would have to go through life without being in love with anyone. What a pity that would be! There must be something wrong with me, thought Malin, staring at her toes, which were sticking out of the water. Why were her brothers making all this fuss? She was never more than just a little in love with anyone. They really had no need to be so anxious.

She sighed and then looked up at the sun and thought that half this lovely day had already passed. And she wondered how her father had got along with the cooking.

But Melker had no intention of spending the day over the hot stove. 'Not when we have food right by our own jetty!' he said to Johan and Niklas. 'We'll have stewed perch for supper!'

He sent the boys to dig for worms and then he sat down on the jetty for two hours without catching so much as a minnow. On the other hand, Johan and Niklas landed one large perch after another and he did not envy them their pleasure. But after a while, he began to look very down in the mouth, for he had warned the boys beforehand that they should not expect their fishing to go that well while he, Melker, was around. He only had to whistle to the fish and they would come. So they were not to be disappointed if he caught more fish than they did. But now there they sat and pulled up fish after fish in front of his eyes, and he caught nothing. It really seemed unfair that he could not get a single bite.

'Not my day,' he said, and stared gloomily at his float.

Johan and Niklas looked almost guilty every time they got a bite. Dad must not be disappointed—that was one thing all the Melkerson children were unanimous about. None of them could bear to see his gay, blue eyes cloud over—and they clouded over so easily and for such childish reasons.

They could see now that he was growing more and more depressed. He had a way of stroking his chin with his hand, which they recognized and which was not a good sign. Finally he threw aside his fishing rod.

'The fish will have to look after themselves,' he said. 'I'm not going to sit here holding my fishing rod any longer.' He lay down on the jetty and pulled his beret down over his eyes. 'If any fish comes along and makes a fuss and wants to be caught, tell him that I'm asleep and he can come back at three o'clock.' Then he immediately fell asleep, and his float went on bobbing up and down. In spite of his sons' heartfelt prayers, no fish came, asking to be pulled up. So they decided to arrange it themselves. Their father must have one fish at any rate. They pulled in Melker's line and put their largest perch on his hook. Then they woke him up with loud shouts of 'Daddy, you've got a bite!'

Melker jumped up and grasped his fishing rod so eagerly that he almost fell into the sea, and he shouted with joy when he drew in his perch. 'Have you ever seen such a fine fellow! He's twice as big as any of yours!'

But this perch did not seem to be making much fuss about being caught. It lay there unnaturally still and Melker looked at it for a long time in silence while his sons regarded him anxiously.

'The poor creature looks stunned,' said Melker. He stroked his chin a few times and suddenly he smiled, like the sun quite unexpectedly bursting through dark clouds. He smiled affectionately at his sons.

'Now I'll go in and cook this perch—and a couple more,' said Melker. 'According to my own excellent recipe. At least that's something I can do better than you!'

Johan and Niklas assured him that he was the world's best fish cook and Melker went off to the kitchen. Malin would have shuddered if she had seen him cleaning the fish. He had a large knife and a small slippery perch, and this combination ought to have resulted in the most frightful blood bath, but the strange thing about Melker was that sometimes he weathered splendidly situations which seemed absolutely ripe for catastrophe.

He was in great good humour. He placed the fish in an enamel saucepan and sang his recipe as if it were an opera.

'Stewed perch à la Melker,' he sang. 'Five fine fishes . . . and then butter . . . plenty of butter, parsley, and dill. A little flour . . . a splash of water . . . just ordinary water . . . and salt according to taste . . . salt according to taste . . . salt according to t-a-a-a-ste!'

It sounded so good that he began to wonder if he had not missed his vocation and ought to have been an opera singer.

Now and again he looked at his water pipe, which was sticking in through the kitchen window, and every time he looked at it, he smiled contentedly. That was something to show Malin when she came home.

Almost immediately, he heard the motorboat arrive at the jetty and he rushed out to the well to show what he had done. As a matter of fact, Malin looked as if she needed to be cheered up. She hung her bathing suit on the line and looked strangely thoughtful, but when she felt Melker looking at her, she smiled. And then she saw the water pipe.

'What in the world is that?' she said, and Melker explained it to her and Krister and Pelle. A simple, first-class arrangement, it was, which from now on would make their life at Carpenter's Cottage so much easier.

'Have you tried it out?' asked Malin.

'Oh, yes—and how have you been getting along?' said Melker. Then he saw that Johan and Niklas had arived—and they knew a thing or two! So Melker told the truth. 'Yes, I have tried it out. Some water leaked on the ground and some onto the kitchen floor, but that will be all right as soon as I've got a trough.'

Melker was beaming all over. He was so delighted with his water pipe and so proud of it that he wanted to stroke it, and he did just that. But just where he put his hand sat one of Pelle's wasps, and when Melker felt the pain of the wasp's sting, he went quite berserk. Twice in the same day was really too much! He uttered a roar that made Krister jump, and looked around for a weapon of revenge. There on the grass lay one of the boys' croquet mallets. He seized it and when he saw the wasp still sitting on the pipe—so pleased with itself—he lifted the mallet over his head and brought it down as hard as he could. Then he stood there, quite paralyzed, on seeing what he had done. He had not killed the wasp. It was probably home in its nest, laughing its head off and boasting to the other wasps. But his pipe, his beautiful water pipe, was shattered in the middle and nothing more than a stump of it hung down from the wire.

At last Melker awoke from his dream, and then he hissed, 'Guess what I'm thinking of doing now?'

'Swearing?' suggested Pelle.

'No, that's ugly and uncivilized. But those damned wasps have got to go from Carpenter's Cottage—or else I go!' He lifted his croquet mallet, but Pelle hung onto his arm and shouted, 'No, Daddy, don't touch my wasps!'

Melker angrily threw the mallet away. He turned on his heel and walked down towards the jetty. It was the last straw— Pelle wanting his father to be perforated with wasp stings! Pelle ran after him to explain and to comfort him and so he did not see Krister's mighty deed.

The wasps' nest was just about high enough to be reached with a croquet mallet if one stretched a little, and Krister thought it would be fun to destroy that big grey mass of wasps. So he took the croquet mallet and aimed a hefty blow at it, but he missed and hit the wall next to the nest. The wasps had never heard such a noise in their lives and they did not like it. The whole army of them came out to avenge themselves. The first person they saw was Melker and they zoomed after him, ready for battle. Melker heard them coming and ran in a zigzag line, bellowing with rage all the time.

'Run, Daddy, run,' shrieked Pelle.

'I thought that was what I was doing,' roared Melker, and charged down towards the jetty.

Krister and Malin and the boys raced after him and Krister

laughed so much that he almost choked—without knowing how much Malin hated him for it.

Melker flailed wildly with his arms to protect himself against his tormentors, but he had already been given a few stings, and in his plight he saw only one way out.

He took a leap straight into the sea and his children saw him disappear below the surface. He intended to remain there for quite a time. The wasps buzzed around and looked for their prey, but all they could find was Krister, standing on the jetty laughing more than ever. But it was strange how quickly he changed his tune when the whole swarm of wasps headed towards him.

'Go away!' he shouted. 'Don't come this way!' But the wasps did not go away. And so Krister too gave a yell and dived head first into the sea. He was more furious than any wasp when he came up again, but Melker, who was treading water a little farther out, greeted him cheerfully. 'Good evening! You out for a walk too?'

'Yes, but I'm on my way home,' said Krister. And with a few more strokes he reached his motorboat. 'Goodbye, Malin!' he called. 'I'm going now. This island's dangerous. Perhaps we'll meet again some day!'

'Not if I can help it,' murmured Malin, but Krister did not hear.

Melker met Tjorven as he came wandering up towards Carpenter's Cottage and she smiled at him. 'Have you been swimming in your clothes *again*? Why are you always doing that? Haven't you got any bathing trunks?'

'Of course I have,' said Melker.

'But I don't suppose you can splash so well when you have them on,' said Tjorven.

'No, it's much better like this,' Melker admitted.

But then came the glorious moment when he was to help his children to the fish stew *à la* Melker.

Malin stood by the kitchen stove and lifted the lid from the saucepan. Oh, how good it smelled and how hungry she was!

'Daddy, you're fantastic,' she said.

Melker had changed his clothes and bathed his wasp stings. Now he was sitting at the kitchen table, once again in high spirits. Life was so rich! He smiled shyly at Malin's praise and said, 'Oh, well, they say that if men really applied themselves to cooking they would do it better than women. Not that I mean *I* . . . but we'll see. Let's taste it, at any rate!'

He served them in turn and said that no one was to begin until each had had his portion, but last of all he served himself. He looked hungrily at the white fish swimming in dill, parsley and butter. He was still smiling as he lifted the first bite to his mouth. But then a desperate little gurgling sound came from him.

Malin and the boys had begun to eat too, and they were sitting as if paralyzed.

'How much salt did you put in?' asked Malin, and put down her fork.

Melker looked at her and sighed. 'According to taste,' he said heavily.

Then he got up and disappeared and went out through the door, the children watching him with anxious eyes. Through the window they saw him sink down by the garden table where he had begun this day with such great expectations. Without a word they all rushed to the door.

'But, Daddy, why are you so upset?' said Malin, when she saw Melker sitting there, his face hidden in his hands.

'Because I'm worthless,' said Melker and looked up at her with his eyes full of tears. 'Live for the day—and what have I done? I've done *nothing* properly. Everything has been a failure,' he said. 'I expect I write bad books too. I can see that now. Yes, don't say a word, I do! Poor children, to have such a worthless father!'

They all threw themselves at him. They hugged him and assured him that no children had a cleverer or kinder or better father than they, and they loved him so much.

'Hmmm,' said Melker. He dried his tears with the back of his hand and then he smiled a little. 'Aren't I strong and handsome too? You didn't mention that!'

'Yes,' said Malin. 'You're strong and handsome too, and if you're that, it doesn't matter if you put a little too much salt in the fish.'

But Johan and Niklas had thrown away the rest of their fish and there was no other food in the house. The shop was closed and they were hungry.

'Is there any bread?' asked Niklas.

But before anyone had time to answer, Tjorven came in with Bosun at her heels and she said, 'Daddy is smoking herrings down on the beach. Would any of you like to come to a party?'

Live for the day—one minute there had been wailing and gnashing of teeth and the next, joy and delight.

They sat on the stones around Nisse's smokehouse and the sun sank in the bay, which flushed with the summer warmth. Nisse gave them golden brown smoked herring, as much as they could eat. Marta gave them butter and potatoes and home-baked rye bread. Melker made a speech. It was a song of praise to friendship and smoked herring, for he felt a surge of gratitude in his breast. Life was beautiful, and think how much could be had on one single poverty-stricken summer day!

'Yes, my friends,' said Melker, 'it's just what I always say—live for the day!'

'And what a lovely day,' said Pelle.

An Animal
for Pelle

Melker loved his children with a fierce, stormy love. Now and then he even thought about them. He was, of course, a writer and when anyone asked him whom he thought about most he would answer, 'Melker thinks of no one but Melker!'

But this was not altogether true, because sometimes he thought about his children. It seemed to him quite incredible that he really had four such beautiful things. And all of them were so different. First there was Malin, his prop and stay. How did she manage to be so wise when she was so pretty? Pretty girls were usually so taken up with their own prettiness that they seemed to have no time to become wise. Malin was different. Of course, he did not know much about the thoughts hidden behind her calm forehead, but he knew that there was wisdom there, and warmth and sound common sense. She was charming too, but as unconscious of it as a flower. Or so it seemed, at least.

Next came Johan. He was the most temperamental of all

the children, the one with the most imagination and also the most restless. He would not have an easy life, for he was too much like his father, poor child! Niklas, on the other hand, was calm, steady, and full of common sense, as he had been from the day he came into the world. He was the happiest and most stable of the whole Melkerson family. Life would be kind to Niklas, Melker was sure of that.

But then there was Pelle. How would he get along? How would life work out for someone who cried because people in a bus looked sad or because he met a stray cat which apparently had nowhere to live? He was in constant fear that people or cats or dogs, or even wasps, were not happy. How would he get along in the long run? And all the other strange things that he brooded over and questioned. Why did one feel like crying when one heard the telephone wires singing and why did wind in the trees sound so sorrowful? And the swish of the waves so dismal? Was it because of all the dead sailors? asked Pelle, with tears in his eyes. But he could be gay too in his own strange way. There were certain things that made him happy. For instance, sitting alone in a boathouse and listening to the rain on the roof, or creeping into a corner of the room when there was a storm, especially in the dusk, and sitting there, listening to the whole house creaking. Niklas tried to get out of him why he liked anything as strange as that, but Pelle only said, 'If you don't understand it yourself, I can't explain it to you.'

He was a naturalist besides, and there was always a great deal for a naturalist to do. For instance, lying on his stomach on the grass, watching all the insects moving around. Lying on his stomach on the jetty, looking down into the strange, green world where the little fishes lived their funny fishy lives. Sitting on the steps of the cottage at dusk and watching the stars come out one by one, trying to spot Cassiopeia, the Milky Way, and Orion. Pelle looked on the whole thing as a series of miracles and he was constantly trying to find out about things. He was dedicated and patient as a naturalist must be.

Melker sometimes felt a twinge of envy when he looked at his youngest son. Why wasn't one able to retain this sense of wonder all one's life?

Then there was Pelle's boundless love of animals. It was really sad that he had never had a dog. He had begun to talk about having one as soon as he was old enough to say 'Bowwow.' He had had goldfish and tortoises and white mice, but never a dog.

Poor Pelle! And then he had come to Seacrow Island and found a dog like Bosun. In Pelle's opinion, Tjorven must be the luckiest person in the world.

'But I would be quite satisfied if I had any kind of animal,' he explained to her. 'I've got my wasps, of course, but I would like to have an animal I could stroke.'

Tjorven was sorry for Pelle, and she was generous. 'You can have a little bit of Bosun. A few pounds!'

'Huh! One of his back legs,' said Pelle, and he went to his father to complain. 'Who wants one of a dog's hind legs? Do you really think that's enough to keep anyone happy?'

Melker was sitting in his little room behind the kitchen and writing, and the last thing he wanted was to think about his children and their needs at that moment.

'We'll talk about it another day,' he said, and waved Pelle away.

Pelle went away gloomily. But leaning up against the cottage wall he saw his fishing rod, which he had been given on his birthday last week. Even a fishing rod can be an experience and this was no ordinary fishing rod—it was the first one in his life. Pelle picked it up—the bamboo felt smooth and good in his hand and a sort of joy spread all through his body. He decided to go down to the jetty to fish. How nice Daddy had been to give him this fishing rod! He had given Tjorven one too, for she happened to have a birthday at about the same time.

So Pelle took his fishing rod and went down to the jetty. This was where Stina found him, and she rushed towards him joyfully. It was very seldom that she was allowed to be alone with Pelle. It was Tjorven who made the rules and decided who should play with whom. How she managed it, no one knew. It was not that she ever said anything in plain words, but things always turned out as she wanted. She, Tjorven of Seacrow Island, could play with whomever she liked, Stina or Pelle, whichever she fancied. Sometimes, when she was in the mood, all three might play together, but what was never allowed was for Pelle and Stina to enjoy themselves without her.

And now, on this warm August morning, without the least

suspicion of any evil in store, she made her way to Carpenter's Cottage and came on the other two, sitting together down on the jetty. She stopped dead and stared at them. They didn't realize it, for they were talking together, Stina laughing and gesticulating with her hands. It had to stop.

'Stina,' shouted Tjorven angrily, 'you aren't allowed on the jetty. Children aren't allowed—because they may fall into the sea!'

Stina started, but she did not turn her head. She pretended she had not heard. If she did not answer perhaps there would be no Tjorven.

So Stina crept a little closer to Pelle and said in a low, confidential voice, 'You'll get a bite soon, Pelle.'

But before Pelle had time to answer, Tjorven shouted again, 'Children aren't allowed on the jetty. Are you deaf?'

And now Stina realized there would have to be a battle, for the issue could not be avoided.

'Then I suppose you're not allowed on the jetty either?'

Tjorven sniffed. 'Huh, you and I are different.'

'Yes, especially you,' said Stina boldly. She had Pelle beside her, so she said things that otherwise she would not have dared to say.

Pelle sat there, looking as if he would much rather be somewhere else, and Tjorven said, 'As a matter of fact, Pelle isn't with you. He's with me.'

'Pelle *is* with me,' said Stina angrily.

Then Pelle realized he must say something. 'I'm with myself.'

He wished Tjorven and Stina were miles away, but now Tjorven had come to sit down on his other side and they all three sat there, looking at the float. At last, Stina said again, 'You'll get a bite soon, Pelle.'

Nothing more was needed to make Tjorven lose her temper. 'It's nothing to do with you. Pelle isn't yours.'

Stina leaned forward and looked her straight in the eye. 'And he's not yours, either—so there!'

'No, I'm my own,' said Pelle.

At that, Tjorven and Stina both fell silent. Pelle belonged to himself, and he sat there, feeling how good that was. No one was going to have even one of his back legs!

But Tjorven knew who Pelle really belonged to and she intended to make this quite clear to him, and so she said, just as Stina had done, 'You'll have a bite soon, Pelle.'

This was obviously not the right thing to say.

'No, I won't,' said Pelle impatiently. 'Stop chattering about it. I can't have a bite because there's no worm on my hook.'

Tjorven stared at him. She was an island girl and she had never heard anything as mad as what Pelle had just said. 'Why haven't you got one?' she asked.

Then Pelle explained. He had tried to put a worm on his hook, but he couldn't because he felt sorry for the worm. The worm had wriggled so much that Pelle had shuddered at the mere thought. Besides, he was sorry for the fish too, which might come and get the hook fastened in its mouth and so . . .

'But why do you sit there fishing then?' asked Tjorven.

Pelle explained even more impatiently. Hadn't he been

given a fishing rod? And anyhow he wasn't the only one who sat there fishing without catching any fish. He had seen people sitting for days on end without getting a single bite. The difference was that they were torturing the poor little worm, and quite unnecessarily. That he did not do, but otherwise he was fishing just like everyone else. Did she understand now?

Tjorven said she understood, and Stina said she understood, too.

Then they sat there and stared at the float for a long time and Tjorven realized that it was a lie to say that she understood. But the sun was shining and it was lovely down here on the jetty, and if only she could make Stina go it would be better still.

'Stina's going to be a waitress when she grows up,' said Pelle. Stina had told him this.

'I'm not,' said Tjorven. She did not really know what a waitress was, but if Stina said she was going to be one, she certainly wouldn't. Stina's mother was a waitress. She lived in Stockholm and sometimes came down to Seacrow Island. She was the prettiest thing Tjorven had seen, next to Malin. But waitresses could be as pretty as they liked—if Stina was to be a waitress, Tjorven would not be one for the world.

'What are you going to be when you grow up?' asked Pelle.

'I'm going to be fat and write books, exactly like Uncle Melker.'

Pelle raised his eyebrows. 'Daddy isn't fat!'

'Did I say he was?' said Tjorven.

'Yes, you did!' shouted Stina.

'You're deaf,' said Tjorven. 'I said that I was going to write books like Uncle Melker and that I was going to be fat. They're two different things.'

Stina had become braver and braver. She believed, quite wrongly, that Pelle was on her side, and so she said that Tjorven was silly. Then Tjorven observed that Stina was much sillier than Jansson's pig.

'I'll tell Grandpa you said that,' shrieked Stina, but Tjorven shouted, 'Telltale! Telltale!'

Pelle shivered with distaste. 'If only they'd leave me in peace,' he muttered. 'It's just one thing after another all the time.'

Then Tjorven and Stina were quiet again. No one said anything for a long time, until Tjorven began to find it boring.

'What are you going to be when you grow up, Pelle?' she asked, just to keep the conversation going.

'I'm not going to be anything,' said Pelle. 'I'll just have hundreds of animals.'

Tjorven stared at him. 'But you must be something!'

'No. I don't want to be anything.'

'Then you needn't,' said Stina ingratiatingly.

Now they were off again.

Tjorven grew angry. 'That's not for you to decide, anyway!'

'Did I say it was?' retorted Stina.

'Go home,' said Tjorven. 'Little children aren't allowed on jetties, I told you.'

'That's not for you to decide either,' said Stina.

Then Pelle shook himself as if he had been sitting on an anthill. 'Well, *I'm* going, anyhow,' he said. 'I can't stay here!'

Melker sat typing in the little room behind the kitchen. His window was open so that he could smell the flowers outside, and when he lifted his eyes from the typewriter he saw a little blue stretch of the bay, which was pleasant. But it wasn't often he had time to take his eyes off the paper. He was in the mood for writing, and when he was in the mood it was best to get on with it.

The worst of an open window was that too many sounds from the outside made their way into his writing world. He heard Malin arguing with Johan and Niklas. She wanted them to go for the milk, but they begged to be let off. Couldn't she send Pelle instead? They were just going off to explore the old wreck at Crow Point with Teddy and Freddy.

Obviously they managed to get around Malin. Melker heard their gay shouts die away in the distance and he was grateful for the silence which came with their departure.

Unfortunately it did not last long. Suddenly Tjorven stuck her nose through the window. She had just left Stina down on the jetty, for when Pelle disappeared, Tjorven hurried away too. She only waited to make it clear to Stina that she could never hope to play with Tjorven ever again, and Stina had said she could think of nothing better.

And now Tjorven had come up to Carpenter's Cottage to try to find Pelle and reason with him, but he was nowhere to be seen. Instead, she discovered her friend Melker through the window of the little room behind the kitchen.

'And you're just writing and writing and writing,' she said. 'What are you writing actually?'

Melker's hands slipped down off the typewriter keys. 'Nothing that you would understand,' he said shortly.

'Wouldn't I? I understand everything,' Tjorven assured him.

'But not this, at any rate,' said Melker.

'Do you understand it yourself, then?' Tjorven wondered.

She leaned against the window sill as if she planned to stay there for the rest of the day, and Melker groaned.

'Are you ill?' asked Tjorven.

Melker said that he felt quite well, but would feel better if she would disappear. And so Tjorven went. But after a few steps she turned around.

'Uncle Melker, do you know what? If you can't write so that I can understand it, you might as well stop writing altogether.'

Melker groaned again, sighed once, and then once more, for he saw Tjorven settle down on a stone, well within sight.

'If I sit here, I won't be in your way, will I?' she shouted.

'No, but you might just as well pull up grass with your toes in your own garden,' said Melker. 'There's more grass there, I believe.'

Of course, it was a very pretty picture, thought Melker—a sturdy little child on a stone among yellow buttercups and grass—but he knew that he could not write a single word as long as he had that child within view every time he looked up.

Then he heard Pelle coming along with the milk bottles, and he shouted to him wildly, 'Pelle! Take Tjorven with you! Here, I'll give you some money so that you can go and buy yourselves ice cream cones at the shop—and you needn't hurry back!'

Pelle had thought that he would have a nice walk all by himself without any womenfolk around. He needed to rest his ears after all that noise on the jetty, but ice cream cones were ice cream cones and of course he didn't mind Tjorven. She was very pleasant to be with when Stina wasn't there.

With tremendous satisfaction, Melker saw them disappearing up the path towards Jansson's farm with Bosun at their heels. He tried to collect his thoughts and had almost succeeded when he heard a little piping sound outside the window and Stina's nose appeared above the window sill.

'Are you writing fairy tales?' she said. 'Write one for me!'

'I am *not* writing fairy tales!' roared Melker, so loudly that Malin jumped when she heard him, although she was halfway to the shop.

Stina did not jump. She only blinked a little. Of course she realized that Uncle Melker was not really very happy, but that was probably because he did not know any fairy tales.

'I can tell you a fairy tale,' she said comfortingly. 'Then you can write it.'

'Malin!' shouted Melker. '*M-a-l-i-n!* Come and help me!'

Stina looked at his typewriter with interest. 'I suppose it *is* difficult to write books, especially the covers. Docs Malin write them?'

'*M-a-l-i-n!*' yelled Melker.

There is no need to hurry, Melker had said to Pelle. What an entirely unnecessary thing to say! One would have thought he knew nothing about children and had never seen Jansson's cow field. It was through this field that one had to go when one went for the milk.

The children walked along a little path between leafy birches, Tjorven, Pelle, and Bosun. There were no cows in the field at the moment, which Pelle was a little sorry about. But there were wild strawberries and flowers, and butterflies fluttering about; there were ants and their ant paths; there were large mossy stones to climb on and a bird's nest that Tjorven knew about in a birch. There was no need to tell them to take two hours to cross the field. There was even a fox's lair, Tjorven said. She had been there with her father early one morning and had seen it run inside the lair.

But now that she wanted to show it to Pelle, she couldn't find it. But Bosun could! First of all he had thought that Tjorven and Pelle were on their way to their secret hut, but as soon as he understood what it was that Tjorven was really hunting for, he looked at her as if he wanted to say, 'Silly little Bumble. Why didn't you ask me first?' And then he led them straight to the lair, right at the end of the field, as well hidden as any fox could wish in a heap of stones.

Pelle shivered with excitement. Down there in the dark passages was a fox. What did it matter if you could not see him when you knew that he was there, with his red coat and his long tail and his shining eyes! That was enough for Pelle.

They went to their secret hut too, as they were not in a hurry. It had been built as a protest against Teddy and Freddy and Johan and Niklas, the secret four. They had a secret hut somewhere and they had said that no one in the world who did not belong to their club would ever know where it was. Tjorven and Pelle had immediately suggested that they should join the club, but that was not allowed either, because they were too small, said Teddy, and the secret hut was far away on another island, a secret desert island, and no one was allowed to go there unless they were twelve years old or over. That was in the rules, said Teddy. Every morning for a couple of weeks, the secret four had taken a boat and rowed energetically away, while Tjorven and Pelle and Stina stood on the jetty, feeling very small indeed.

'We aren't too small,' said Tjorven. 'We'll make our own secret hut.'

And they had built one in Jansson's cow field. Even Stina had been allowed to help.

But two days later while they were sitting there being secret, Niklas had come and stuck his nose in. It was a lovely hut, he said, and very secret—although it could be seen every time anyone went to get the milk.

He had laughed a little and without meaning to had made their hut seem rather worthless, just a couple of boards and an old rug, where it was no fun to be at all.

But on this day there was no end to their enjoyment, for

when they at last reached the farm, Farmer Jansson was just going to take a couple of his cows over to Great Island.

Pelle went quite wild when he saw the cows and without thinking dumped the milk bottles in front of the farmhouse door.

'Oh, Uncle Jansson, can we come with you?' he cried.

He had never seen a cow ferry before in his life and he had never seen cows on a boat either. It was only on Seacrow Island that wonderful things like that happened. Tjorven had the feeling that she more or less owned the island and so it was thanks to her that there were fox's lairs and cow ferries. So she begged Uncle Jansson too, for she thought it would be a good thing to give Pelle a little extra pleasure when all it meant was being together with a couple of cows. Farmer Jansson was rather dubious, as he thought Bosun would take up about as much room as half a cow, but Tjorven assured him that Bosun could make himself so flat that he would take up no room at all, and then she led Pelle in triumph to the cow ferry.

There was not much room, in fact, and Pelle had a cow right against his face, but he thought it was very comfortable. He patted her damp muzzle and she licked his fingers with her rough tongue. Pelle laughed and looked blissfully happy.

'I would like to have a cow,' he said. 'I would like this one. Her eyes are so loyal.'

Tjorven shrugged her shoulders. 'All cows look the same,' she said.

Pelle never had a cow, either on that day or on any other day. But something quite fairytale-like happened to him. It began on the island, close by a rabbit hutch and a fisherman's cottage. By that rabbit hutch stood Knut Österman, a redheaded, thirteen-year-old boy, a friend of Tjorven, and the happy owner of three white rabbits, the sight of which excited Pelle so much that he could hardly speak.

'The ferry will be going back to Seacrow Island in an hour,' said Farmer Jansson, before he let Tjorven and Pelle loose on the island. 'If you aren't on the jetty when I come, you'll have to swim home.'

'Don't worry,' said Tjorven, and then she took Pelle with her to see Knut Österman, the owner of the rabbits. Pelle thought him the luckiest boy in the world.

'How about yourself?' said Knut, when Pelle had stood for a long time, worshipping the rabbits. 'Rollo, on Little Ash Island, has some rabbits for sale.'

From what Knut said, it seemed the simplest thing in the world to buy rabbits whenever one felt inclined. Pelle drew a deep breath. Could you really buy a rabbit as easily as all that? What would Daddy say, and what would Malin say? And then where could he keep his rabbit? Thoughts rushed through his head, but then he suddenly remembered something and the light in his eyes faded just as quickly as it had been kindled. 'I haven't any money.'

'Yes, you have,' said Tjorven. 'The ice cream money—and if I tell Rollo on Little Ash Island that it's enough, it will be enough.'

'But—but—' stammered Pelle.

'Take our boat,' said Knut. 'You can row there in five minutes.'

But that was something they were not allowed to do. Neither Pelle nor Tjorven was allowed to go out in a boat alone.

'Only five minutes!' said Tjorven. 'That's almost nothing!'

She arranged everything. Pelle was paralyzed and could raise no objection. She dragged him to Knut's boat and before Pelle knew exactly what was happening, she had rowed him over the narrow channel to Little Ash Island and introduced him to Rollo as a prospective buyer of rabbits.

And there *were* rabbits—long rows of rabbit hutches behind Rollo's house were filled with black, white, grey and spotted rabbits of all sizes. Pelle pressed his nose against the wire netting and smelled the wonderful smell of rabbit, hay, and dandelion leaves. He stood in front of every single cage and looked into the eyes of every single rabbit. But in one cage sat a lonely little white and brown rabbit, eating his dandelion leaves energetically.

'That one,' said Pelle. And that was all he said. He just looked at the rabbit and wondered how it would feel to hold it.

'He's the ugliest of the whole lot,' said Tjorven.

Pelle looked tenderly at the little brown-spotted creature.

'Is he? But his eyes are so kind,' he added.

Rollo was an old bachelor, who lived alone on his island and made his living by fishing and rabbit breeding. Once a week he went over to Grankvist's shop and bought his coffee and whatever else he needed, so he had no more been able to avoid Tjorven than anyone else in the islands.

Now she stood there in front of him with Pelle's money in her hand. 'You can have all this for that one,' she said, and pointed at the brown and white rabbit. 'Yes or no?'

'Oh, all right,' said Rollo uncertainly in the face of such a shameless piece of bargaining.

Then Tjorven pressed the money into his hand. 'Thank you. I knew you would.'

She quickly opened the rabbit hutch, pulled out the rabbit and put it into Pelle's arms. 'There you are!'

Rollo laughed.

'You can do business all right, young Tjorven. But you wait until I go to buy my coffee next week!'

Pelle held the rabbit. He shut his eyes and felt how soft it was. And suddenly, almost as if it hurt, came the realization that this incredible happiness was his. This was the most wonderful thing that could happen to anyone, and it had happened to him!

'Yes, that one will make a good stew when he's a bit older,' said Rollo.

Pelle turned pale. 'He will never be a stew—never!' he said violently.

'What do you want him for then?' asked Rollo.

Pelle pressed the rabbit close. 'For my own! I'm going to have him for my own!'

Rollo was not hardhearted. He agreed that you could keep

a rabbit for that reason too, although he himself had never thought of it. He thought it nice to see a boy so happy just because he had a scrawny little rabbit, and he became quite excited himself. He found a wooden box for Pelle to put the rabbit in, and went with him down to the jetty where Tjorven was already sitting at the oars.

'It's very warm today,' said Rollo, wiping the perspiration from his forehead. 'You're lucky, Tjorven, that you haven't got far to row.'

Tjorven looked knowingly at the clouds that had gathered on the horizon behind Little Ash and said gloomily, 'It's going to thunder!'

Yes, it certainly was a good thing that they did not have far to row. She was as brave as anyone, but she had one weakness. She was afraid of thunder, although she did not like admitting it. And she had scarcely begun to row before she heard the first faint roll.

Pelle did not hear it. He was sitting in the boat with the wooden box on his knee, looking in through the netting at his rabbit. His very own rabbit. It would need very heavy thunder to rouse him. But just then came a really loud clap, which made him look up. He saw Tjorven sitting there, looking as if she were going to cry, and he asked in surprise, 'Are you afraid of thunder?'

Tjorven fidgeted in her seat. 'No,' she said, 'not really— only sometimes—only when it's thundering.'

'Oh, there's nothing dangerous in it,' said Pelle, and felt proud that for once he was braver than Tjorven. Of course,

131

he did not like sitting in a kitchen all night, listening to the thunder, but he was not afraid of it, although he was afraid of a good many other things.

'Teddy says it isn't dangerous, too,' said Tjorven, 'but when it's thundering, I hear the thunder say, "I *am* dangerous"—and then I believe the thunder more than Teddy.'

Scarcely had she said this than there was another clap, which really did sound dangerous. Tjorven shrieked and put her hands over her face.

'Oh, look out! The oars!' said Pelle. 'Look at the oars!'

So Tjorven did. She looked at the oars and they were floating quite quietly on the water, both of them, and were already several yards away from the boat.

Tjorven had lost oars many times before and that did not frighten her; but now there was thunder as well. She did not want to sit at sea in an open boat, unable to get to land. She started to shout for Rollo and Pelle helped her. They could still see him. He was going up the hill towards his rabbit hutches, but he did not turn when they shouted to him.

'Are you deaf?' shrieked Tjorven. Quite obviously he was. Soon he was out of sight.

Pelle wondered nervously if this was what was called a wreck and if he would have to die now, just when he had got a rabbit.

'Not if you go on sitting in the boat till she drifts ashore on Knorken,' said Tjorven.

Around Great Island and Little Ash Island the islets lay scattered as thickly as raisins in a fruit cake. One of them was called Knorken and anyone with any sense could see that they could not possibly be wrecked, as their boat had just decided to drift ashore there in a suitable little creek. Tjorven steered it in by splashing with the bailer.

They had just managed to pull the boat up on shore when the rain came. It was like a wall over the grey-blue water and was approaching quickly. In a few seconds it would be over them like a flood.

'Run,' said Tjorven and she led the way, running across the beach towards the sheltering trees behind. Pelle raced after her as quickly as he could with his rabbit hutch in his arms and with Bosun pushing him at the back of his knees to help.

Then came a shout from Tjorven. A shout of joy. 'The hut,' she shouted. 'We've found the hut!'

And they really had. There it was, the secret hut they had heard so much about all summer. There could not be a finer hut on any other island in any other archipelago anywhere. It was hidden between thick, leafy branches and was built almost like a real house. The walls had been made of tightly packed moss and branches and the roof was of moss—a hut ought to look just like that! And they could not have found it at a better time. For now the rain burst over the little island of Knorken. They sat in the hut and looked out between the branches at the rain whipping up the sea.

'And here we are, absolutely dry,' said Tjorven happily. 'I'll really have to thank Teddy and Freddy when I get home.'

'We will never get home,' said Pelle, and strangely enough he did not feel frightened as he said it. For sitting in this hut with the rain pouring down outside was even better than sitting in a boathouse. And besides he had a rabbit—that was enough to make up for everything. He opened the box and patted his rabbit.

'You're not afraid, are you?' he said. 'You needn't be, because I'm here.'

Tjorven sat there, shining with contentment. It would be fun to get home and talk to Freddy and Teddy about the secret hut. She was really looking forward to that. And she was not at all afraid that they would have to stay on the island till they died. She was not afraid of anything any longer now that the thunder had stopped and the rain would soon stop too. You could play in this hut, thought Tjorven. You could pretend that you were shipwrecked and were thrown up on a desert island like that Robinson Crusoe Freddy had told her about. He must have had a hut just like this one. Pelle could be Friday. Who would be Robinson went without saying, but she meant to be a Robinson with a cosy little household, one who had strawberries for supper. She could see that the grass was thick with strawberries outside. If only Friday had been like ordinary people he could have taken Teddy's old fishing rod, which was standing outside the hut, and gone down to the sea and landed a couple of perch. For when you're shipwrecked you must eat the whole time, said Tjorven. But Pelle said he would rather die of hunger than torture any more worms today or any other day.

'Well, I suppose we will have to have just strawberries, then,' said Tjorven and went out in the wet grass.

Pelle took his rabbit with him and went down to the sea, not to fish but to try to get away from their shipwreck. He had found an old newspaper in the hut and if he stood on the shore and waved it as hard as he could then perhaps someone on Great Island would see it.

Pelle waved until his arms ached but it was no use. He was just as wrecked as before. He felt that by now it must be more than an hour and Uncle Jansson had most likely taken his cow ferry and gone back home to Seacrow Island. Probably he was angry, and they would all be very angry at home when they were told that Tjorven and Pelle had gone out to sea without permission and were lost.

It was a grim thought, but he had a rabbit and that made up for *almost* everything.

The water lapped, blue and glittering, for now the sun was shining again. Pelle sat down on a stone with his rabbit in his arms. Then he suddenly thought it would be a good idea to christen it.

'You can't just be called "my rabbit." You must have a real name, you know.' He thought for a long time and then he dipped his hand in the sea and christened the rabbit.

'You shall be called Yoka, Yoka Melkerson.'

It felt even better to have a rabbit which had a name. Now it was not just any little rabbit but a special one called Yoka. Pelle tried it out to hear how it sounded.

'Yoka. My little Yoka.'

But then Robinson called his man Friday, and he went obediently. Robinson had arranged some clover in a glass jar

135

on the sugar box which was the table and had put out the red strawberries on the green leaves, for this was a housewifely kind of Robinson, who shared his strawberries equally with his servant.

When they had eaten Tjorven said, 'That was good, but now I think we'll go home.'

Pelle almost lost his temper. Why did Tjorven say such stupid things, when she knew they could never get away from here?

'Of course we can get away from here,' said Tjorven. 'I can put a motor on the boat.' And she called, 'Here, Bosun!'

Pelle knew there was no dog in the whole world like Bosun. He had been together with him the whole summer and admired him for all the wonderful things he could do. Bosun could play hide-and-seek and he could work the seesaw. He could find things and he could retrieve things; once he had even retrieved Stina when she had fallen into the sea. But what he did now was more wonderful than anything else, thought Pelle. If only Daddy and Malin had been there to see it. If only they could have seen Bosun swimming along, pulling the boat behind him! The rope was fastened to his collar and he swam calmly and steadily straight to Great Island, while Pelle and Tjorven sat there like royalty without having to lift a finger. What a dog!

Tjorven did not think it was anything out of the ordinary, but Pelle sat back in the boat and loved Bosun so much that his heart almost burst.

'He's cleverer than a human being,' said Pelle.

The next moment he saw something which made him shout. 'Look, there are the oars!'

And so they were. They were bobbing gently, close to a little rock.

'What luck,' said Tjorven, when she got hold of them. 'Knut would have been very angry if we had come back without the oars.'

Then her face suddenly darkened, it was almost as if she were afraid of the thunder again. 'I know someone else who'll be angry now, and that's Uncle Jansson.'

He had a violent temper, she knew, for she was well acquainted with everybody on the island. Uncle Jansson could sound like the thunder when he was angry and Tjorven would have preferred not to see him just now.

'But I bet he went back to Seacrow Island ages ago,' said Pelle, 'and surely that's far better.'

They landed at the Great Island jetty. Tjorven set Bosun free and tied up the boat. And when Bosun had shaken off the water he looked at Tjorven with his wise, rather sad eyes as if to say, 'Little Bumble, is there anything else you want me to do?'

Tjorven took his great head between her hands. 'Bosun, do you know what? You're my own darling little soppy dog.'

There was nobody to be seen; no Knut, no Uncle Jansson. But the cow ferry was still there and that must mean that Uncle Jansson was rushing around furiously, looking for them.

They stood there on the jetty and felt miserable. Then they saw someone coming down the hill from the Östermans'. It was Uncle Jansson. Tjorven shut her eyes anxiously. Now they had nothing to do but wait for the scolding.

Uncle Jansson was so out of breath when he reached the jetty that he could scarcely speak.

'You poor children,' he said, 'here you are, still waiting for me! I *am* sorry—but I had to mend a fence first, you see, and then it began to rain and then I went in to see the Östermans and stayed there for a chat. You poor little children. Have you been waiting long?'

'Oh no, not very,' said Tjorven. 'But it doesn't matter!'

After four hours' work Melker put the cover on the typewriter contentedly and arranged the manuscript on the table. Then Pelle suddenly arrived outside the window.

'Why, here's our Pelle with the milk!' said Melker. 'You've been quick.'

But Melker was wrong. It wasn't 'our Pelle with the milk,' it was 'our Pelle' without the milk. The milk bottles were still outside Farmer Jansson's back door. But Pelle had something else with him, something which was hidden below the window sill.

'Dad, you did say I could have an animal soon, didn't you?'

Melker nodded. 'Yes, we really must think about that.'

Then Pelle put his rabbit on the table in front of him and Yoka, terrified, sent the manuscript pages flying all over the place.

'What do you think of this one?' asked Pelle.

Malin had a good deal to say when Pelle and Tjorven came into the kitchen and showed her Yoka.

'Darling Pelle, we are going back to town in a week. What are we going to do with Yoka then?'

But she had no need to be anxious about that. Uncle Jansson had promised that Yoka could live on his farm until it was summer again and Pelle came back.

This was a great moment in Pelle's life. He was proud of his rabbit, so proud that he seemed to send out a glow all around him. And it was even more fun when Johan and Niklas, Teddy and Freddy came rushing into the kitchen and wanted to look at it. Even Tjorven grew a little jealous.

'I should like to have a rabbit too,' she said.

'You can have a bit of him,' said Pelle. 'One hind leg!'

'Where did you get him?' said Johan eagerly. He thought he would like to have a rabbit.

'Oh, some place—where I went,' said Pelle.

No one except Knut and Rollo knew anything about their boat expedition, and Pelle and Tjorven had wisely decided to keep it a secret from the rest of mankind. It was a difficult decision. For it meant that Tjorven would not be able to talk about the secret hut with Teddy and Freddy, and she had looked forward to it so much.

Now she sat on top of the woodbin in the kitchen of Carpenter's Cottage and saw how the secret four were crowding around Pelle's rabbit. Pelle was fully occupied, showing off his rabbit; otherwise he would have seen the dangerous glint in Tjorven's eyes.

'Ho, yes,' said Tjorven suddenly. 'Keep everything secret!'

'What do you mean by that?' asked Freddy.

Tjorven smiled a wicked smile. 'Don't you ever go to your secret hut nowadays?'

The secret four looked at each other—they had almost forgotten the hut. Just at that moment they were very busy with the wreck out at Crow Point and they had no time to think about huts. They explained this to Tjorven.

'Then you might as well tell me where it is,' said Tjorven.

But Freddy repeated that the hut was to be a secret forever and no one who was not twelve years old and therefore included in the secret club could possibly know where it was.

Tjorven nodded her agreement. 'That's right! Keep everything secret!'

Then she stared out the window, looking as if she saw something very, very far away.

'There are lots of strawberries this year,' she said. 'I wonder if there are any on Knorken.'

The secret four looked hastily at each other and there was anxiety in their eyes, though they tried to keep it a secret, of course. But Tjorven saw it clearly enough and it made her feel completely satisfied with her day.

Pelle saw nothing but his rabbit. She could not expect anything from him and anyhow it was time for her to go home.

But down near Söderman's cottage she saw Stina. She was out pushing her new doll's pram. Only people whose mothers were waitresses in Stockholm had lovely things like that. Tjorven rushed over to her.

'Are you out for a walk with Lovisabet?' she said. 'Shall I help you?'

Stina beamed at her. 'Yes, of course.'

Tjorven pushed the doll's pram backward and forward along the jetty as far as she could go and then she lifted out the doll.

'Dear little Lovisabet, I suppose you would like to come out and have a look around,' she said, and sat Lovisabet comfortably with her back against a post.

'No, Lovisabet,' said Stina anxiously, and took a firm hold of the doll. 'Children aren't allowed out on jetties, surely you know that.'

But Tjorven calmed her. 'Yes, she is, when her mother is with her and Aunt Tjorven too—then she is.'

The Odd Thing About Summers

The odd thing about summers, wrote Malin in her diary, *is that they are over so quickly.*

Before the Melkersons really felt they were settled in, their first summer on Seacrow Island had come to an end, and it was time to go back to town.

'I can't think of anything more crazy,' said Niklas. 'Why do the schools have to begin again in the middle of the summer holidays? Can't you write to the school supervisors, Daddy, and tell them to change such a stupid habit?'

Melker shook his head. 'The school supervisors are as hard as nails. It's you who must just adapt yourself,' he said.

It feels as if we got here only a moment ago, wrote Malin in her diary, *and now we have to leave everything. It seems very hard. Pelle must leave his rabbit and his strawberry patches, Johan and Niklas their huts and fishing rods, their swimming and their sunken wrecks, Daddy his bay in the dawn light and his Carpenter's Cottage. As for me, what have I to leave? My summer meadows, my apple trees, my*

142

mushroom patches, my woodland paths and the silent evenings. No more sitting on the steps of Carpenter's Cottage watching the path of moonlight across the dark bay. No more swims beneath a night sky bright with stars. No more nights in my attic room lulled to sleep with the cradle song of the waves in my ears. It will be hard. And the people here who have been our friends, we must leave them too. How I shall miss them!

But we are going to have a farewell party, Daddy decided that, and I have been spending my days thinking out the menu. We will have a mushroom omelette and delicious little rissoles, and a cream cake with our coffee.

Melker was delighted with his party; he wanted to finish with fireworks, which he said would be the high spot of the summer, but Malin would not have it for she remembered the time when Melker had set off all the firecrackers at the same moment.

'Yes, the high spot of the summer, I can well believe that,' said Malin, 'but there are going to be no fireworks here until the last ones have been completely forgotten.'

She said that cream cake was a much more soothing finish, and they ate it out in the garden on a warm August evening with the bay as bright and smooth as a mirror. 'Everything more summery than ever!' said Niklas.

Pelle, Tjorven, and Stina sat on the steps of Carpenter's Cottage and Malin allowed them as much cream cake as they could possibly eat. Pelle enjoyed himself, but he, like Melker, considered that fireworks would have been more fun.

'Yes, but what if you had seen Daddy explode and go sailing away over the bay with his hair on fire?' said Malin. 'And, anyway, wasn't the cake good?'

'Malin, do you know what?' said Tjorven. 'It's so fantastically good that you have to smack your lips when you eat it.'

'Goodness!' said Malin. 'I would have been quite happy just to hear that it was good.'

'But that would have sounded as if we were talking about ordinary bread!' objected Tjorven.

Söderman drank three cups of coffee, although he knew it was not good for his stomach, but he needed something to comfort him, he said, now that Malin was going away for a bit.

'Yes, if it would help I would have a whole bathtubful,' said Björn, holding out his cup to Malin. His eyes were gloomy and she tried not to look at him.

'With most summer visitors,' said Nisse, 'it's generally fun when they come and when they go, particularly when they go. But Carpenter's Cottage without the Melkersons will really seem empty!'

'I know you will be coming back next summer,' said Marta.

It was then that Melker had his bright idea. 'Why couldn't we come to Carpenter's Cottage for Christmas? Ha, ha! Who is the world's greatest idea man? Melker Melkerson! I've taken the cottage for the whole year for safety's sake.'

There was a shout of joy from the children and Malin turned eagerly to Marta and Nisse.

'Would that be possible? Could we live in Carpenter's Cottage in the middle of the cold winter?'

'If we begin to light the fires in the middle of October, it will be all right,' said Nisse.

Melker declared that he could not have the whole of Carpenter's Cottage, for which he had paid rent, standing empty for the rest of the year. One must have value for money and must spend Christmas here even if one's ears are frozen stiff.

He took hold of Tjorven and danced around and around with her. 'With a hey and a ho and a hey-nonny-no, we'll have a happy Christmas Eve together-o!' he shouted. 'And not only at Christmas but now, this very evening,' said Melker, 'because we are going to meet again in a couple of months. I want to see happy faces around me—did you hear what I said, Bosun?' he asked sternly, because Bosun lay looking sadder than ever. 'Malin, give him a piece of the cake and see if that helps,' said Melker.

Bosun ate the cream cake, but it had no effect on his sad face.

'Although he thinks it's fantastically good anyhow, I know that,' said Tjorven.

Pelle sat on the steps with his head in his hands. He felt as gloomy as Bosun looked. Everything came to an end, cream cakes and summers and perhaps life itself for all he knew.

But strangely enough a little bit of cream cake had been left over and when the party came to an end the plate stood there as a treat for all the wasps. Lucky wasps! They could

145

stay in Carpenter's Cottage, for little wasps had no need to go back to town and go to school.

However, they did not get their cake. Tjorven had discovered it and she immediately shooed away the wasps. She had eaten three pieces of cake already but this one looked better than any of the others, with its little pink marzipan rose on the top, and Tjorven wanted it. She looked around to see if Malin was there because she was not used to taking things without permission, but Malin had disappeared with Björn, and Uncle Melker was nowhere to be seen either.

In fact there was absolutely no one to ask, and at any moment someone else might come and see the cake and want it too, so she must act fast. And Tjorven put her hands together and prayed.

'Dear God, may I take the piece of cake?' And she answered herself with the deepest bass voice she could muster, 'Yes, you may!'

And then the cake was finished and the party was over. The summer was over too . . . wasn't it?

No, the summer was not over just because the Melkersons had left the island. Warm September days came with the humming of wasps and the fluttering of butterflies. Quiet October days came, as clear as crystal. The boathouses down on the jetties mirrored themselves in water so still that it was almost impossible to know what was the actual thing and what was the mirror picture. But Tjorven knew and she explained it to Bosun.

'What you see upside down are boathouses too, but they belong to mermaids, you see. And they swim in and out, playing together, the whole day.' Tjorven played hide-and-seek with Bosun in the boathouses that were not upside down. She would have been very lonely without him, with Teddy and Freddy at school every day, and with Pelle and Stina far away in distant Stockholm, where she herself had never been and which she knew nothing about. But she had Bosun and she filled her days with the solitary child's strange, wonderful games. She did not feel lonely.

And slowly the autumn darkness sank down over Seacrow Island and the people who lived there. The lights shone out of the windows in the evening, small, solitary lights in the midst of the coal-black darkness. So few people lived out here on the island, and when the darkness came and the autumn storms whipped around their houses and the sea lashed furiously against their jetties and boathouses, there were one or two among them who wondered why they lived in the uttermost part of the sea; but they knew they could not live anywhere else.

The boat from the town came only once a week. There were no summer visitors on board; nobody except the crew, but Nisse went down to fetch his goods and stood waiting without fail, for the boat to arrive. And Tjorven waited too with Bosun beside her in all weathers—even though sometimes it was pitch-black when the boat eventually arrived and even though there was no Pelle on it.

But Pelle wrote letters, because he was back in school and

he could write with capital letters. He did not write to Tjorven but to Yoka, although it was Tjorven who had to go to Yoka on Uncle Jansson's farm and tell him what was in the letter after Freddy had read it to her.

'DEAR LITTLE YOKA,' wrote Pelle, 'HOLD OUT; HOLD OUT—I'M COMING SOON.'

One morning when Tjorven woke there was ice on all the puddles in which she had paddled the day before. For a long time she had great fun, crushing the ice to pieces under her boots. But the following day there was still more ice and it grew colder and colder until one night even the bay was frozen.

'I have never seen ice so early,' said Marta.

The icebreaker had to come and make a channel for the boat and it still took ten hours to work its way through the ice to the outlying islands.

And then at last it was Christmas. The Grankvists' shop was full of Father Christmas advertisements and all the people from all the islands around crowded in to buy Christmas fare. Teddy and Freddy had Christmas holidays and helped in the shop. Tjorven was in the way everywhere.

'Only a few days now to Christmas Eve,' she said, 'and I can't waggle my ears yet!'

She saw a lot of Söderman at this time and he had told her that Father Christmas particularly liked people who could waggle their ears—because it looked friendly, so Söderman claimed.

He was able to do it, but he was going to Stockholm to

spend Christmas with Stina and who would be left to waggle their ears in a friendly manner at Father Christmas out here on Seacrow Island?

'It will have to be you, Tjorven,' said Söderman, and Tjorven practised patiently and perseveringly.

Three days before Christmas the steamer *Seacrow I* came through the ice channel with the Melkerson family on board. They all stood at the rail, staring at their summer island, which now lay white and silent, engulfed in snow and surrounded by ice, strangely beautiful and unfamiliar with white roofs on all the boathouses and empty jetties where no boats were moored. It was their summer island but they did not recognize it.

But they could see Carpenter's Cottage among the snowy apple trees. Smoke was rising from the chimney and Melker had tears in his eyes. 'It feels like coming home, at any rate,' he said.

And there stood Nisse Grankvist on the ice beside the channel, and now Teddy and Freddy were rushing down and there was Jansson arriving in his sledge with Söderman and Tjorven. A thin little clang of bells reached their ears and Pelle responded with his whole body. It was Christmas now and he would soon see Yoka again. And Bosun—there he was! Pelle's eyes lit up when they caught sight of him. Tjorven waved and shrieked but he did not notice it. He saw no one but Bosun.

'Everything is quite different from summer,' Johan and Niklas decided. Not Teddy and Freddy, of course; they shouted and yelled and squawked like cormorants and were, thank goodness, the same as ever. But otherwise it was like coming to a different world. Neither Johan nor Niklas gave a thought to what it would be like to live in this world in the midst of snow and ice, alone and cut off from civilization. They regarded all this wintry difference as something exciting and adventurous, arranged more or less for their pleasure.

The boat at last came to a stop. It could not get right in to the jetty and they had to climb down onto the ice by a ladder.

'At last we've reached the North Pole,' said Johan. 'All members of the expedition disembark!'

He climbed down the ladder first and the others followed. Then they saw Björn coming across another ladder which had been laid right across the steamer channel. It was a shaky and rather precarious bridge, but it was the sort of bridge one had to use if one lived at Norrsund and wanted to get over to Seacrow Island, and Björn had obviously wanted to get to Seacrow Island today.

'Why have you come? Something special?' Söderman asked disagreeably.

But Björn did not answer, for now he saw Malin. 'With a hey and a ho and a hey-nonny-no! We'll have a happy Christmas together-o!' shouted Melker and grabbed hold of Tjorven, but she dragged herself loose because she wanted to go with Pelle and so she must hurry.

Pelle had no time to say hello to anyone but Bosun. Then he ran across the ice to the jetty as fast as his legs could carry him, and as quickly he ran down the whole of the village street.

Tjorven could not keep up with him. She shouted angrily to him but he did not stop and she saw him disappearing in the dusk far in front of her. But she knew where she would find him.

'Yoka, little Yoka, here I am. I've come back to you!' Pelle was sitting with his rabbit in his arms when Tjorven walked into Jansson's cowshed. It was so dark that she could hardly see him, but she heard him prattling to his rabbit, almost as if Yoka had been a human being.

'Pelle, guess what I can do,' said Tjorven eagerly. 'I can waggle my ears now.'

But Pelle did not listen to her. He went on talking to Yoka and she had to say it three times before he bothered to answer her.

'Let me see,' he said at last.

And Tjorven stood in the sparse light by the window and began. She made the wildest grimaces and then she asked hopefully, 'Was that all right?'

'No,' said Pelle.

He did not understand why it was important to waggle one's ears, but Tjorven explained to him how much Father Christmas liked people who could. Then Pelle laughed loudly and said that, to begin with, there was no Father Christmas and that meant that he could not like people who could waggle their ears any more than he liked other people. So it would be much better for her to learn something more useful, whistling for example. Pelle could whistle, and with Yoka tenderly clasped in his arms he whistled 'Good King Wenceslas' to him and to Tjorven too, if she cared to listen.

151

Pelle did not know what he was doing when he said his piece about Father Christmas. Tjorven's childish belief was dealt a tremendous blow. Could it be true that there was no Father Christmas? As Christmas Eve approached she became more and more afraid that Pelle might be right and by the time she sat at breakfast on Christmas Eve, eating her morning porridge, her disbelief and despair had gone so far that she had more or less lost faith in Father Christmas. It was no fun at all. What sort of Christmas Eve was this going to be? No Father Christmas and—and, besides that, porridge for breakfast! She pushed her plate away from her in disgust.

'Eat up, little Bumble,' said her mother kindly. She did not understand why Tjorven was so gloomy. It was this sort of porridge that Father Christmas liked best, she assured her.

'Then he can have mine,' said Tjorven miserably. She was furious at that old Father Christmas who half did not exist, and half wanted you to eat porridge and waggle your ears, and she said crossly, 'Eating and believing in Father Christmas seem to be the only things a kid is supposed to do.'

Nisse realized that something was wrong. He almost always understood when things were wrong with Tjorven and could work out the reason, and when Tjorven looked him straight in the eyes and asked, 'Is there a Father Christmas or isn't there?' he knew that all the enchantment of her Christmas Eve would disappear if he answered, 'No, he doesn't exist.' So he showed her the old wooden bowl that his own grandmother had filled with porridge every Christmas Eve and put out at the corner of the house for Father Christmas.

'What if we did that too?' said Nisse. 'Shall we put your porridge here in the bowl and put it out for Father Christmas?'

Tjorven brightened as if a candle had been lit within her. Of course there was a Father Christmas if Daddy's grandmother had believed in him. And how delightful that he really did exist and came creeping around the house on Christmas Eve. It was a good thing too that he liked porridge so that you didn't have to eat it yourself. Everything was all right now and she would tell Pelle.

She did not meet him until it was getting dark, when they all stood together down on the icy jetty of Carpenter's Cottage and watched Father Christmas' sledge appearing from out on the ice. He had a torch to light his way and looked just as Father Christmas should look. He had Jansson's horse and sledge, Tjorven could see that, but of course Father Christmas had to borrow a horse when he had so many Christmas presents to carry.

Even Pelle was struck dumb. His eyes grew larger and larger and he pressed himself closer to his father. Father Christmas threw two sacks of presents onto the jetty, one for the Melkersons and one for the Grankvists. It was all done as quickly as when the crew aboard the steamer threw goods ashore, and then the sledge disappeared in the darkness.

Pelle stood wondering whether there actually was a Father Christmas after all and then he saw Johan laugh and wink at Niklas and he became almost angry. Did they really think that he was just a baby and that they could make him think whatever they liked? But whether or not there was a Father

Christmas, it was great fun to stand here in the darkness and hear the sledge bells and see the light from the torch disappearing out in the bay and have a whole sackful of Christmas presents besides.

In fact it was wonderful to be Pelle during these winter days on Seacrow Island. Malin watched him going about shining with happiness and one evening when they were alone in the kitchen she asked him why he was enjoying himself so much. Pelle crept up onto the kitchen sofa and thought for a moment and then he told Malin what was such fun.

'For example,' he said, 'going out first thing in the morning when there's new snow and helping to shovel a way to the well and the woodshed. Seeing the tracks of different birds in the snow. Putting the Christmas wheatsheaf up in the apple tree for all the sparrows, bullfinches, and tits. Having a Christmas tree which you've brought from the woods yourself. Coming home to Carpenter's Cottage as dusk is falling when you've been out skiing, and stamping off the snow in the hall, and coming in and seeing the fire burning in the kitchen grate, and seeing how the kitchen looks with all the lights. Waking up in the morning while it's still dark and hearing Daddy making a fire in the stove. Lying in bed and watching the light flicker behind the shutters of the stove. Crossing the attic in the evening and feeling a little frightened of the dark, but only a little! Going out on the ice right to the edge of the steamer channel and feeling a little afraid. Sitting in the kitchen and talking to Malin—like now—eating buns, drinking milk, and not being afraid at all. Oh, and of course, sitting in Jansson's cowshed and talking to Yoka—that's almost the greatest fun of all. But have you heard that the fox took one of Jansson's hens again last night?' he asked Malin.

Pelle was afraid of that fox. For two consecutive evenings he had taken hens from Jansson, and a fox who took hens could also take rabbits. That was a dreadful thought. The fox was creeping about everywhere. Of course, it was the fox which had eaten Tjorven's Christmas porridge, although she thought it was Father Christmas. What did Malin think? wondered Pelle.

'Perhaps the fox, and perhaps Father Christmas,' said Malin.

Pelle lay awake for a long time that evening and was anxious about his rabbit. Of course, he had Yoka safely in the cowshed, but foxes were cunning, particularly when they were hungry.

Foxes should be shot, thought Pelle. He was not generally so bloodthirsty, but now he lay in his bed and in his mind's eye saw the fox leaving his lair in the cow field and creeping across the quiet snow towards Jansson's cowshed.

Pelle began to perspire as he lay there, and he slept fitfully all night.

Next morning he happened to meet Björn, who was coming from the forest with a newly shot hare. Pelle shut his eyes to avoid seeing the poor little hare. Why didn't Björn shoot that stupid fox instead? Uncle Jansson would be very glad if he did. Björn thought so too when he heard what had happened.

'We must put an end to that rascal. You can tell Jansson that I'll try tonight.'

'What time shall we come?' Pelle asked eagerly.

'We?' said Björn. 'You won't be coming at all. You'll be lying in your bed asleep.'

'I certainly won't,' said Pelle.

He did not say this to Björn, but to Yoka a little later, for the wonderful thing about Yoka was that he could not make any objections.

'Don't be afraid if you hear a shot tonight,' said Pelle, 'because I'll be with you, you can be sure of that.'

And he was, but he had very nearly broken his promise to Yoka. He had lain blinking his eyes to keep himself awake until Johan and Niklas had gone to sleep and then he had crept out through the kitchen door, with Daddy and Malin sitting in front of the fire in the sitting room with the door open to the kitchen. It was a miracle that they had not heard him.

And then he had gone out into the moonlit night and had run along a snowy road, absolutely alone, to the dark cowshed which was not at all as homely as it usually was. He had crept in silently, afraid that Björn might see him. He was really afraid as he felt his way over to Yoka. 'Oh, little Yoka, I am here after all!'

A cowshed at night is a strange place. It is silent; the cows are asleep, but one hears noises. Now and then a chain rattles when a cow shifts a little. Now and then a hen cackles, as if she were dreaming about the fox. Now and then you can hear Björn fixing his gun and whistling quietly behind his shutter. The moon shines in through the window and there is a path of moonshine across the floor. The farmyard cat glides over it and is immediately swallowed by the darkness again, and you can see only his yellow eyes shining. Poor farmyard rats, if they are out tonight. And poor Yoka, if Pelle were not there to protect him from the fox. He presses Yoka close to him and enjoys feeling how soft and warm he is, wondering how long it will take. Perhaps, just now, at this very moment, the fox is creeping across the snow towards Jansson's farmyard.

At any rate it is just now, at this very moment, that Melker goes up to tuck in his boys. In Pelle's bed he finds no Pelle but a piece of paper and a message written in large capital letters: I AM OUT SHOOTING FOXES FOR JANSSON.

Melker took the paper down to Malin. 'What do you think about this? Can Pelle be out shooting foxes for Jansson in the middle of the night?'

'No, certainly not,' said Malin firmly.

You get sleepy, sitting in a cowshed with a warm rabbit in your arms. Pelle was just about to fall asleep when suddenly he started. He heard Björn cocking his rifle and in the moonlight he could see him over beside the shutter in the wall. He saw him lift the rifle and aim.

Now—now, the fox is coming, and now he is going to die, his life is over. He will never return to his lair in the cow field and it is Pelle who has arranged it all!

With a shriek Pelle put the rabbit hastily back and rushed out to Björn. 'No, no, don't shoot!'

Björn was absolutely furious. 'What are you doing here? Get out of the way—I'm going to shoot.'

'No,' cried Pelle and clung to his legs. 'You mustn't! Foxes have to live too!'

And certainly no fox died that night for Pelle's sake. There was no fox out there in the moonlight, but instead Malin on her skis. Björn turned white. Think what would have happened if he had shot, if Pelle had not stopped him!

'It was a good thing you came,' said Pelle to Malin when he lay in his bed again. He had promised never to go on a fox hunt at night again and Malin had assured him that the fox could not take Yoka as long as he was securely fastened in his hutch.

But now Pelle lay fidgeting. There was something that troubled him even more than the fox. 'Malin,' he said, 'are you going to marry Björn?'

Malin kissed him, laughing. 'No, I'm not,' she assured him. 'The fox can't catch Yoka and Björn can't catch Malin as long as we each stay in our little hutch.'

Winter days were short and dusk came early. During the long evenings everyone collected in the kitchen, which was the warmest spot in the cottage. To tell the truth, it was the only really warm place in the whole of Carpenter's Cottage.

The nights were cold. The boys slept in their attic in warm pyjamas and sweaters. Melker fared well in his little room off the kitchen, but Malin had to move down to sleep in the kitchen.

'Two attics needing fires will not do,' said Malin and she enjoyed herself on her kitchen sofa. 'The only drawback is that one never gets to bed early in the evenings,' she said, 'because everyone is cluttering up the kitchen.'

Nisse and Marta came there for an evening cup of coffee and a chat. Teddy and Freddy sat there playing Casino with Johan and Niklas. Tjorven and Pelle drew and played. Bosun lay in a corner and slept, Malin knitted, Melker sang and chatted and was generally happy.

Outside it was the coldest of winters. Cold stars shone over the icy bay and the cold hit you as you turned the corners. Then it was delicious to settle down in a warm kitchen. Pelle beamed and filled the stove with wood; this was all just as it should be, with everyone sitting together, warm and cosy, singing and talking. Until at last he grew so sleepy that he heard everything in a kind of hum and tottered to bed.

Otherwise, Pelle spent most of his time in Jansson's cowshed. Not only with Yoka. He helped Uncle Jansson to clean it out and he came home smelling so strongly of cowshed that no one could go near him. Malin had to put aside a pair of old ski pants and an ancient cast-off jacket as cowshed clothes, which Pelle had to take off in the hall as soon as he got indoors.

'Then we will burn them when we leave,' said Malin.

'No, I'll take them with me to town,' said Pelle, with unexpected fervour. Malin was about to destroy something that he had thought out and a little shyly he explained to her what it was. 'I want to keep them in a special cupboard,' he said, 'and when I miss Yoka badly I can go there and smell them.'

Tjorven went with him to Jansson's cowshed once or twice, but finally she got tired of it. 'I don't want to be with cows the whole time,' she said.

Instead she skied. She had been given a pair of skis for Christmas and she struggled about the island perseveringly. When she fell she found it difficult to get up by herself, so she lay there, kicking her legs like a beetle, until Teddy or Freddy helped her onto an even keel again. But they were very seldom around nowadays. They spent most of their time with Johan and Niklas, being 'secret' again. They had a secret snow castle, which anyone with eyes in his head could see down by Crow Point. They spent most days there, but sometimes they grew tired of it and set out on long ski tours across the ice to other islands, or else they fished for herrings with Söderman, who was at home now and swore he would not go to town again for a long time.

Everyone was busy with his own affairs and Tjorven continued to be a rather solitary Tjorven, with Bosun as her dearest companion. One very cold day when the sky was icily green over Seacrow Island, and the whitebeam by Carpenter's Cottage was white with hoarfrost, Malin came home from a ski trip and found Tjorven crying on the little hill behind Söderman's cottage. She generally only cried when she was angry, but this was an unhappy crying because her feet were so cold that they ached and she was overcome by that feeling of desertion which comes when one has been wandering about in the snow for hours and has suddenly noticed how terribly cold one is. Söderman's cottage was locked up, and there was no one at home either there or at Carpenter's Cottage, and Teddy and Freddy had forgotten that they had promised to look after her while Mummy and Daddy were in Norrtälje. So when she saw Malin, the tears, which till then had only been a lump in her throat, suddenly welled out of her eyes.

Malin picked her up and carried her home to Carpenter's Cottage and sang to her as she carried her. And when they arrived in the kitchen of Carpenter's Cottage, Malin did something very strange, something fantastically strange, thought Tjorven.

'But you can't undress and go to bed in the middle of the day,' said Tjorven.

'Yes, you can, especially when little children have to have their toes warmed. It's the best way,' Malin declared.

They both lay comfortably on Malin's sofa, and it was warm, like heaven for anyone who had been wandering about in the snow for four hours. Tjorven's eyes began to shine.

'Can you feel my toes?' she asked, and Malin assured her with a shiver that she could for they were certainly the coldest child's toes that had ever been thawed out on this kitchen sofa.

Tjorven could not get over her surprise at Malin's strange behaviour. Now and then she laughed, as she thought that it was quite unlike anything else she had ever done.

'But you shouldn't go to bed in the middle of the day,' she said again.

'Yes, you should—if your hands and feet are full of snow and your eyes are full of tears, you certainly must,' said Malin.

Tjorven yawned. 'Don't sing that sad little song you've just been singing. Sing one that makes toes warm.'

Malin laughed. From where she lay she could see the frost flowers on the window and the pale winter sun, which shone so coldly through the branches of the whitebeam and which would so soon go down and leave Seacrow Island in the darkness and creaking cold. To be sure, they needed songs that would make their toes warm! So she began:

> *Gently blows the summer breeze,*
> *The cuckoo calls among the trees—*

and then she stopped, for she felt a violent longing for summer, so violent that she could not go on. But she did not need to, because Tjorven was asleep.

Two Enchanted Princes

One spring day Tjorven fell into the sea from the steamship jetty. She had lived in the belief that she could swim at least five strokes, but now she realized that she was wrong. Still, she was not afraid, for before she had time to be, Bosun had pulled her out and by the time Nisse came running, she was already on the jetty, wringing water out of her hair.

'Where's your life jacket?' asked Nisse sternly.

'Daddy, do you know what?' said Tjorven. 'When Bosun's with me I don't need a life jacket.' She flung her arms around Bosun and put her wet head close to his. 'Bosun,' she said tenderly, 'you are my own darling little soppy dog.'

Bosun looked seriously at her and, if it was true that he could think like a human being, perhaps he was thinking, Little Bumble, I would die for you if you wanted me to. You have only to say the word!

Tjorven patted him. Then she laughed contentedly. 'Daddy, do you know what?'

But Nisse stopped her. 'No, Tjorven, no more 'Do you know whats' before you have been home and changed your clothes.'

'Oh, but I only wanted to say that now I've fallen into the sea three times—and Stina has only fallen in twice!' And Tjorven went off, pleased that she would be able to show herself off to Stina.

On the slope in front of his cottage Söderman was tarring his boat. He was about to refloat it. The whole of Seacrow Island was engaged in spring-cleaning. The sea was free of ice once more, and all the boats were being made ready. The whole island was enveloped in the smell of tar and paint and the continual smoke from burning leaves. But stronger than all the other smells was the smell of the sea. Söderman felt it in his nose and he felt the spring sun warming his back. His boat looked splendid, he was feeling very content, but his brain was beginning to get tired, for Stina was sitting in the sun beside him, telling him fairy tales which seemed never to come to an end. Poor Söderman, it was impossible for him to keep track of which prince was turned into a wild pig and which was turned into an eagle. But Stina kept questioning him at regular intervals and she would stand for no mistakes. 'Guess who was enchanted then!'

But then Tjorven appeared in front of her, as wet as a mermaid.

'Guess who's fallen into the sea!' said Tjorven.

Stina gazed at her silently. She did not know that falling into the sea was something to boast about, but when she saw how triumphant Tjorven looked, she said, 'Guess who will fall into the sea on Sunday!'

'Not you, at any rate,' said Söderman. 'If you do I'll send you straight back to town when the Melkersons go.'

The Melkersons had brought Stina with them when they came. They had come out for a few days' spring visit, for Melker continued to believe that one could not have the whole of Carpenter's Cottage standing empty when one had paid for it. And besides, never was Seacrow Island more beautiful than at this time of the year, when the birches had their first tender leaves and the whole island was a sea of white anemones.

'Oh, my goodness, our Swedish spring!' Melker would say. 'It's cold and bare, but it's so beautiful that it pulls at the heartstrings!'

Tjorven certainly felt that the spring was cold. She was shivering and now she wanted to go home and get dry clothes. But as she passed the jetty of Carpenter's Cottage, Uncle Melker was sitting there in his boat, working away at the old motor, so Tjorven stopped.

Melker liked talking to Tjorven. 'It's the most amusing thing I know,' he confided to Malin. 'It's a pity you can't hear us. Our conversations are really interesting. But we talk best when we're alone.'

They had an interesting little conversation now as Melker tinkered with his motor. 'Uncle Melker, I fell into the sea,' said Tjorven, but Melker only grunted. He was tugging at the starting rope and he had probably been at it for a long time, for his face was red and his hair was sticking up in all directions.

'You haven't got the knack, Uncle Melker,' said Tjorven.

Melker looked up to her as she stood there on the jetty and gave a little smile. 'Oh, haven't I?'

'No, you must jerk it like this,' said Tjorven and showed him what he should do, with a smart movement of the arm.

'Listen, I'll jerk you unless you go away,' said Melker.

Tjorven blinked, surprised at such an ungrateful answer. 'I thought you would be pleased if I helped you.'

Melker turned around and went on with the motor. 'Yes, I am glad—very glad—very glad indeed,' he assured her and pulled the rope in time with his words. But the motor only muttered *phut, phut* and then stopped.

Tjorven shook her head. 'I'm sure you're a handyman, Uncle Melker, but perhaps you don't understand motors. Wait a minute and I'll show you!'

But Melker roared, 'Go away! Go and jump into the sea again or go and play with Pelle. Go on!'

Tjorven looked hurt. 'I *will* go and play with Pelle, but I must go home first and change my clothes, you realize that, don't you?'

Melker nodded agreement. 'Do that! Put on everything you have! Preferably two or three bodices, buttoned up behind!'

'Bodices!' said Tjorven. 'We aren't living in the Stone Age.'

That was what Teddy always said about anything old-fashioned.

Melker did not hear her, for now the motor had begun to

say *phut, phut* again. He looked beseechingly at it, but in vain. When the motor had said its last *phut*, it fell absolutely silent.

'Uncle Melker, do you know what?' said Tjorven. 'I hope you're better at writing books, because you're no good at this. Where is Pelle, anyhow?'

'With his rabbit hutch, probably,' roared Melker, and then he folded his hands in an attitude of prayer. 'I pray to God that he is at his rabbit hutch and that you will go to join him there.'

'Why do you want God to be at the rabbit hutch?'

'Pelle!' roared Melker. 'It is Pelle who is supposed to be at the rabbit hutch, and then you, above all, you!'

'No, you *said* that you prayed to God that He would be at the rabbit hutch,' Tjorven began. But Uncle Melker looked wild and so, to calm him, she said quickly, 'It's all right. I'm going now!'

Melker's prayer had been heard. Pelle was at his rabbit hutch and Tjorven went to find him when she had changed her clothes. Yoka had been given a fine hutch. 'Made by Melker with his own hands,' Melker boasted when it was finished. Pelle had helped him, although Melker had warned him, 'You will only bang your fingers.'

'No, I won't,' said Pelle. 'Tjorven will hold the nail.' Melker had never thought of that.

'Why do you always bang your thumb?' asked Tjorven when Melker had got in two bangs, one after the other.

Melker sucked his thumb. 'Because you, my little Tjorven, are not holding the nail for me.'

But it was a fine rabbit hutch when it was finished. One which would be fun for a rabbit to live in, thought Pelle. He was so happy that he seemed to shine when he brought Yoka from Jansson's farm and put him in his new home.

The whole thing was placed behind the lilac hedge in a protected corner where Pelle could sit by himself and be the world's happiest rabbit owner. The hutch was made of wire netting and had a door with a catch at one end, so that he could take Yoka out if he wanted to hold him in his arms. Yoka had his own little house at the other end—a box with a round hole in it.

'You can sleep in there when it rains and turns cold,' Pelle explained to him.

He was sitting with the rabbit in his arms when Tjorven arrived. Together they fed him and Pelle explained to Tjorven the art of looking after rabbits, as she was to take care of Yoka when Pelle went back to town.

'And I'll never forgive you if you don't feed him properly,' said Pelle. 'And you must make sure he doesn't run away.'

But Pelle ought to have seen to this himself, for before he had finished speaking Yoka jumped out of his arms and ran away through the lilac hedge. Pelle and Tjorven quickly ran after him. So did Bosun, with a little bark.

'Now then, Bosun, you are not to touch Yoka,' shouted Pelle anxiously as he ran. It was the stupidest remark Tjorven had heard for a long time.

'Bosun never touches anyone, you ought to know that by now. He just thinks we're playing.'

Pelle was ashamed, but he had no time at that moment to beg Bosun's pardon. Now he had to get hold of Yoka.

Behind Carpenter's Cottage Malin, Johan, and Niklas were beating blankets and when Yoka arrived Johan threw a blanket over him. Yoka squirmed under the blanket, which billowed like an angry sea. But out came Yoka finally and with three happy jumps he had disappeared around the corner.

It was Stina who caught him. She was sitting there with Hop-ashore Charlie when she saw Yoka rush past. She had caught him by the time Tjorven and Pelle arrived, breathless.

'How clever of you to catch him,' said Pelle. He sank down on Stina's front steps with Yoka in his arms and looked at him as tenderly as a mother looks at her newborn child. 'It's nice to have your own animal,' he said. Tjorven and Stina agreed.

'Especially a raven,' said Stina. And then she said triumphantly, 'He can say it now!'

'Say what?' asked Tjorven.

'He can say "Go to blazes!" I've taught him.' It was obvious that Pelle and Tjorven did not believe her and Stina grew angry. 'Just wait! You'll hear! Charlie, say "Go to blazes." '

The raven put his head on one side but remained silent. But after Stina had talked with him for a long time he let out two small croaks. Only someone with a lively imagination could have turned it into 'Go to blazes' but Stina had a lively imagination.

'Did you hear?' she said joyfully.

Tjorven and Pelle laughed, but Stina said, 'Do you know what I think? I think that Charlie is an enchanted prince, because he can talk.'

'Go on,' said Pelle. 'Have you ever heard of a prince who said 'Go to blazes'?'

'Yes, this one,' said Stina and pointed at Charlie.

In the fairy tale that she had just told her grandfather, there were no less than three enchanted princes. They had been turned into a wild pig, a whale, and an eagle, so why couldn't a raven be an enchanted prince?

'No, it's only toads who are enchanted princes,' said Tjorven.

'That's all you know,' said Stina.

'It's true. Freddy read it to me. It was about a princess who kissed a toad and then he became a prince—bang—just like that!'

'I'll try that some time or other,' said Stina.

Pelle sat laughing. 'What would you do with the prince if you had one?' he asked.

'He could marry Malin,' said Stina.

Tjorven thought this an excellent suggestion. 'Then she wouldn't have to be absolutely unmarried any more.'

They could not have thought of anything to annoy Pelle more. 'To blazes with all your enchanted princes,' he said. 'Come on, Yoka. Let's go.'

Tjorven and Stina looked after him for a long time.

'He doesn't want Malin to get married ever,' said Tjorven. 'Perhaps it's because he hasn't got a mother.'

Stina grew serious and she wrinkled her forehead thoughtfully. 'Why is his mother dead?' she asked.

That was not easy to answer. Tjorven meditated. She

did not know why people died. 'I guess it's like that hymn,' she said at last. 'It just happens that way.' And she sang to Stina:

All the world's an isle of sorrow,
Here today and gone tomorrow.

'It's very sad, isn't it?' said Stina.

Pelle put Yoka into his hutch and then had a lovely evening all by himself, devoted entirely to spring ditches. He loved spring ditches; there was so much to look at, insects and plants of many different kinds. But almost the most amusing part of a spring ditch was to try to jump over it and see if he could do it in one jump. Sometimes he did not make it, and so Pelle was covered with mud right up to his forehead when he returned home that evening.

By that time Melker was sitting in Carpenter's Cottage kitchen with the motor, which he had taken to pieces, in front of him on the table. He meant to adjust it so that it would never say *phut, phut* and nothing more again, and he thought that perhaps a thorough cleaning would improve it. But, strangely enough, all the little nuts and screws had a habit of disappearing just when he needed them and Melker became just furious each time it happened.

'Have you been eating my screws?' he asked Johan and Niklas, who were hanging round the table, looking on, and after a couple of these unfair remarks Johan said, 'Come on,

Niklas, let's go to bed. Daddy can stay here and look after his screws by himself.'

And as soon as they had gone, Melker found what he had been looking for.

'Why, here's the little fellow I've been looking for,' he said.

Just at that moment Pelle came in, covered with mud and very tired, and Malin said, 'And here's another little fellow I've been looking for—but what a sight you are, Pelle!'

So it was not only the motor that was cleaned in the kitchen of Carpenter's Cottage that evening. Malin got out the big tub, put Pelle in it, and began a real scrubdown.

'You needn't bother about my ears,' muttered Pelle. 'I washed them on Saturday.'

But Malin answered that she wouldn't be held responsible for such ears as Pelle's. 'Aunt Marta might be coming for coffee tomorrow and if she saw your ears—'

'Malin, couldn't you—let's wait and see if she's really coming first,' suggested Pelle.

Malin turned, laughing, to Melker. 'Are all little boys as dirty, do you think? Were you like this when you were little?'

Melker sat surrounded by his screws, humming contentedly. 'I *have* got the right knack . . . Tjorven will soon see . . . Dirty? Me?' Then he said, 'No, I was a very clean little boy, I remember.'

Pelle looked dreamily at his father over the edge of the tub. 'Yes, of course you were a clean little boy, Daddy.'

'What makes you so sure of that?' asked Melker.

'Because you were so good in every way. You always did

as you were told and your reports were always so good. You never told lies or did anything wrong.'

'Did I say that?' said Melker, and laughed loudly. 'Then I must have begun to tell a few fibs in my old age.'

Afterwards, when he was sitting on Malin's knee wrapped up in a big towel, Pelle remembered Stina's silly suggestion about the enchanted prince that Malin was going to marry. He looked at her searchingly, wondering if she was sorry that she was 'absolutely unmarried,' as Tjorven put it.

There had been great news as soon as they had come out to Seacrow Island this time. Björn had got engaged to a girl on one of the other islands and Pelle had anxiously asked Malin if she was sad. But Malin had laughed and said, 'No, it was the best thing that could happen, and I told him so at Christmas.' But still it was not altogether certain that she liked being 'absolutely unmarried'!

'There—my little motor's finished. Absolutely clean,' said Melker, and screwed in the last screw as he sang. 'She works perfectly now. I'll show you.'

It was in Pelle's bathtub that the motor was to show whether it worked perfectly or not. It did. It worked so perfectly that the water sprayed out on all the walls and Melker, who was leaning over the bathtub, had the first wave, straight in the face.

'Oh dear,' said Melker. And then he added hastily, 'Malin, I'll dry it all up for you.'

But Malin said she was thankful to have the whole kitchen washed down so unexpectedly and that she did not mind drying it up at all. 'Just let Pelle go to bed first. Are you cold?' she asked him, when she saw Pelle standing there, shivering.

'I'm as cold as an Eskimo,' said Pelle, and he was cold even when he got into bed. 'I think you must have aired my blankets too much,' he said. 'It's dreadfully cold!'

'Change the subject,' muttered Niklas sleepily.

Pelle lay still in his narrow bed, trying to warm up a little patch for himself. 'It would be nice to have a warm rabbit in my bed,' he said.

Johan stuck up his head. 'A rabbit, did you say? That's just like you,' he said, sinking back onto his pillow and immediately falling asleep.

Pelle lay awake. He was anxious about Yoka, so anxious that he could not sleep. Just think if there was frost tonight and Yoka was shivering in his hutch. He himself had begun to get warm and it seemed unfair that rabbits should have only small, cold boxes with a little hay in which to sleep.

Pelle sighed a few times. At last he could stand it no longer. He got out of bed and climbed onto the ladder outside the window, left there after one of Melker's many roof expeditions. He clambered out into the chilly spring evening and ran with chattering teeth to his rabbit hutch. No one saw him when he got there or when he came back with Yoka in his arms. No one except the fox perhaps, who was out on a little evening walk around Seacrow Island.

Yoka was by no means as grateful as Pelle had expected. He struggled wildly when Pelle tried to put him into his bed.

That was no place for a rabbit to sleep, he thought, and he took a wild leap.

Malin and Melker were down in the sitting room when they suddenly heard a shriek from above. They hurried upstairs and found a terrified Niklas, sitting up in bed and trembling in every limb.

'There are ghosts up here,' he said. 'A horrible furry ghost jumped on me.'

Melker patted him soothingly. 'That's what's called a nightmare. There's no need for you to be frightened.'

'Some nightmare,' muttered Niklas. 'He jumped right on my face.'

But under Pelle's eiderdown, held tight in his arms, lay the little nightmare, only waiting for the next opportunity to get up and play ghosts again.

When the whole house was asleep, Pelle climbed out into the night again and put Yoka back into his hutch.

'I just can't have you in my bed,' he said.

Soon a new spring day dawned over Seacrow Island—a day which no one would ever forget. For it was on this day that Moses came to the island and started a whole chain of events. Moses was a baby seal that Westerman found out on the island, caught in a net, and brought home with him to Seacrow Island, as he knew that the sea eagles attacked deserted baby seals.

'Westerman is the biggest mischief-maker on this island,' Marta would say. Now and then quarrels broke out in the shop when the islanders were collected there and it was always the same—it was always Westerman who started it and kept it going. He was a restless soul. 'Like water swirling around stones,' his wife would say. 'And he simply doesn't realize it,' she explained to anyone who would listen. He was a fisherman and a hunter and he hated any other sort of work, although he had a farm, which his wife mostly had to look after. It was hard work and she grumbled sometimes. He often had money troubles too and he always went to Nisse Grankvist at the shop for help. But lately Nisse had refused. He did not want to lend money to someone who never paid when he should.

Tjorven was standing on the jetty when Westerman came back from the island that morning and she shouted with excitement when he put down a complaining little baby seal, with black, damp eyes, in front of her. It was the sweetest thing she had ever seen. 'Oh, how sweet he is,' exclaimed Tjorven. 'Can I pat him?'

'Certainly,' said Westerman, and then he said something quite unbelievable. 'You can have him if you like.'

Tjorven stared at him. 'What did you say?'

'You can have him—if your father and mother will let you, of course. I'll be only too glad to be rid of him. You can feed him until he's big enough to be of some use.'

Tjorven caught her breath. As a matter of fact Westerman was not one of her favourite people, but just now she felt that she adored him. 'Oh,' she said, and wondered how you could say thank you for anything so marvellous.

'I'll make you a cross-stitch pot-holder. Would you like that?'

Westerman did not realize that Tjorven meant to give him the greatest gift that she could possibly make and he said, 'Well, I can't exactly say that I'd like one, but you take the seal anyway, because I just don't dare go home to the wife with a baby seal.'

Then Westerman went away and Tjorven stood absolutely overwhelmed. 'Bosun, it's crazy! We've got a seal,' she said.

Bosun nosed the seal. He had never seen anything like it before, but if Tjorven wanted to have it, he would make friends with this strange little creature which lay growling at him.

'Now, don't frighten him,' said Tjorven and pushed Bosun aside. Then she shouted as loudly as she could, 'Come here, come here, everybody! It's absolutely crazy! I've been given a seal.'

Pelle was the first to arrive and he was trembling with excitement when he saw the baby seal and heard this amazing news. Tjorven had been given that fantastic grey-spotted little bundle that squealed and growled and wriggled about on the jetty with its strange little flippers!

'Oh, how lucky you are,' said Pelle from the bottom of his heart, and Tjorven agreed.

'Yes, it's quite fantastic. I always have such good luck!' But she still had to persuade her mother and father what a good thing it was to own a seal. Soon everyone was on the jetty, admiring the baby seal.

'We'll soon be able to open a zoo on Seacrow Island,' said Melker. 'I'll see if I can find a couple of cheap hippopotamuses.'

But Marta said that on no account did she want a seal in the house. Nisse was not certain either. He explained to Tjorven what a lot of trouble she would have in feeding him. He needed as much milk as a calf, and pounds of fish when he was a little older.

'He can have fish from us,' said Stina. 'Can't he, Grandpa?'

Tjorven looked at her parents. 'But he's been *given* to me,' she said. 'It's just like having a baby, surely you see that.'

Teddy and Freddy both agreed with her.

'And when you have a baby, you don't begin talking about how much milk it must have and how difficult it will be to feed it,' said Teddy.

They begged and pleaded with Marta. Johan, Niklas and Pelle helped. They promised to make a pool for the seal where he could swim during the day. There was a big cleft in the rock behind the boathouse and if that was filled with fresh sea water the seal would have the finest pool he could wish for.

'And he could stay in the boathouse during the night,' said Freddy. He would be no trouble at all, they all said.

The baby seal gave out small helpless shrieks now and again and Stina said triumphantly, 'Listen, he's calling 'Mummy'!'

'And that's me,' said Tjorven and caught the baby seal in her arms. It looked as if he felt comfortable for he pushed his nose in her face and his whiskers tickled her so she laughed.

'I know what he'll be called,' said Tjorven. 'Moses! Because Westerman found him exactly as the princess found Moses in the bulrushes. Do you remember that, Freddy?'

'Not that I have ever thought Pharaoh's daughter was quite like Westerman, but Moses is a good name,' said Melker.

As everybody seemed to take it for granted that Moses was to stay, Marta agreed at last. 'Well, you can keep him until he's big enough to look after himself,' she said, and all the children shouted for joy.

'Do you know what I think?' said Stina. 'I think Moses is an enchanted prince who has come up out of the sea.'

'You and your enchanted princes,' said Pelle. 'Prince Moses, how's that?'

Tjorven sat on the jetty and Moses lay on her lap. She stroked him and he nosed her hands so that she felt his whiskers, and then she laughed again until she was shaking with laughter.

Bosun stood watching. He stood quietly for a long time, looking at Tjorven with his usual sad gaze. Then he suddenly turned and went away.

Tjorven had a very busy spring with both Yoka and Moses to look after. Pelle wrote letter after letter from town, telling her to look after his rabbit properly. GIVE HIM A LOT OF DANDELION LEAVES, he wrote, and Tjorven complained to Stina, 'A lot of dandelion leaves, Pelle says! I've never seen a rabbit who is always so hungry.'

But Yoka was at least a very quiet animal and was perfectly content with dandelion leaves and water. He did not cry when he was left alone. He did not crawl about everywhere, pulling down tablecloths or nosing out saucepans or tearing Daddy's Sunday paper to pieces. Moses did all these things, Moses who should have been in his pool during the day and in the boathouse during the night. Moses did not want to stay either in the pool or in the boathouse. He followed Tjorven wherever she went. Wasn't she his mother? Didn't she give him his bottle containing warm milk and oil? As that was so, he wanted to be with her all the time. He squealed and protested when Tjorven locked him into the boathouse in the evening and once when he was making more noise than usual she took him into her room—Mummy was off with Mrs. Jansson, so she could not forbid it.

Bosun usually slept on a mat beside Tjorven's bed. He had slept there every night since he was a puppy. But when Moses came and began to crawl back and forth over the floor, Tjorven said, 'Bosun, you must sleep with Teddy and Freddy tonight.'

It was some time before Bosun understood what she meant. Not until she took hold of his collar and led him out of her room did he understand.

'It's only for tonight, Bosun,' said Tjorven.

But when Moses realized how comfortable it was to sleep in Tjorven's room, he would not be satisfied with any old boathouse. Next evening when Tjorven locked him in, he squealed so loudly that it could be heard all over Seacrow Island.

'People will think we're torturing him,' said Teddy. 'He had better sleep with Tjorven.'

Marta hesitated a little, but at last she gave in. It was

difficult to resist a little seal who looked at you with his wise, charming eyes exactly as if he understood everything.

That evening Bosun went and lay down in Teddy and Freddy's room of his own accord and continued to do so after that. He stopped following Tjorven wherever she went. Perhaps he was afraid of walking on Moses. Nowadays he spent most of his time by the steps leading to the shop, with his head between his paws as if he were asleep, and he only looked up when anyone went into the shop.

'My own darling little soppy dog, how sleepy you are these days,' said Tjorven and patted him. But then she would have to go off to pick dandelion leaves for Yoka and see to warm milk for Moses. It was such hard work to look after the animals, even if Stina did help her sometimes.

'You've only got Hop-ashore Charlie,' said Tjorven, 'but I've got two animals to look after—and Bosun, of course.'

Stina did not think it was at all a good thing that she only had Hop-ashore Charlie. She could not feed him with a bottle as Tjorven fed Moses, lucky Tjorven! Stina helped her pick dandelion leaves for Yoka and hoped every time for the reward she longed for—to be allowed to feed Moses with the bottle. But Tjorven was adamant. She wanted to feed Moses herself. She said that he was not happy otherwise. Stina was allowed to sit and look on, although her fingers itched to take the bottle away from Tjorven, whether Moses was happy about it or not.

But better days dawned for Stina. Her grandfather owned a few sheep, which he was allowed to keep in Westerman's field. At this time of year they had their lambs and Stina went with her grandfather every day to see if any lambs had been born.

'Come along, sheep,' shouted Söderman. 'Come along, so that I can count you and see if I am any richer.'

One of his ewes did all she could to increase his riches. One day she had no less than three lambs in the little shed that Söderman had put up as a shelter for his sheep.

'She hasn't got enough milk for all of them,' said Söderman. 'One of them will be bound to suffer.'

Söderman was right. For several days he and Stina saw how the youngest of the lambs grew weaker because he was not strong enough to fight for milk with the other two.

Finally Söderman said, 'We must try with the bottle.'

Stina jumped. Sometimes the most unexpected and wonderful things happened after all. She made her grandfather go to the shop with her in a hurry which Söderman thought was excessive. After all, the lamb was not at death's door; but at Stina's order he bought a baby's bottle exactly like the one that Tjorven had for Moses, and Stina smiled happily. Now she would be equal with Tjorven at last!

Tjorven was feeding Moses when Stina arrived with a full baby's bottle in her hand.

'What do you think you're doing?' asked Tjorven.

Moses had a reserve bottle which he was given if he was particularly hungry, and Tjorven thought that this was what Stina had dared to bring, without asking her permission.

'Moses is full up. He doesn't want any more,' said Tjorven.

'Who cares,' said Stina. 'I've got other things to think about.'

Tjorven lifted her eyebrows. 'What, for instance?'

'I'm going to feed Tottie, so there,' said Stina importantly.

Tjorven was silent with surprise. 'Who on earth is Tottie?' she said at last.

And as soon as she had been told, she ran with Stina to Westerman's field and eagerly helped her feed the little lamb, although she generously allowed Stina to hold the bottle.

Tottie soon became as tame as Moses, and Stina took him milk several times a day. Sometimes she let him out in the field and took him with her for a little walk. He followed her just as devotedly as Moses followed Tjorven.

'It's a real sight,' said Nisse Grankvist, when he came out on his steps and saw Tjorven and Stina come towards him with Moses and Tottie behind them. And then he bent down and patted Bosun. 'And how are you getting on? Are you lying here all sad because you aren't allowed to go with them and play?'

But Stina and Tjorven sat down on the steps and fed their animals and discussed which of them was the sweetest.

'At least a seal is a seal,' said Tjorven, and Stina could not deny that.

'But a lamb is much sweeter,' said Stina. And then she added, 'I think that Tottie and Moses are both enchanted princes.'

'Nonsense,' said Tjorven. 'Only toads are that—I've already told you.'

183

'That's what you say,' said Stina. She sat silent and thought. Perhaps it wasn't possible for an ordinary lamb in Westerman's field to be an enchanted prince, but Moses, who had been found in a fishing net, why, that was just like in the fairy tales.

'I think, anyhow,' said Stina, 'that Moses is a sea king's little boy who has been bewitched by a bad fairy.'

'No, he's *my* little boy,' said Tjorven and hugged Moses.

Bosun lifted his head and looked at them. And if it was really true that he could think like a human being, perhaps he thought, just like Pelle: To blazes with all enchanted princes!

Does Malin Really Not Want a Husband?

Now our apple trees are in flower, wrote Malin in her diary. *They stand around our house in their pink loveliness and sometimes some of their blossoms snow down over the path leading to our well. Our apple trees, our house, our well—marvellous! It isn't ours at all, but I like to pretend it is, which seems strangely easy. At this time a year ago I had not even seen Carpenter's Cottage and yet it feels as if it is our home on earth. Oh, you gay carpenter, how I love you for having built this house, if it was you who did, and thank you for planting apple trees around it. How can I ever be grateful enough that we are allowed to live here and that it is summer again?*

'How about it, Daddy?' she asked Melker. 'Have you been just as clever this year and signed a contract for the whole year?'

'Not yet,' said Melker, 'I'm waiting for the man Mattsson. He's supposed to be coming here one of these days.'

And while they were waiting for Mattsson, the Melkersons prepared their Carpenter's Cottage for the summer. They raked all the leaves in the garden together, they beat the rugs and aired the bedclothes, they cleaned windows and scrubbed floors and put up fresh curtains. Niklas blacked the iron grate and Johan painted the kitchen chairs blue. Melker made a bookshelf for the family's varied summer reading and put up pictures which he had brought with him from town. Malin gave the kitchen sofa a new cover and Pelle just walked around, enjoying everything. The furniture that was too ugly for use was put in the boathouse and Pelle arranged it into an ugly little room, so that it would feel that there was someone who still cared for it, and, besides, he wanted to sit there with Yoka when it rained.

'It feels as if we're creating something,' said Malin looking about her summery house. 'Now I just want masses of flowers.' And she put out the happy carpenter's wife's old pottery jars and filled them with lilac, and finally she wandered out into Jansson's cow meadow, where the wild lilies of the valley grew, and picked whole handfuls of them.

On the way home she met Tjorven and Stina, who were walking along under the birch trees, chattering merrily away. They fell silent when they saw Malin, for she looked so pretty as she came to meet them with her hands full of lilies.

'You look like a bride,' said Tjorven.

Stina's eyes brightened immediately as a favourite thought awoke within her. 'Aren't you ever going to get yourself a bridegroom?'

Tjorven burst into loud laughter. 'A bridegroom? What's that?' she said.

'It's something you have at a wedding,' said Stina uncertainly.

Malin said she would like a bridegroom some time, but at the moment she thought she was a little too young. Tjorven stared at her as if she could hardly believe her ears.

'Too young! You? You're as old as the hills already!'

Malin laughed. 'Of course you've got to find somebody you really like first.'

Both Tjorven and Stina admitted that there were very few bridegrooms on Seacrow Island.

'But you might be able to find an enchanted prince,' said Stina eagerly.

'Are there any?' asked Malin.

'Yes, all the ditches are full of them,' said Stina. 'Because all frogs and toads are enchanted princes, Tjorven says.'

Tjorven nodded. 'You only have to kiss one and—bang —there's a prince for you!'

'That sounds simple enough,' said Malin. 'If that's all you have to do, I'll try to find one.'

Tjorven nodded once more. 'Yes—before it's too late.' And she went on, 'I will get married before I'm all that old, at any rate.'

'To an enchanted prince?' asked Malin.

'No, I'm going to marry a plumber,' said Tjorven. 'Daddy says they make lots of money nowadays.'

Stina wanted to marry a plumber, too, hastening to add, 'Because I want to be exactly like Tjorven.'

'Then there will be at least two happy plumbers,' said Malin, and she turned to go. 'If you see an enchanted prince,' she said, 'tell him I've just tottered home on my two old legs.'

Then Tjorven took Stina's hand and they both ran off between the birches, singing loudly.

They intended to pick lilies of the valley, just like Malin, but before they had begun something wonderful happened. They found an enchanted prince for Malin—for they found a frog! Just imagine! He was sitting at the side of the road, looking thoughtful.

'Come on, we must find Malin and get her to kiss him.'

But Malin had disappeared. They went all the way back to Carpenter's Cottage with the little frog, but when they got there Uncle Melker said Malin had gone to Söderman's to buy herrings.

'Then we'll go there,' said Stina, but there was no Malin there either. She had bought her fish and gone.

'Let's go down to the jetty and wait,' said Tjorven. 'But unless she comes soon, she'll have to go without her prince because I'm beginning to get tired of this frog.'

It appeared that the frog was at least as tired of Tjorven as she was of him, for when she carefully opened her hands to let Stina have a look, the frog took a long jump onto the jetty and would have fallen over the edge if Stina had not caught it just in time.

A strange sailboat lay by the jetty, but there was no one to be seen, either on board or anywhere else. The sun shone and it was warm and boring sitting there waiting, thought Tjorven. She was not the patient sort and she was used to inventing ways out of boring situations.

'I know,' she said. '*We* can kiss the frog. That will make him into a prince just as well, and then we can take him to Malin and he can do the rest himself.'

Stina thought this sounded sensible. Of course, it was most unpleasant to kiss frogs, but she would do anything for Malin. Evidently the frog did not like being kissed. It struggled wildly to get free, but Tjorven held it firmly and Stina drew a deep breath and shut her eyes.

'Do it,' said Tjorven, and Stina did. She kissed the frog. But the stubborn creature refused to turn itself into a prince.

'Well, I'll try,' said Tjorven. She put a little more strength into her kiss, but it still had no effect.

'Stupid prince, he doesn't want to come,' said Tjorven. 'Off you go then!'

She put the frog down on the jetty, and happy at his unexpected release, he took a long jump right over the edge of the jetty and down into the sailboat. And bang! There the prince was, exactly as in the fairy tale. He came hurrying out of the cabin and jumped up onto the jetty and stopped right in front of Tjorven and Stina, with a little brown puppy in his arms. A prince if ever there was one!

Tjorven and Stina stared at him with eyes that grew rounder and rounder. He was not dressed as he should be, of course. He wore an ordinary shirt and an ordinary jacket and ordinary blue trousers, but otherwise he really looked princelike, with his blue eyes, white teeth, and fair hair like a golden helmet. Yes, he would do very well for Malin.

'I thought he would at least have a crown on his head,' whispered Stina.

Without taking her eyes off the prince, Tjorven said in a low voice, 'I suppose he only wears it on Sundays. Oh, how pleased Malin will be!'

Only then did Tjorven think about Pelle. *He* would not be pleased about this. In fact he would be furious with them for finding a prince for Malin. And there was Pelle now, and behind him was Malin! Tjorven whispered to Stina, 'Now it's beginning to get exciting.' And they opened their eyes still further, for it was not every day one could see Malin meet a prince.

It was quite obvious that the prince liked Malin. He looked at her as if he had never seen anything like her before, and Tjorven and Stina exchanged satisfied glances. They felt it was to their credit that Malin was so lovely and so soft and that her hair and dress blew so prettily around her, and now it appeared that the prince had thought of saying something to her.

'Now he's beginning to pay court,' whispered Tjorven.

But the prince was not quite so quick off the mark as all that. 'I've heard that there's a general store here on Seacrow Island,' he said to Malin. 'Do you know it?'

Yes, Malin knew it, and she was just going there herself. If he would like to go with her, she would show him the way.

'Oh, can I look after your puppy while you go?' begged Pelle.

Enchanted princes were a bore, but enchanted princes

who had little brown puppies were easy to put up with. And, besides, Pelle did not know that he was speaking to an enchanted prince.

'He thinks he's just an ordinary man,' whispered Tjorven to Stina. 'So we needn't tell him what we've done.'

Still, it felt a little like treason. Tjorven looked at him guiltily, but he did not notice it. For the moment Pelle saw nothing but the little brown puppy.

'What's his name?' Pelle asked eagerly.

'He's called Yum-yum,' said the prince, 'and my name's Petter Malm.' This last remark was to Malin.

'Petter—what a name for a prince!' whispered Tjorven and then she took Stina's hand. 'Come on, let's follow them and see what happens.'

The prince gave the puppy to Pelle. 'All right, you look after Yum-yum carefully while I'm away,' he said kindly. And before Pelle could answer, Malin said, 'Oh, I assure you he'll do that.'

Then Malin went off with her prince. Tjorven and Stina followed them, giggling, to the shop, and there, to their great surprise, they heard the prince ask for half a pound of hamburger meat.

'Do princes really eat hamburger?' asked Stina, aghast.

'No, he probably wants it for his little pigs at home in his palace,' said Tjorven.

They kept as close to Malin as they could, so that they would hear every word the prince said to her. That he did not want to leave her was obvious.

He and Malin stood for a long while outside the shop, talking. He said that he had rented a little cottage on Great Island, and now he had borrowed a boat and was out sailing. But he would soon be coming back to Seacrow Island, he said, for the shop they had there was really a very good one.

'A good shop, oh yes!' said Tjorven to Stina. 'And a good Malin too, eh?'

At last Malin said she could not stay talking any longer and then the prince said goodbye. He walked backwards, as if he wanted to look at her for as long as possible, and he swung his paper bag and said, 'Well, I'm off with my hamburger, but I'll be back when I've eaten it, and I eat quickly, and mind you're standing on the jetty then, looking like a lovely summer day.'

'Did you hear that?' said Tjorven. 'That's what's called princely talk, you know.'

'We've got another frog in the well now,' Pelle said to Malin when he went to bed that evening. 'I found one in Petter's boat and he said I'd have to take it away because frogs don't like sailing.' Pelle sat up straight in bed and went on, 'He likes animals just as much as I do. And he's a scientist. He looks after animals all the time and finds out everything about them. I want to be something like that when I grow up.'

Pelle, who had always said he was going to be nothing at all, had now suddenly heard that there were professions which tried to find out everything about animals. And it was like letting a flood of light into a great darkness, for silently Pelle, seven years old, had been worrying about his future. How were things to go for him, who didn't want to do anything when he grew up? Now he wanted to do something and he felt relieved.

'Petter does really interesting work,' he declared. 'Malin, guess what he does. He has fastened little radio sets onto some seals, to find out what they do under water and where they swim to and all that . . .' Then he suddenly threw his arms around Malin. 'But, oh, Malin, if only I could have a puppy! It's all right with Yoka, but he has to sit in his hutch all the time. Just imagine how wonderful it would be to have a puppy like Yum-yum, who followed me wherever I went!'

'I would like you to have a puppy too,' said Malin. 'But you must make do with Yoka for the time being.'

'And with Bosun and Tottie and Moses,' said Pelle.

Bosun was still the world's most wonderful dog to Pelle and when he had arrived at Seacrow Island this time Bosun had welcomed him with loud barks. He knew who was the world's greatest Pelle too and nowadays he followed him everywhere. Sometimes Moses did too and sometimes even Tottie. Pelle wandered about like an animal tamer and when Tjorven saw it she became violently jealous, not because Moses followed Pelle, but because Bosun did. Then she would throw herself on the neck of her dog and roll around with him, saying, 'Bosun, you are my own soppy little dog, you know that, don't you?' And Bosun would look at Tjorven as if he thought, Little Bumble, I want nothing better! And immediately he would leave Pelle to follow Tjorven again, but then Moses would come floundering along and push in between them.

Moses had become quite spoiled lately and sometimes even Tjorven thought he was a nuisance. One evening she had been stupid enough to take him up on her bed, and after that he would not sleep in his sleeping box any more, only on Tjorven's feet. It was no good trying to push him off the bed because he always climbed up again. Tjorven would try to push him down.

'We lie there, pushing each other the whole night,' she said, and her mother shook her head. 'That seal ought never to have been allowed in the house!'

But nowadays Moses liked to swim in his pool and since Johan and Niklas and Teddy and Freddy had nailed up a fence around it, Tjorven could keep him shut in there whenever, for some reason or other, she wanted to move around freely without a baby seal floundering along behind her.

But Moses still demanded a great deal of her time and attention and love, and when she played with the baby seal Bosun went off and lay down by the steps of the shop. Especially if Pelle was nowhere about. Especially if Pelle was sitting down on the jetty and playing with Yum-yum, which he often did.

If you live on Great Island, it is absolutely necessary to visit Seacrow Island pretty often, for that's where the shop is. And if you have a little brown puppy you have only to lay to at the quay and Pelle Melkerson will come rushing down to play with it. And when Pelle Melkerson is playing with the puppy, he answers every question without even noticing that he is answering.

'Where's Malin today?' you ask, for example.

'She's sitting on the steps at home, cleaning herrings,' says Pelle Melkerson.

Or: 'She's off swimming with Teddy and Freddy.'

Or: 'I think she's in the shop.'

And when you have found out what you want to know, you leave your puppy in Pelle Melkerson's care and rush away to meet Malin quite by accident, and every time you get to know her a little bit better. And every time you become a little bit more in love. *More* in love? As if that were possible! As if it had not happened the very first time you'd seen her, standing here on the jetty.

One Wednesday in June, a never-to-be-forgotten Wednesday, Petter Malm found Malin in the shop, and not only her. He found a seal. Amazing though it may sound, he found a baby seal crawling around on the floor, playing with two little girls. So Pelle Melkerson had not been boasting when he had said there was a tame seal on the island.

The shop was full of people and Moses was enjoying himself. He bit at all the trousered legs, especially Tjorven's, and she defended herself, laughing. 'No, Moses, stop, or Mummy will say that you mustn't be let loose!'

'Is that your seal?' asked Petter with a smile.

'Yes, of course,' said Tjorven.

'Then I don't suppose you want to sell him?'

195

'Not on your life,' said Tjorven. 'Anyhow, what do you want a seal for?'

'Not me,' said Petter, 'but my institute.'

Insti . . . ? What strange words princes used.

'A zoological institute where I work,' the prince declared, and Tjorven was no clearer about it even then.

'Work!' she said afterwards to Stina. 'What lies he must be telling. Princes don't have jobs. But I suppose he wants Malin to think he's an ordinary man.'

Petter patted Moses. 'I bet he's a good playmate,' he said.

And he himself played with Moses until he had to leave, which strangely enough, happened exactly when Malin had finished her shopping. 'I'll carry your basket to Carpenter's Cottage, even if you don't ask me in for tea or coffee or something,' he said to Malin.

'I'll ask you in for a cup of tea,' said Malin, 'kind soul that I am. Come along!'

Just at that moment Westerman came out of the shop and shouted to Petter, 'Sir, can I have a word with you?'

Petter turned when he heard the rough, rather thick voice, and saw who was calling him: a very coarse-looking man of wild appearance.

'What do you want?' Petter asked, surprised.

Westerman moved away from Malin, so that she would not hear what they were saying. 'I was in the shop when I heard you say you would like to buy that seal,' said Westerman as politely as it was possible for a wild man to speak. 'Actually it's my seal, to tell the truth. I found him out on the island.

How much could one get for him?' He edged up close to Petter and stared at him eagerly.

Petter drew away. He did not want to do any business about seals just now. The only thing he wanted was to catch up with Malin and he said hastily, 'Oh, well, a couple of hundred crowns perhaps—but I can't decide on the price. And besides I must know first of all who the seal really belongs to.'

'It belongs to me,' Westerman shouted after him.

And that was exactly what he said to Tjorven when she and Stina came out of the shop with Moses at their heels.

'Listen, I want my seal back,' said Westerman.

Tjorven stared at him without understanding. '*Your* seal! What do you mean?'

Westerman looked a little awkward and spat as far as he could, to show that he was not in the least embarrassed. 'I mean just what I say. You've had him long enough now, and he's my seal and I'm thinking of selling him.'

'Sell Moses? Are you mad?' shouted Tjorven.

But Westerman explained to her. Hadn't he said that she could have the baby seal only until he was big enough to be of use?

'You can go to blazes with all your lies,' yelled Tjorven. 'You said I could have him altogether! You *said* that!'

Westerman must have been ashamed somewhere in his greedy soul, and that made him more abrupt than ever. There was no need for him to ask Tjorven's permission, he said. He was free to sell his own seal and it was going to be sold and there was nothing more to be said about it, as Westerman needed the money badly. If Tjorven would not see reason he would go and talk to her father.

'I'll do that myself, anyhow,' retorted Tjorven, crying from vexation.

'Stupid!' said Stina, kicking out at him with her thin little leg as Westerman went off.

'You wait till I talk to Nisse,' he said.

Tjorven stood gasping with rage. 'Never,' she shouted. 'You won't ever have Moses!'

Then she began to run. 'Come on, Stina, we must find Pelle.' She could not speak to Daddy and Mummy just now, because the shop was full of people, but in time of need Pelle was a person one could turn to. Tjorven knew that. He must know of this dreadful thing that was going to happen.

Pelle shook his head dolefully. 'Talking to your father won't do any good,' he said. 'You can never prove that Westerman promised that you could have Moses altogether, and then Uncle Nisse won't know what to do.'

Stina agreed. 'Well, then, he'll have to go and ask Aunt Marta.'

But Pelle shook his head again. There was only one way, he said, and that was to hide Moses somewhere where Westerman could not find him.

'Well, where?' asked Tjorven.

Pelle thought for a moment and suddenly he knew. 'In Dead Man's Creek,' he said.

Tjorven looked at him full of admiration. 'Pelle, do you know what?' she said. 'You think of better things than anyone else.'

Pelle was right. Of course he was right. Mummy and Daddy must not be involved in this. If Westerman went to them afterwards and asked for Moses, they would be able to answer quite truthfully, 'We don't know where he is. Look for yourself!' And that would be difficult for Westerman. Oh, how difficult it would be!

In the old days, hundreds of years ago, the village on Seacrow Island lay by a creek on the island's west side. But once, when Sweden was at war with Russia, the Russians had come and burned the whole village. After that the inhabitants of Seacrow Island had built their new houses for safety's sake on the opposite side of the island. Now nothing of the former village was left except for a few very old grey boathouses edging the little creek, where once fishing boats and trawlers had lain by the jetties and where the ancestors of the present village people had put their nets out to dry on the bare rocks. Now there were no ships there except one old deserted trawler, which had found its last anchoring place in the creek. The children called it Dead Man's Creek, and dead it certainly was— silent and dead. There was a strange stillness over the place, and Pelle sometimes went there on his solitary wanderings. He would sit for hours, leaning against a sunny·boathouse wall watching the dragonflies hovering softly in the breeze and counting the rings in the water when some fish or other moved below the smooth surface.

Dead Man's Creek was a place full of peace and dreams for Pelle. But there were some people who thought the stillness was terrifying, almost ghostlike. It was easy to imagine that the blackest of secrets were hidden in the deserted boathouses, and people very seldom went there. No one would look for Moses here. In a boathouse in Dead Man's Creek he would be safe.

Tjorven had a little cart in which she pulled Moses if she had a long way to go with him and hadn't the patience to wait for him as he crawled along, and now they had a long way to go. So they put him into the cart with all the herrings that Stina had managed to beg from her grandfather.

The secret four, who were kicking a ball about behind Carpenter's Cottage, saw them setting out, and Teddy shouted to Tjorven, 'Where are you going?'

'We're only going for a little walk,' answered Tjorven. 'No, Bosun, you had better stay at home,' she said, when the dog came towards them. A walk usually meant long wanderings through fields and woods and it was something Bosun could never resist, but he stopped when Tjorven told him to. He stood still for a long time, looking after her, Pelle, and Stina, with Moses in his cart. Then he went back and lay down in his usual place beside the steps. His head sank down on his paws and he looked as if he was asleep.

A winding, half overgrown road led to Dead Man's Greek and Westerman's farm lay about halfway there. As they could not take the cart over a field, they had to go past the house with Moses. It was dangerous, but unavoidable.

'If he sees us that will be the end,' said Tjorven as they passed Westerman's gate. 'He'll take Moses away. Please, Cora, keep quiet!' This last remark was made to Westerman's dog, who was standing inside the hedge, barking. All they needed was for Westerman to come out to see why Cora was barking.

'Yes, that would be the end,' agreed Stina.

Westerman did not appear. Only his wife was there, standing with her back to them, hanging up washing on a line outside the house, and happily for them she had no eyes in the back of her head.

They also went past Westerman's field where Stina's grandfather kept his sheep, and Stina called to Tottie. He came immediately, thinking that he was going to be fed.

'Oh, I was only coming to say hello to you and to see that you were all right,' said Stina.

Moses enjoyed riding in his cart all the way to Dead Man's Creek and apparently thought he was out on a little joy ride, but when he was suddenly put into a strange boathouse he began to understand that this was an underhand trick and he did not intend to put up with it. He uttered one of his angry squeals and it sounded horrible in the empty stillness of Dead Man's Creek.

'Moses, you're making such a noise that it can be heard over the whole island,' said Pelle reproachfully.

All three of them sat on their heels around the baby seal in the darkness of the boathouse, stroking him and trying to get him to understand that all this was for his own good.

'It's only for a little while, you know,' said Tjorven. 'It will all turn out all right some way or other, and then you can come home again.'

How it was to turn out all right Tjorven could not for the life of her see, but most things seemed to sooner or later and no doubt this time would not be an exception—she hoped.

And so Moses gradually settled down with his mouth full of herring.

'You've never lived in a better boathouse,' said Tjorven. 'You'll be very happy here.'

'Although it *is* horrible here,' said Stina, shivering. 'I feel almost as if there were ghosts about.' There was a strange semidark daylight in the boathouse that she did not like, but the sun came through cracks in the wall and she could hear the water lapping outside. 'I'm going out for a minute,' she said, and opened the heavy door, which groaned as she pushed it. Then she disappeared.

What Stina thought so horrible Pelle thought very homely. It gave him a sensation he enjoyed so much that he felt it all over his body.

'I'd like to live here myself,' he said, looking around at the rubbish which the last owner had left in his boathouse. There were tattered fishing nets, a willow basket, a dilapidated old fish box, ice picks, bailers and oars, a laundry basket and a clothes beater, a rusty anchor, an old-fashioned toboggan with wooden runners and, farthest away in a corner, an old cradle with a name and a date carved on it. 'Little Anna,' said the carving. He could not read the year.

'I expect it's a long time since Little Anna lay in that cradle.'

'Where do you think Little Anna is now?' asked Tjorven.

Pelle thought for a moment. He stood for a long time, looking at the old cradle and thinking of Little Anna.

'I expect she's dead by now,' he said reverently.

'No, don't say that—it's sad,' said Tjorven. 'Oh, well,' and she began to sing:

> *All the world's an isle of sorrow,*
> *Here today and gone tomorrow,*
> *Only dust remaining.*

Pelle pulled open the door and rushed out into the sunshine. Tjorven followed after him as soon as she had said goodbye to Moses and promised him on her honour to bring him herrings every day.

Outside, Dead Man's Creek lay dreaming in the afternoon sun. Pelle took a deep breath, and then a kind of madness seemed to take hold of him. He gave a shout and began to run. In and out of the boathouses he raced, as if possessed. He jumped on crumbling jetties and slippery planks until Tjorven grew frightened, although she followed him and jumped just as recklessly as he did. Onto the shivering boards in the darkness of the boathouses they ran, where the water lay black beneath them. Pelle jumped about in a sort of silent fury, saying nothing, and Tjorven was silent too. She was frightened, but she followed him without hesitation.

Afterwards they sat on a jetty in the sun, and then Pelle said, 'Where's Stina?'

They remembered now they had not seen her for a long

time. They called her, but there was no answer. Then they began to shout. Their cries echoed around Dead Man's Creek and then died away, leaving a terrifying silence.

Pelle went white. What had happened to Stina? What if she had fallen into the sea from some jetty and had been drowned? 'Little Stina' and 'Little Anna'—anyone could die, he knew that.

'Oh, why didn't I bring Bosun with me?' said Tjorven with tears in her eyes.

They stood there in agony and anxiety, and then they suddenly heard Stina's voice. 'Guess where I am!'

They did not have to guess, for now they could see her, high up in the crow's-nest of the old trawler, and they wondered how in the world she had got there. Tjorven was furious and dried her tears angrily.

'You stupid little girl!' she yelled. 'What are you doing up there?'

'Trying to come down,' said Stina miserably.

'Is that why you climbed up?'

'No, to look at the view,' said Stina.

'Well, look at it now,' said Tjorven. What a silly thing, she thought, to go climbing about looking at views instead of getting drowned. Of course it was lucky that she wasn't drowned, but she should not have frightened them like that.

'Didn't you hear us when we called?' said Tjorven furiously.

Stina was ashamed of herself. She had heard them calling of course, but it was fun to see that they could not find her. Stina had been playing hide-and-seek, although Pelle and

Tjorven did not know it. And now the fun was over, she knew that.

'I can't get down,' she called.

Tjorven nodded grimly. 'Well, then, you'll have to stay where you are and when we bring Moses his herrings we'll put one on a fishing rod and hand it up to you.'

Stina began to cry. 'I don't want any herrings. I want to get down, but I can't.'

It was Pelle who took pity on her, and he had a difficult task. It was easy enough to climb up to the crow's-nest but when he got there he understood what Stina meant when she said, 'I want to get down, but I can't.' But he took a firm grip round Stina's middle, shut his eyes and climbed down, promising himself that never would he go any higher than the kitchen table at home in the future.

As soon as Stina was back on solid ground she was as lively as usual. 'There's a wonderful view from up there,' she said to Tjorven.

But Tjorven just gave her a look, and Pelle said, 'We must hurry home. It's almost six o'clock.'

'It can't be,' said Stina. 'Grandpa said I was to be home at four o'clock, and I'm not.'

'Your own fault,' said Tjorven.

'Well, I don't suppose Grandpa will notice a couple of hours more or less,' said Stina hopefully.

But she was mistaken. Söderman was with his sheep, giving the lambs fresh water, and when he saw Stina come skipping along, he said, 'What in the world have you been doing all day?'

'Nothing special,' said Stina.

Söderman was not a stern grandfather. He only shook his head. 'It takes a long time for you to do nothing special.'

When Tjorven got home she saw her father down on the jetty and ran down to him.

'Well, here's our Tjorven at last,' said Nisse. 'What have you been doing all day?'

'Nothing special,' said Tjorven, exactly like Stina.

And Malin got the same answer out of Pelle. He came into the kitchen after the whole family had sat down to supper.

'No, I haven't been doing anything special,' said Pelle. And he really meant what he said.

When one is seven years old, one lives dangerously. In the land of childhood, that wild and secret country, one can be on the verge of complete disaster without thinking it is 'anything special'.

Pelle made a face when he saw what they were having for supper—fish and spinach. 'I don't think I want any food,' he said.

But Johan raised a warning finger. 'Don't be fussy! We're all helping here. It's Daddy who cooked the supper. Malin has been sitting talking to her newest sheik,' he said.

'For three hours,' said Niklas.

'Now, now, now,' said Melker. 'We'll leave Malin in peace.'

But Niklas would not stop. 'I only wondered what you could possibly sit and talk about for three hours.'

'The weather, of course,' said Johan brightly.

Malin smiled and patted Johan's shoulder. 'He's not a

"sheik" and we didn't talk about the weather, isn't that strange? But he thinks I'm sweet, you know.'

'Of course you're sweet, Malin, my dear,' said Melker. 'Aren't all girls?'

Malin shook her head. 'No, Petter doesn't think so. He said that if girls these days knew what was best for them they would all be much sweeter.'

'You only have to tell them,' said Niklas. 'Be sweet or I'll give you what for!'

Malin looked at him and laughed. 'It'll be fun to be a girl when you're a few years older. Eat up now, Pelle,' she said.

Pelle looked lovingly at Melker. 'Did you really cook the supper, Daddy? How clever you are!'

'Yes, I thawed it all by myself,' said Melker, in a housewifely sort of way.

'Couldn't you have thawed something else?' asked Pelle, turning up his nose.

'Listen, my dear boy,' said Melker. 'There are certain things called vitamins, which I expect you have heard of—A, B, C, and D, in fact the whole alphabet—and we all have to have them in our food!'

'What vitamins are there in spinach?' asked Niklas, eager for information. But that Melker could not remember.

Pelle looked at the green mess on his plate. 'I think there must be piles of smelly vitamins in this,' he said.

Johan and Niklas laughed, but Malin said sternly, 'No, Pelle, we do not speak like that in this house.'

Pelle said nothing, but when after supper he went out to

his rabbit hutch with his hands full of dandelion leaves, he said to Yoka encouragingly, 'It's all right—there aren't many smelly vitamins in these.'

He took Yoka out of his hutch and sat with him on his lap. He sat with him a very long time, but then he heard Malin come out on the step and call something to her father which Pelle was not pleased to hear.

'Daddy, I'm going out,' called Malin. 'Petter is waiting for me. Can you see to putting Pelle to bed?'

Pelle hastily pushed Yoka into his hutch. Then he raced after Malin.

'Won't you be at home to say good night to me?' he asked anxiously.

Malin hesitated. Petter's holiday was over and this was his last evening and after that she might never see him again. Not even for Pelle's sake could she stay at home this evening.

'I can say good night to you here and now,' she said.

'No, you can't,' said Pelle crossly.

'Yes, I can, if I make up my mind to it.' She kissed him violently, a whole row of small, quick kisses which she planted here, there, and everywhere, on his forehead, on his ears, on his soft brown hair. 'Good night, good night, good night. I could, you see!' she said.

Pelle laughed, but then he said sternly, 'Don't be back too late anyhow!'

Petter was sitting down on the jetty, waiting, and as he sat he too was being kissed. But not by Malin. Tjorven and Stina had seen him as they were out on a little evening promenade with the doll's pram and Lovisabet, and when Tjorven saw the enchanted prince she was gripped by holy wrath. Wasn't it his fault that Moses was lying all alone in his boathouse in Dead Man's Creek? When one produced enchanted princes, one did not actually mean that they should go around buying baby seals.

'Stupid,' she said to Stina. 'Why did you suggest that we should kiss that frog?'

'Me?' said Stina. 'But it was you!'

'No, it wasn't,' said Tjorven.

She looked angrily at the prince they had found for Malin. He really looked rather good with his dark-blue jacket and shining hair, but he could look as nice as he liked, it was a great disaster that he was there at all. Tjorven thought hard. She was used to finding ways out.

'What about . . .?' she said. 'But no, that won't do.'

'What?' asked Stina.

'What if we kissed him once more? Then he might turn into a frog again, you never know.'

Petter sat there, not knowing what was in store for him. He was gazing towards Carpenter's Cottage with eager eyes. Surely Malin would be coming soon? That was the only thing he was occupied with just now. Not until they stood immediately in front of him did he see the two little girls he had previously met in the shop.

'Sit still and shut your eyes,' said Tjorven.

Petter laughed. 'What's all this about? Is it a game?'

'We won't tell you,' said Tjorven grimly. 'Shut your eyes, I said.'

Malin's prince shut his eyes obediently and they kissed him angrily, first Tjorven and then Stina. And then they ran away as quickly as they could. They did not stop until they were a safe distance from him.

'Well, it looks as though we'll have to put up with him,' said Tjorven glumly. And then she shouted to the prince who would not become a frog, 'Go to blazes!'

Girls were certainly not as sweet as they ought to be, thought Petter. He looked in astonishment at the two small terrors who had just kissed him, but then he saw Malin coming, as lovely as a June evening, and he quickly shut his eyes.

'Why are you sitting with your eyes shut?' said Malin, flicking him on the nose. He opened his eyes and said with a sigh, 'I was only trying it out. I thought it was probably the custom here on Seacrow Island for all girls to kiss a man sitting quietly with his eyes shut.'

'Are you crazy?' said Malin. But before Petter had time to explain it, Tjorven shouted to her, 'Malin, do you know what? Just you beware of him. He's really a frog!'

That evening Bosun returned to his place beside Tjorven's bed and when the whole family came as usual to say good night to their youngest, she told them why Moses was no longer there and what a spoilsport Westerman was.

'He's just like that Pharaoh in Egypt,' said Tjorven. 'You remember, don't you, Freddy, when they had to hide all those Moseses?'

'Where have you hidden your Moses?' both Teddy and Freddy wanted to know.

'That's a secret,' said Tjorven.

Secret Teddy and secret Freddy, after all there were others who could have secrets!

'I keep everything secret,' said Tjorven. 'You won't ever know where Moses is—not ever!'

Her father looked thoughtful. 'But this business with Westerman must be cleared up somehow.' Then he scratched Bosun's neck. 'Well, Bosun, at any rate you're happy now.'

Tjorven jumped out of bed and looked Bosun deep in the eyes. 'My own little soppy dog,' she said tenderly. 'Now let's both go to sleep, you and me.'

But perhaps this was too great a joy for Bosun to bear. He slept restlessly and at about twelve o'clock that night he woke Tjorven and wanted to go out. Drunk with sleep, she opened the door for him.

'What's the matter with you, Bosun?' she murmured. But then she staggered back to bed and was asleep by the time she reached it.

Bosun wandered out into the June night, which with its pale light makes both people and animals restless. Malin saw him when she came home. For she was standing at the gate of Carpenter's Cottage, saying good night to Petter. Sometimes such things take about two hours and June nights are not made for sleep. As Petter had said—they were so short and there was so much to talk about.

'I have met a lot of girls,' Petter assured her. 'I've liked some of them—a lot. But I've never been seriously in love before, so much in love that you feel almost as though you must die of it. That has only happened to me once.'

'And perhaps you're still in love with her,' said Malin.

'Yes, I am still in love with her.'

'Is it long since it happened?' asked Malin, and there was anxiety and disappointment in her voice.

'Let me see.' Petter looked at his watch and then he reckoned, 'It's exactly ten days, twelve hours, and twenty minutes. There was a bang and I was done for. You can see it in my log book, if you like. You'll see "Today I met Malin." Quite simple.'

Malin smiled at him. 'But if it happened so quickly, perhaps it won't last long. Bang—and it will all be over.'

He looked at her seriously. 'Malin, I'm the steady type, believe me.'

'Are you?' said Malin. Just at that moment they heard a dog barking and Malin murmured, 'What's the matter with Bosun, I wonder?'

Whether it is a June night or not, one cannot stand at a gate forever. Petter kissed Malin and slowly she left him and went towards the house. He stood, looking after her, and she turned back to him.

'I think you can write something else in that log book,' she said. 'Today Malin met Petter.'

And then she disappeared into the shadows between the apple trees.

'June nights are not made for sleep,' Petter had said. There

212

were several others who thought so too. But finally they all returned home. Bosun came home just as Malin was saying her last good night to Petter, and the fox that lived in Jansson's cow meadow also returned to his hole.

And Söderman, who could never sleep when the nights were light, had just been on a nightly round of his sheep and he came home, carrying Tottie in his arms.

There was one more creature who had been out wandering that June night—Yoka. Pelle had not fastened his hutch door properly and Yoka had been out for a walk too—but he, alas, did not come home!

Sorrow and Joy

Sorrow and joy go hand in hand—some days are black and full of misery and generally they come when least expected.

Next morning Söderman came into the shop to see Nisse and Marta. He was unhappy, for he had sad news to tell.

'Last night I went on the rounds among my sheep as I usually do and what did I hear? A dog barking and my sheep baaing—and from a good way off I could see them running back and forth as though they were being chased. And when I got to the field, who do you think I met, rushing wildly away? Well, Bosun!'

Söderman looked as if he thought the earth would open under him when he said this, but Nisse looked at him blankly.

'Oh, really—and who do you think was chasing the sheep?'

'Didn't you hear what I said? It was Bosun! And I've got Tottie at home with one of his legs bitten.'

'You can hear a lot before your ears fall off,' said Marta. 'But you'll never get me to believe that Bosun chases sheep.'

Nisse shook his head. It was hardly worth answering such an absurd accusation. Bosun, the world's most gentle dog.

You could put any child or kitten or lamb right under his nose and he would not touch it.

But Söderman stuck to his accusation, and just then Malin came in to buy potatoes with Westerman immediately behind her. He had meant to talk to Nisse about Moses, but he changed his mind.

'It might just as easily have been Cora who was out last night,' said Nisse when he saw Westerman.

There were only two dogs on Seacrow Island, Westerman's Cora and Tjorven's Bosun.

But Westerman declared angrily that he, unlike some others, kept his dog tied up, and Malin was able to confirm that it was true. At any rate Cora had been outside her kennel as usual and had barked when she and Petter passed by at about eleven o'clock yesterday evening.

'And besides,' said Malin unwillingly, 'I saw Bosun when he went out last night and when he came back. And I heard him barking, I'm afraid.'

Söderman looked anxiously at Nisse. It was not pleasant to have to bring such a tale of woe.

'Bosun hardly ever barks, you know that, Nisse. And, as I told you, I saw him coming straight out of the sheep field.'

Nisse swallowed. 'If it's as you say, there's only one thing to be done.'

Then Marta began to cry. She made no attempt to hide her tears, and she cried bitterly as she thought of someone who would take it even harder than herself. How were they to tell Tjorven?

Tjorven was not at home just then. She was running around looking for Yoka. Everybody was helping Pelle hunt for his rabbit, which had disappeared. Johan and Niklas, of course, and Teddy and Freddy and Tjorven. They looked everywhere but they could not find Yoka. Pelle hunted and cried and was angry with himself. Why hadn't he closed the hutch properly last night? Why had he been in such a hurry? You should never be in a hurry when you've got a rabbit.

They found Yoka at last. It was Teddy who found him. She screamed when she saw the little rabbit lying lifeless under a bush not far from the sheep field.

'No,' she screamed. 'No!'

Someone had come up behind her. She turned her head and saw it was Pelle. Then she shouted still more wildly, 'Pelle, keep away!' But it was too late. Pelle had already seen. He had seen his rabbit.

They stood in a helpless ring around him. None of them had ever been so close to bitter sorrow, and they did not know what to do when anyone looked as Pelle looked now.

Johan cried. 'I'll get Daddy,' he mumbled and ran as fast as his legs would carry him.

Melker also had tears in his eyes when he saw Pelle. 'My poor little boy.'

He picked him up in his arms, and carried him home to Carpenter's Cottage. Pelle did not cry, he only hunched up closer and hid his face with closed eyes against his father's shoulder. He never wanted to see anything in the world again.

'Here today and gone tomorrow.' He choked. His own rabbit,

the only animal he had. Why hadn't it been allowed to live? Pelle lay on his bed with his face hidden in the pillow and then at last he cried, a quiet, miserable sort of crying which cut Malin to the heart. She sat beside him, feeling quite helpless. No one was dearer to her than this weeping little boy, who lay there so thin and small, far too small to bear such a great sorrow. It was terrible not being able to shield him, at least a little, from what was hurting him so much. She stroked his hair and told him why she could do nothing to help.

'That's the way life is, you see. Sometimes it's very difficult. Even a child, even a little boy, sometimes has to endure something that hurts, and has to go through it all by himself.'

Then Pelle sat up in bed, his face white and wet with tears. He threw his arms around Malin. He clung to her, and said in a hoarse voice, 'Malin, promise me you won't die until I grow up!'

Malin promised solemnly that she would do her best not to. And then she said to comfort him, 'We can buy you another rabbit, Pelle, you know.'

Pelle shook his head. 'I *never* want another rabbit but Yoka!'

There was someone else who was crying, not silently like Pelle, but loudly and wildly so that it could be heard a long way off.

'It's not true!' shrieked Tjorven. 'It's not true!' She hit her father for saying it. He could not say such dreadful things, that Bosun—no, not possibly!—had bitten Tottie and killed Yoka. No, never, never! Poor Bosun, she would take him with

217

her and run away, far, far away. Yes, she would—and never come back again. She would hit anyone on the head who said anything like that to her.

In a rage she kicked off her shoes and looked for someone she could throw them at—not Daddy—someone, anyone, she did not know who, and so she picked up her shoes with a shriek and flung them at the wall. 'I'll give it to you! I'll give it to you!' she shouted.

She stood there mad with rage. Then she saw that Daddy had tied up Bosun by the steps, and she panted, 'Do you mean to say you're going to keep him tied up always?'

Nisse sighed. 'Tjorven, my poor little girl,' he said, crouching on his heels in front of her, as he always did when he wanted to make her listen properly. 'Tjorven, now I have to tell you something which will make you very miserable indeed.'

Tjorven broke out into still wilder sobbings. 'I'm miserable already.'

Nisse sighed again. 'I know that—and it's difficult for me too. But, you see, Tjorven, a dog who hunts sheep and kills rabbits can't be allowed to live any longer.'

Tjorven stood quite still, looking at him. It was as if she had scarcely taken in what he had said, but at last she ran from him with a cry of grief.

She rushed to her bed and flung herself down on it, and there, with her head hidden in the pillow, she lived through the longest and most bitter day of her life.

Teddy and Freddy went about with their eyes swollen

with crying. They grieved as much as Tjorven did, but when they saw her lying there they were full of compassion. Poor Tjorven, it was far worse for her. They sat down beside her, tried to say something that would comfort her, but it was as if she could not hear, and they got only two words out of her: 'Go away!'

So, crying, they left her. Marta and Nisse also tried to talk to her but they could not get any answer either. The hours passed. Tjorven lay on her bed, dumb and immobile. Now and again Marta opened the door a crack, looked in and heard a little moan, otherwise all was silent.

'I can't bear this any longer,' said Marta at last. 'Come on, Nisse, we must try again!'

And they tried in every way that love and despair could suggest to them.

'Little Bumble,' said Marta. 'Would you like to go to visit Gran? Would you like that?'

There was no answer, only a little dry sob.

'Or what if we bought a bicycle for you?' said Nisse.

Another sob and nothing more.

'Tjorven, isn't there *anything* you want?' said Marta at last in despair.

'Yes,' mumbled Tjorven. 'I want to die.' She sat up in bed and suddenly words came with a rush. 'It's all my fault. Because I haven't cared about Bosun as I did before. I've only cared about Moses.'

She had thought it all out, she had thought and thought —and that must be it. It was her fault. Bosun had never done anything wrong before, and if it was really true that he had bitten Tottie and Yoka it was because Bosun was unhappy himself and no longer cared what he did.

'Yes, it's my fault,' sobbed Tjorven. 'It would be better if you shot me and not Bosun.'

Then she sank back on her pillows again. For a short moment she remembered Moses over at Dead Man's Creek, but he belonged to another world and she did not want to think about him. She thought of one thing only. She longed for Bosun until her whole body ached. He was standing tied up by the steps and soon Daddy would take his rifle and go into the woods with him.

'Bring me Bosun,' she mumbled with her face in her pillow.

Nisse looked unhappy. 'Tjorven, dear, wouldn't it be better if you didn't see Bosun just now?'

Then Tjorven roared, 'Bring Bosun!'

Teddy brought him and Tjorven turned them all out of her room. 'I want to be alone with him.' And then she was alone with her dog. She threw her arms around his neck and wailed. 'I'm sorry, Bosun. I'm sorry, I'm sorry!'

He looked at her with eyes which showed nothing but an eternal loyalty, and perhaps he was thinking, Little Bumble, I don't understand any of this, but I don't like your being unhappy.

She took his great head between her hands and looked him straight in the eyes, trying to find the answer to all the incredibly grim things that had happened. 'It *can't* be true! Oh, Bosun, if only you could speak and explain everything!'

And poor Moses, locked in his boathouse in Dead Man's Creek, who had time to think of him? No one but Stina. She had been crying too, about Tottie and Yoka and Bosun. Everyone on Seacrow Island had been crying that day. But Tottie would soon be well again, Grandpa had said, and even if everything was one big misery, Moses ought not to be left to die of hunger.

Pelle and Tjorven are just lying there, crying and crying, so I must look after Moses, she thought. 'Give me some herrings, please, Grandpa!'

She was given her herrings in a basket and off she went. Söderman went on with what he was doing. Then Westerman arrived. He was furious with Nisse because of what he had said about Cora.

'Blaming my dog!' he said angrily to Söderman.

He had lost all desire to speak to Nisse about the seal—about who was its owner and was not its owner. He realized there was only one thing to do and that was simply to take the seal and keep it hidden until he could get hold of that young man who apparently was a prospective purchaser of seals. But where was the seal? Its pool was empty and it was nowhere else either as far as he could see and he had been looking all morning.

'Do you know where the children have put the seal?' he asked Söderman.

Söderman shook his head. 'It can't have disappeared altogether because Stina has just been here, asking for herrings for it.'

As soon as he had said that, he remembered something Stina had told him: that Westerman wanted to take Moses away from the children and sell him.

'But you've got nothing to do with the seal now,' said Söderman. 'Surely you have a little shame in you!'

Westerman swore and went. He was angry with the children and with Nisse Grankvist and Söderman and with every single person here on the island. The whole of Seacrow Island could go up in smoke for all he cared. He dawdled homeward. Then he saw Stina a little way in front of him, with her herring basket on her arm. That hurried him up. With long strides he caught up to her.

'Where are you going, Stina?' he said gently, for now he had to be cunning.

Stina smiled at him with a friendly smile. 'You're just like the wolf.'

Westerman did not understand. 'The wolf? What wolf?'

'Red Riding Hood and the wolf. Do you want to hear the story?'

Westerman did not want to hear the story. But Stina was Seacrow Island's most enthusiastic storyteller and Westerman had to listen while she told him the story of Little Red Riding Hood from start to finish. Not until then could he get a word in sideways.

'Who are those herrings for?' he asked.

'They're for Mo—' began Stina, but then she stopped herself, for she remembered now whom she was talking to.

Westerman did not give up. 'Who did you say they were for?'

'Grandma,' said Stina firmly. Then she giggled and added, ' "What a big mouth you have, Grandma," said Little Red Riding Hood. "All the better to eat herrings with," said Grandma. What do you say to that, Mr. Westerman?'

She gave Westerman her most impudent smile and then she ran away.

But she was just as innocent as Red Riding Hood, who showed the wolf the way to her grandmother's cottage. Stina went straight to Dead Man's Creek without so much as turning her head. If she had done so she might have caught a glimpse of Westerman as he followed stealthily after her. In fact, there was really no need for him to take the trouble to hide. No one could have been less on the watch than Stina, and now she was in a hurry to get to Moses.

Moses hissed at her as soon as she came through the door, but he was silent when he saw his herrings. Stina sat beside him and stroked him while he ate.

'Perhaps you're wondering why I've come by myself,' she said. 'But I won't tell you because it would only make you sad.'

Sad? Who wasn't sad! Moses did not like this boathouse and he did not like being alone, so now that Stina had come he did not intend to let her go, and he knew how to keep her. He had only to sit on her. So as soon as he had finished eating he floundered up on to her knee. There he settled down, and he hissed at her when she tried to push him off. If he had to stay in this boathouse she should stay too! Stina felt her legs giving under her and she grew frightened. Who knew how long Moses meant to sit there? Perhaps until Midsummer! Then they both would starve, both she and Moses, and that was not a pleasant thought. So she said beseechingly, 'Dear Moses, do get off me.' But Moses refused. She tried to push him down again, but he only hissed.

Then she saw there was still one herring left in the basket beside her and that saved her. She took it and held it high in the air so Moses could not get it, and then threw it with all her strength into a corner. Moses floundered after it, but squealed with fury when he came back and saw there was no longer any knee for him to sit on.

'Goodbye, Moses,' said Stina, shutting the door. She fastened the catch and went away very pleased with herself. She looked neither to the right nor to the left and so she did not see Westerman, who was hidden in a corner between two boathouses.

But even if Stina was as innocent as Little Red Riding Hood—what luck it was that she had taken the herrings to Moses just when she did and that he sat on her for as long as he did and that she passed the sheep meadow just at the moment she did; otherwise, she would never have seen the fox. A large, hungry fox which had not managed to get what he wanted last night, no lamb, not even a rabbit, because a ferocious dog had chased him back to his lair.

He was hungrier than ever now and thought at least he would get a lamb, but then Stina turned up and began screaming to high heaven. This frightened him out of his wits and he slunk terrified through a hole in the hedge, across the road and between the pine trees on the outskirts of the wood.

Like a shining red streak he shot past the feet of old man Söderman, who had come to see whether Bosun had done any more damage to his sheep than he had noticed last night.

'The fox,' shrieked Stina. 'Oh, Grandpa, did you see the fox?'

'Did I see him!' said Söderman. 'That was the largest rascal of a fox I have seen in my life. That must have been what worried my sheep last night.'

'And then you go and say it was Bosun,' said Stina accusingly.

'Yes, then I go and say it was Bosun,' said her grandfather, scratching the back of his neck. He was old and very slow-thinking. How did it all hang together? he wondered. He *had* seen Bosun last night. And he had never heard of a fox daring to go right into the middle of a herd of sheep, but apparently there were some that did. One, at any rate. Were the fox and Bosun working together? Were they both hunting sheep? No, that couldn't be it. And suddenly Söderman understood—he was not as stupid as all that. The fox had chased Tottie last night and Bosun had chased the fox. Bosun had protected his sheep, that was what he had been doing, and as a reward Söderman had accused him and made it seem that . . .

'Stay here,' he said to Stina, 'and shout if you see the fox!'

He must get hold of Nisse—at once. He ran as he had not run for many years and at last arrived at the shop, panting and short of breath.

'Nisse, are you there?' he called anxiously, and then Marta came out, her face swollen with crying.

'No, Nisse has gone to the woods with Bosun,' she said. Then she covered her face with her hands and rushed inside again.

Söderman stood there as if he had been wounded. Then he began to run again. He groaned and ran and soon he could run no more. But he *must* find Nisse before it was too late.

'Where are you, Nisse? Don't shoot!'

It was absolutely silent in the woods. Far away a cuckoo called, but then he fell silent, too. Söderman ran along, hearing only his own panting and his own anxious cries.

'Where are you, Nisse? Don't shoot!'

He got no answer. Söderman kept on running. Then there was a shot. Söderman stopped dead and grasped his chest with his hands. He had come too late. It had happened! He would never be able to look Tjorven in the eye again! Söderman stood still and shut his eyes. Then he heard steps and looked up. Nisse was coming with his gun over his shoulder and beside him—Söderman stared and his jaw dropped to his chest. For beside Nisse padded Bosun!

'Wasn't that you—firing?' stammered Söderman.

Nisse gave him an anguished look. 'God help me, Söderman, I can't do it! I must ask Jansson to do it, but he's out shooting black-backed gulls today.'

Sorrow and joy go hand in hand and sometimes everything can change in the time it takes to sneeze. That day it only needed a panting old man with tears in his eyes to tell about the fox in his sheep field.

Nisse hugged Söderman. 'No one has ever made me happier than you, Söderman!' And never has a happier man come home from the woods with his dog than did Nisse Grankvist.

He is happy, but even so he will lie awake tonight and remember that unhappy moment in the woods. Most of all he will remember Bosun's eyes as he sat among the pines, waiting for the shot. Bosun *knew* what was going to happen and he gazed at Nisse submissively, sadly and faithfully. The memory of that gaze will keep Nisse awake tonight, but for the moment he is happy and he shouts to Tjorven, 'Tjorven, come here! Come here, little Bumble. I've got something to tell you that will make you very happy!'

Operation Moses

'I can't stop crying,' said Tjorven in surprise. She was sitting on the kitchen floor pressed tight against Bosun, and Bosun was eating steak. He had been given a whole pound of prime steak and everyone had asked his forgiveness. Now the whole family sat in a ring around him, adoring him and patting him, and everything was heavenly, thought Tjorven.

'But, just imagine, I can't stop crying!' she said angrily and dried away her tears with her fist.

She remembered all that she had thought during those last few grim hours. She had been quite wrong. Bosun would never chase sheep, however unhappy he felt about Moses. He was just as good, whatever happened. But she had been right too, and things would stay right in the future. Everything would be as before, before Moses came and muddled everything up.

Oh yes, Moses! She wondered how he was over in his boathouse, and suddenly she remembered Yoka. And Pelle, poor Pelle, why couldn't he be happy too if she was happy? Everybody should be happy now.

And Pelle was naturally very pleased when he heard that

Bosun was innocent, as pleased as one can be when they are absolutely in despair. He had grieved about Bosun as much as over his own rabbit, and it was a comfort to know that it was not Bosun who had killed Yoka.

'I feel much better now that I know it wasn't Bosun,' he said to Melker. But then he turned his head and said in a low voice, 'Although Yoka felt just the same, whoever it was who did it.'

At night he dreamed about Yoka, a living Yoka, who came leaping up to him, asking for dandelion leaves. But morning came and there was no Yoka any more. Not even his hutch was there. Johan and Niklas had taken it away so that Pelle would not see it. How nice they were, his brothers. Niklas had given him a little model boat which he had built, and Johan had given him his old sheath knife. Pelle was so grateful that he could have burst. Still, it was a sad morning and he wondered, if it was always going to be like this, how he was ever going to endure the long days.

That evening they buried Yoka in Jansson's cow meadow in a little glade with saxifrage in the grass and high birches around it.

HERE LIES YOKA

Pelle had carved this on a bit of wood and now he knelt, pressing down the turf on Yoka's grave, while Tjorven, Stina, and Bosun looked on. It would be lovely for Yoka here with saxifrage swaying over him and the thrushes singing for him in the evening, exactly as now.

Tjorven and Stina wanted to sing. It was always done at funerals. They had buried dead birds many times and they had always sung the same hymn that they now sang for Yoka.

All the world's an isle of sorrow,
Here today and gone tomorrow.

'No, let's not sing that one,' said Tjorven hastily. What was the matter with Pelle? He was sitting on a stone with his back to them and they could hear small, strange sobs. They looked at each other and Stina said anxiously, 'Perhaps he's crying because the world is an isle of sorrow.'

'But it isn't,' said Tjorven. And she shouted to Pelle, 'No, Pelle, the world isn't really an isle of sorrow. It's only something we're singing for Yoka.' On no account did she want there to be any more crying. In some way or other she must make Pelle happy, and suddenly she knew how to do it. 'Pelle, I'll give you something if you will promise not to be sad any more.'

'What?' said Pelle morosely, without turning around.

'I'll give you Moses!'

Then he turned around and stopped crying. He stared unbelievingly at Tjorven, but she assured him, 'Yes, I'll give him to you for your very own.'

And for the first time since that moment of sorrow when Yoka had disappeared, Pelle smiled again. 'How kind you are, Tjorven!'

She nodded. 'Yes, I am. But then, of course, I have Bosun.'

Stina beamed. 'Now all of us have got animals again. But we must go and tell Moses, mustn't we?'

They were all agreed about that. Moses must know to whom he belonged; besides which, he needed food, the nuisance.

'Goodbye, little Yoka,' said Pelle tenderly. And then he ran away without looking back.

And suddenly it was as if a cramp had let go of him. Suddenly he was another Pelle, a wild, excited, happy boy, who jumped and ran the whole way to Dead Man's Creek and finally threw himself on the ground and rolled down the slope towards the boathouse.

'Are you so happy just because I've given you Moses?' asked Tjorven.

Pelle thought. 'I don't know. Perhaps. But it's so sad to be sad that you can't stay like that for as long as you'd like.'

'Wait till you see Moses,' said Tjorven and opened the door to the boathouse.

They stood and stared, aghast, into emptiness. There was no Moses there. He had disappeared.

'He's run away,' said Tjorven.

'Run away! And fastened the latch on the door by himself?' said Pelle.

Moses had not run away. Someone must have taken him.

Tjorven turned to Stina. 'Did anyone see you when you came yesterday?'

Stina thought. 'No, nobody, except Westerman. He wanted to hear the story of Little Red Riding Hood.'

'Anyone can take you in,' said Tjorven.

'Oh, that Westerman, what a robber!' Tjorven kicked Moses's sleeping box so hard that it flew over to the wall. 'I'll pull out all his hair. He's a thief. I'll shoot him,' she shrieked in rage.

'I know what we'll do,' said Pelle. 'We'll steal Moses back. I bet you he's put him into his boathouse, and I bet there's a latch on that door too.'

Tjorven's rage abated. 'Tonight—when Westerman is asleep,' she said eagerly.

Stina was eager too, but there was one thing that worried her.

'But what if we go to sleep before Westerman?'

'We won't do that,' Tjorven assured her, threateningly. 'Not when we're as angry as all this.'

Stina was obviously not angry enough, for she could not keep awake. But Tjorven and Pelle could and, what was stranger still, no one saw them when they crept out.

There had been a fox hunt on Seacrow Island that evening. Everybody had gathered together to frighten the fox out of his lair and they had managed to frighten him, but no fox was shot. For when they got him in a tight corner out on Crow Point and he saw no other way out he slunk into the water and swam away. He was a fox who was used to getting away and it was not far to the nearest island. Nisse Grankvist fired after him, but missed.

Pelle was pleased when he heard this. 'Why shouldn't a fox live too?' he said. 'And on the island he's gone to there aren't any rabbits or sheep or hens, anyhow.'

'So he'll have a tough time,' said Tjorven, contented. 'The nasty creature, why should he kill Yoka?'

'He only did it because he was a fox,' Pelle explained to her. 'And he had to behave like a fox, you see.'

'Well, he may be a fox, but that needn't stop him from behaving like a human being,' said Tjorven and refused to understand the fox.

But . . . behave like a human being? Like Westerman for example? Would that be much better? Stealing a poor little baby seal just to sell him! But he wasn't going to get away with that, Tjorven asserted. 'If only Cora doesn't bark,' she said.

But Cora did. She stood outside her kennel and barked as loudly as she could when she saw Tjorven and Pelle creeping past her. But Pelle had planned on this beforehand and had brought a bone for her, which he now held out, speaking kind words, and after that she was quiet. But it was anxious work, in any case, for they did not know whether anyone would come out to see why she had been barking. They lay for a long time hidden behind the lilac bush at the gate and waited, but when no one came they crept cautiously into the garden. Up on a rise stood the house, which they would have to pass to get down to the boathouse. All was silent and dark. The house lay like a black, threatening square with the light night sky behind it. No one appeared.

'They are sleeping like logs,' said Tjorven. But she spoke too soon, for suddenly a light appeared in a window and Tjorven gasped. Mrs. Westerman had just lit the oil lamp over the table. They ran frantically straight towards the window and threw themselves down on the ground. In a panic, they lay there and waited. Had she seen them or hadn't she? Perhaps she had been standing in the darkness before she lit the lamp, had looked out from behind the curtains and seen them come in through the gate. No one could really hide himself on a light June evening on this little hilly promontory, where there was not so much as a bush to crouch behind.

But when Mrs. Westerman did not come out they began to take courage. She could not possibly see them unless she leaned out and looked down on them, and that they hoped she would not do—because if Mrs. Westerman began to bark they would not be able to silence her with a bone, they knew that. They hardly dared to move or whisper, scarcely to breathe. They could only lie still and listen. They could hear Mrs. Westerman moving about inside. The window was open and she was so close that they could have stretched up over the window sill and said hello, had they wished to. Suddenly she began to read aloud to herself. Tjorven groaned. It would have been all right if she had read something out of the daily paper, but to lie here as quiet as a shrimp and have to listen to things she did not understand was more than she could bear.

Pelle did not understand it either, but it sounded like something out of the Bible. She had a monotonous voice, but she read without hesitation and Pelle listened. Suddenly there came some words which stood out from all the other meaningless ones and began to shine, as words could shine for him sometimes.

'If I take the wings of the morning, and dwell in the

uttermost parts of the sea,' read Mrs. Westerman. Then she sighed before she went on.

Pelle did not pay any attention to what came afterwards; it was just those words he could not forget. And he murmured them silently to himself.

'If I take the wings of the morning, and dwell in the uttermost parts of the sea . . .' Like Carpenter's Cottage, for example. That was a dwelling in the uttermost parts of the sea. And that was where you wanted to be when you were at home in the town. Just think, if only one had the wings of the morning and could fly there across the water, how wonderful that would be! To your dwelling in the uttermost parts of the sea—to Carpenter's Cottage!

Pelle was so absorbed in his thoughts that he did not notice that Mrs. Westerman had stopped reading until Tjorven poked him. What would happen now? She put out the lamp and it was dark inside. And suddenly Pelle heard someone breathing heavily just above his head. He did not dare look up, but he realized that Mrs. Westerman was standing at the open window. It was terrifying, lying there hunched up, just listening and waiting. Now—now she would see them, he was sure of it. But just when he felt he could not endure it a second longer, she shut the window with such a slam that they both jumped, and then everything was quiet. They lay still for a time and heard their own hearts beating, and then they ran quickly, bent almost double, around the house and down to the boathouse.

'Moses, are you there?' whispered Tjorven.

And it was obvious that Moses was there for he wailed like a ghost. Tjorven opened the door.

Stina shivered when they told her everything the next day. How Moses squealed and how they got hold of him and how Westerman came out in his shirt sleeves and swore at them just as they were going out of the garden gate, and how Cora barked, and how they finally got Moses into his cart, and how they rushed home to Carpenter's Cottage with him while Westerman shouted after them, 'You wait till I catch you, Tjorven!'

'It was a good thing I wasn't with you,' said Stina. 'I would have died on the spot.'

Moses had slept beside Pelle's bed that night. Johan and Niklas were amazed but not at all displeased when they woke next morning and saw their new roommate.

'I *must* keep him here, so that Westerman won't come and take him,' explained Pelle. 'But now you must help me to talk to Daddy.'

His father certainly had objections. 'It's all right for Tjorven to give you Moses,' said Melker, 'but it's not a good thing for you two and Westerman to be carrying on a sort of gangster warfare, stealing seals from each other at night.'

They all tried to figure out a better way. The whole family was sitting around the breakfast table and they could hear Moses floundering around up in the boys' room.

Malin was not particularly pleased about her new lodger, but for Pelle's sake she had to put up with him. Pelle needed

Moses just now, she understood that, and Westerman would have to be made to understand too.

'It's only money he wants,' said Johan. 'Can't you give him a few hundred crowns, Daddy, so that Pelle can keep his seal?'

'Give him a few hundred crowns yourself,' said Melker. 'We must all help.'

'You aren't generally at much of a loss when it's a question of earning money. *You* get going!'

So they got going. Every child on Seacrow Island wanted to take part in what Melker called Operation Moses. It was like a game. Suddenly it was much more fun to weed strawberry beds and carry water and bail out the boats and tar the jetties and carry luggage for summer visitors when one knew that with every penny earned, the sum that was going to buy Moses free from Westerman increased.

Westerman sneered when he came into the shop and heard about Operation Moses. 'That's all right by me,' he said. 'It doesn't matter to me who buys the seal. But two hundred crowns I must have this week, otherwise I'll sell him elsewhere.'

'Go to blazes, Westerman,' said Tjorven, straight out.

Westerman threw a few coppers to her. 'A little help for Moses,' he said. 'I think you'll need it. I don't expect you'll collect two hundred crowns by Saturday, and I'm not waiting longer than that.'

'Oh, go to blazes,' said Tjorven once more for safety's sake. But she took the coppers and put them in Moses's savings box, which stood on the counter.

'No, Tjorven, we don't talk like that,' said Nisse sternly,

and then he turned to Westerman. 'You really are a skunk, Westerman, do you know that?'

But Westerman only grinned.

Operation Moses continued, growing more intensive every day.

'You see, Moses? I've got blisters on my hands for your sake,' said Freddy, after she had been beating rugs a whole morning.

But Moses lived his own life and paid no attention to anyone. He was quite indifferent to Operation Moses. Obviously he had not got along very well during his solitary sojourns in various boathouses. He was scarcely recognizable, he was so nervous and restless. Almost bad-tempered. He squealed and hissed more than ever, and sometimes he even tried to bite.

'He isn't exactly the kind of animal I like having in the house,' said Malin, but she did not let Pelle hear her saying this.

Pelle adored Moses in the same way he had adored Yoka, and when Moses hissed at him he only patted him.

'Poor little Moses, what's the matter? Aren't you happy with me?'

But nowadays it did not seem that Moses was happy anywhere. He would not stay in the boathouse nor in his pool. He preferred to be down by the water's edge, but Pelle did not dare leave him there for long, for Uncle Nisse had warned him, 'Keep him in his pool, otherwise he'll run away one of these days.'

And Pelle kept Moses shut up in the pool and wondered sadly what it would be like to have an animal which did not want to run away. Yoka had run away—to his own cost—but Pelle had hoped it would be different with a seal. Poor Moses, why was he so restless?

Tottie's leg was almost well again but he had not moved back to the sheep meadow. He followed Stina wherever she went and Bosun again followed Tjorven. He had not done so immediately, for he was not a dog who pushed himself forward before he knew whether he was wanted. He had gone quietly to his usual place beside the steps until Tjorven came and threw her arms around him.

'Now then, Bosun, you are not to lie here any more, ever again!'

Then he had followed her and from that moment he had never left her side.

Wherever Tjorven and Stina went their animals followed them. But Pelle had no one following him.

'Although, of course, he is your seal,' said Tjorven.

Pelle looked thoughtful. 'I'm beginning to think that Moses belongs to himself,' he said.

And then it was Saturday, the day when Westerman was to have his two hundred crowns.

There was a feeling of nervousness in the Seacrow shop, for now the money was to be counted. The shop was full of people. This was something which had interested the whole island. None of the islanders envied Westerman a penny. To

239

treat Tjorven, *their* Tjorven, so badly—he should never have done it! They were all agreed on that.

Westerman felt this and so he looked more cocksure than usual when he came into the shop, exactly at the time arranged, and pushed his way to the counter. Behind it stood all the children in a row, glaring at him. All the Melkersons and all the Grankvists. Tjorven glared at him most angrily of all. It was the limit that Westerman should be paid for a seal that he had given her and which had cost her so much in milk, herrings, and care.

Westerman grinned at her and was full of jokes. 'How nice you look, Tjorven! You think you're going to have a seal now, don't you?'

'We shall see,' said Nisse and opened the savings box, pouring the money out on to the counter. The whole shop was absolutely silent as he began to count. No one made a sound. Nothing could be heard but the clink of money and Nisse's mumbling.

Pelle had climbed up on a margarine box behind the counter. It was horrible to hear that clinking. What if there wasn't enough money? Poor Moses, what if Westerman took him and sold him to Petter?

Then he had a thought which hurt him a little. Who said it would be so much worse for Moses? Perhaps it was more fun to swim about in the sea with a radio apparatus on you than to splash in the pool on Seacrow Island. Though, of course, the very best thing for a seal, thought Pelle, was to swim about in the sea, absolutely free, without any radio apparatus or anything, just like an ordinary seal among other seals.

In the middle of his thoughts he heard Uncle Nisse's voice. 'One hundred and sixty-seven crowns and eighty öre.'

A murmur of disappointment went through the crowd in the shop and everyone glared at Westerman as if it were his fault that there was not enough money in the savings box. Nisse looked him straight in the eyes.

'I suppose you'll be willing to bargain a little?'

Westerman looked straight back at him. 'Do you usually bargain with your customers?'

Then suddenly Tjorven stood in front of Westerman. 'Westerman, do you know what? I never asked you for that baby seal. You gave him to me. Do you remember that?'

'Don't begin that all over again,' said Westerman.

Tjorven eyed him from top to toe. 'You really are a skunk, Westerman, did you know that?' she said.

But then Marta took charge. 'No, Tjorven, you really mustn't talk like that!'

'But that's what Daddy said,' said Tjorven, and everyone laughed.

Westerman turned red with fury. He could stand anything but people laughing at him.

'Where's the seal? I'll take him now!'

'Don't try that, Westerman,' said Melker, who until now had not said a word. 'I'll pay the difference.'

But now Westerman was really enraged. 'No, don't bother. I've got a better customer.'

And then a strange thing happened, for just at that moment the door opened and into the shop came none other than

Westerman's other customer, Petter Malm. Malin's prince had arrived, and when she saw him she began to tremble. She had been longing for him ever since he had left, most of all during those days of despair with Pelle. Then she had longed for him so hard that she felt he must sense it wherever he was. And now there he stood. He had come back. It must mean that he had been longing for her too.

'Do you live in this shop?' asked Petter. He took her hands and he sounded very happy, for he had looked for her in vain at Carpenter's Cottage. Now he had found her, and her eyes were warm and sparkling as she gazed at him. But her first words to him sounded like a reproach. 'Petter, must you really have a seal?'

Before Petter had time to answer, Westerman went over to him, grinning smugly. Now the islanders could stare as much as they liked. He would show them that Westerman knew how to do business.

'You've come at the right moment, sir,' he said. 'You can buy that seal now. Three hundred crowns and we'll call it a deal!'

Petter Malm smiled at him in a friendly way. 'Three hundred—isn't that a lot for a seal? I don't think I can pay as much as that.'

Tjorven and Stina gave him a look which showed what they thought of him. Oh, why had they kissed that frog!

'Oh, well, say two hundred then,' said Westerman eagerly.

Petter continued to smile in a friendly way. 'Really? I can have him for two hundred crowns! That's cheap. But I don't really want a seal at the moment.'

'Don't want a seal!' Westerman gasped. 'But you said . . .'

'No, thanks. I told you—I don't want a seal at the moment,' said Petter Malm. 'Not this particular seal, at any rate.'

Then jubilation broke loose in the shop on Seacrow Island and Westerman stormed furiously towards the door. But Nisse shouted after him, 'You can take this money anyhow and be content with it!'

But by now Westerman was tired of everything to do with the business of seals and he was ashamed of himself, too, not because he had been greedy, but because they were all standing there, thinking that he was. So he didn't want the money or the seal. In fact, he didn't want anything, except to get away from the shop and avoid seeing a single person who lived on Seacrow.

'Take your old seal, Tjorven,' he said. 'I don't care about him or any of you.' Then he disappeared.

But then Pelle came to life. 'No, he must have the money. Otherwise I will never feel that Moses is really my seal.' And he took hold of the bag into which Nisse had put the money and rushed after Westerman. They all waited in excited anticipation, and after a time Pelle came back very red in the face.

'Well, he finally took it, because he said he needed it.'

Malin stroked his cheek. It was a caress full of tenderness. 'Then, Pelle, it's your seal altogether now.'

'Now perhaps we can finally have a bit of rest!' said Teddy.

Malin wrote in her diary about all these events: 'Peace be to Moses as he swims in the sea! Pelle let his seal loose yesterday

243

evening. Daddy, Petter, and I came down to the jetty just as it happened, and there he stood with blank eyes, looking after his seal, which he could still see as a little spot far out in the bay.

' "But why, Pelle, why in the world?" asked Daddy.

'And Pelle answered in a hoarse little voice, 'I don't want any animal of mine pining to be somewhere else. Now Moses is where he *ought* to be.'

'I got a lump in my throat and I saw that Daddy swallowed once or twice. We were quite quiet.

'But Tjorven and Stina were there too, and Tjorven said, 'Pelle, do you know what? It wasn't any good my giving you that seal, because now you haven't got an animal at all.'

' "Only my wasps," said Pelle, sounding even more miserable.

'It was then it happened. Oh, Petter, I will be grateful to you for it as long as I live! Petter was standing with Yum-yum in his arms and suddenly he said in that quiet way in which he says everything, 'But I don't think it's right that Pelle should have nothing but wasps. I think he should have Yum-yum.' And he went up to Pelle and put the puppy in his arms. 'Yum-yum won't pine to be somewhere else,' said Petter.

' "No, because that puppy will have a very good time," said Tjorven when she finally realized what had happened.

'Pelle stood there quite pale, looking first at Petter, and then at Yum-yum. He did not say thank you—he didn't say anything. But I behaved in a way which I could not understand myself when I thought about it afterwards. I rushed at Petter and kissed him, and when I had done that, I kissed him again—and then again! It looked as if Petter liked it.

' "Who'd have thought a little puppy could do so much," he said. "Why didn't I bring a whole kennelful?"

'Tjorven and Stina stood there looking at us, very much amused. I think they thought it an interesting scene, but then Tjorven said, "Don't kiss him too much, Malin. You never know, he may turn into a frog again."

'Young children really have some very strange ideas in their round little heads, and I can't imagine where they get them from. But both Tjorven and Stina seem to think quite seriously that Petter is an enchanted frog-prince out of a ditch. Stina's poor little head is absolutely full of enchanted princes, Cinderellas, and Little Red Riding Hoods and I don't know what else. And when she saw Moses disappearing out in the bay she said to Tjorven, "I believe that Moses is the Sea King's little boy, anyhow. That's Prince Moses swimming out there!"

'I earnestly hope that Prince Moses is just as happy now as Pelle imagines he is.

' "Pelle, you'll find that Moses will come back to visit you sometimes," said Petter. "He's a tame seal anyhow and he may suddenly decide to take a little trip to Seacrow Island again."

' "If the Sea King allows him to, he may," said Stina.

'Well, whether the Sea King allows Moses to come or not, Pelle is a very happy Pelle at the moment. And I am a very happy Malin, even though Petter went back to town when *Seacrow I* steamed away a little while ago. But, at any rate, at last I know how it feels! And it really does feel as if you'll die of it. How long can one go on feeling like that? Petter says that he's steadfast and true. Am I steadfast as well? How can I know? But I hope I am. I believe I am. One thing is certain, at any rate. Pelle needs a steadfast Malin and he must have that whatever happens. Pelle likes Petter—how could he not like him? But at the same time he is, as usual, a little afraid, and when he lay in bed last night with Yum-yum beside him, so happy that the air seemed to shine around him, he suddenly became serious and threw his arms around me, and said, "You are my Malin, aren't you?"

'Yes, my dear little brother, I am. And although Tjorven and Stina think I am already too old to have an enchanted prince, I think the prince can wait for me a couple of years. And he has said he will.

'Now a new June night is beginning over Seacrow Island. And now I am going to sleep. But tomorrow I will wake and be as happy then as I am now. I think!'

Tjorven Earns
Three Crowns

On Monday morning Pelle woke up early because Yum-yum was whining, and he took him into his bed. With his nose burrowed under Pelle's chin the puppy went to sleep again, but Pelle did not. It would be madness to sleep when he could lie awake and know that this soft, warm little thing that he had close to him was Yum-yum, his own puppy. How wonderful that you could be so completely happy! In the middle of all this happiness he remembered Moses. It seemed a little unfair that he did not miss him as much as he should have.

'But,' he explained to the sleeping Yum-yum, 'Moses doesn't miss me either, I'm quite sure of that. He's swimming around, playing with the other seals and enjoying himself like anything.'

A moment later he thought of Yoka, too. That hurt a little. Not so much for Yoka's sake, perhaps, but because it reminded him of what could happen when the world sometimes became an isle of sorrow. He pushed away these thoughts, which was not difficult, for at that moment Yum-yum woke up and was immediately full of life. He nosed Pelle's face and licked him, worried his pyjamas, and barked and jumped around on the bed. And Pelle laughed. It was a laugh so full of happiness that Malin stopped making toast downstairs just to enjoy it.

What might not happen on a day that began with a boy's happy laughter and with such lovely weather? Last week had been unbearable, with nothing but wind and rain and cold—and then suddenly a wonderful morning like this one. Malin decided to serve breakfast outside in the garden.

Her father was dressing in his room behind the kitchen and he sang as he did so.

'You mustn't sing on an empty stomach,' Malin shouted to him, 'or you'll cry before evening. Didn't you know that?'

'Utter nonsense,' said Melker, and he came out into the kitchen, singing. 'Don't you think we've cried enough?' he said. 'There really has to be an end to all this weeping and wailing!'

Together they prepared for breakfast on the garden table. Malin stood in the kitchen and handed out the things to Melker through the window. When everything was ready, Melker looked around. 'And where are my three hungry boys?'

The two eldest came up from the shore. They had been out early, fishing. They had not caught anything, but sitting there in the morning sun made them feel that the hours were not being wasted, and anyhow it gave them an appetite for breakfast.

'Oh, Malin, you have made waffles!' Niklas looked at his sister and the waffles with great satisfaction.

'Yes, I've made them out of gratitude to this Monday morning, just to make everything as lovely as possible.'

Melker nodded in agreement. 'Yes, it's a wonderful morning and a wonderful breakfast table, laid by Melker himself. Waffles, chocolate, coffee, toast, butter, cheese, marmalade, jam, and wasps. What more could anyone ask?'

'Did you invite the wasps too?' asked Johan.

'No, those little devils came of their own accord. What a pity we have to put up with that wasps' nest this year too!'

Melker shooed away a couple of wasps from the marmalade jar. But even if Pelle was sitting with the world's most wonderful puppy on his knees there was still room in his heart for all other animals, and he said reproachfully, 'You leave my wasps alone, Daddy! They want to live at Carpenter's Cottage too. Can't you understand that—just like we do!'

And, of course, Melker understood all about wanting to live in Carpenter's Cottage. They all understood that.

'It's odd how very fond one gets of this tumbledown old dump,' said Malin.

The wall behind her, the red Carpenter's Cottage wall, gave out a warmth that was not only due to sunshine, Malin was convinced. She thought of the house almost as a living being, a secure and warmly alive being, which had taken them all to its heart.

'Tumbledown—oh, come, it's not exactly that,' said Melker. 'The walls need repairing here and there, but the house is built of sound old weathered timber. There's some rot, of course, but if it were my house, I would soon fix that and make it into such a splendid place that it would astonish you all.'

If I had a dwelling in the uttermost parts of the sea and put a new roof on it, thought Pelle, that would be something!

'And then this site,' said Melker. 'You could never find its equal anywhere.'

And there they sat with their waffles, looking at each other and at their site and their Carpenter's Cottage and thinking that everything was absolutely marvellous. The jasmines were in flower, sending out their sweet perfume; the wild roses were full of pink buds, ready to burst at any moment; the grass was green and soft and sloped gently down towards the shore, where the seagulls screeched. Yes, it was absolutely marvellous—everything.

'And to think that an ordinary, simple carpenter could position his house so perfectly,' said Melker, 'with exactly the right view, making it look as if it had just grown up out of the ground by itself, and giving it a garden like this one!'

'Are you sure, Daddy—it is certain, isn't it?—that we'll live here always?' said Pelle. 'In the summer, I mean?'

'Oh yes, of course,' said Melker. 'Mattsson is coming today. He telephoned and told them so at the shop, so we will have our new contract at last.'

While the Melkersons sat finishing their breakfast Tjorven was out for a little morning walk with Bosun. She went down to the jetty to feed the swans. They came every morning and she gave them dry bread. There was a swan father and a swan mother and seven grey balls of children. As she stood there, a large motorboat, which she did not recognize, came in towards the jetty. There were three people on board. One of them she knew to be Mattsson, who always came once or twice a year. The other one, a large fat man wearing a yachtsman's cap, she did not know. He was driving the boat and she did not think he had ever been to Seacrow Island before. Nor had the girl who was sitting beside him.

'Throw me the rope,' said Tjorven, and Mattsson threw it to her and she moored the boat.

'Clever girl,' said the man with the yachting cap, when he had jumped ashore. 'That's a splendid knot!'

Tjorven laughed. 'Knot! It's only a half hitch.'

'H'm,' said the man with the yachting cap. 'And where did you learn that?'

'I've always known it,' said Tjorven.

Then he took two shining coins from his pocket and gave them to her. She stared at them in amazement, and then she smiled at him.

But by now he was no longer paying any attention to her. 'Come on, Lotte,' he shouted, and the girl jumped ashore.

She was very pretty, thought Tjorven, with her slim, light blue jeans and shining brown hair, which was obviously permanently waved. Lucky girl, to be allowed to have her hair done, although she was only about as old as Teddy. But she looked sulky and did not pay any attention to Tjorven. She had a little white poodle in her arms and Tjorven looked around for Bosun. It might be fun for him to meet a poodle.

But Bosun had gone off along the shore and was halfway to Crow Point.

Mattsson was on his way to Carpenter's Cottage, Tjorven realized that. But why he had the other two with him she simply could not understand, nor did she care. She followed them, anyway, because she was on her way there to call for Pelle.

'Ah, there you are at last, Mr. Mattsson,' said Melker when he saw the visitors. 'Come on in, and we'll clear the table so that we can sign the papers here.'

Mattsson was a small, nervous, self-important gentleman, and he wore a suit that made Malin shudder. It was striped and quite horribly ugly, she thought, but surely it couldn't be just because of his suit that she felt so antagonistic towards him and the two others.

Mattsson introduced his friends. 'This is Mr. Karlberg and his daughter—they would like to have a look at Carpenter's Cottage.'

'Certainly,' said Melker. 'But why do they want to?'

Mattsson explained that it was just that Mrs. Sjöblom wanted to sell Carpenter's Cottage. She was old and was tired of renting it and so . . .

'Wait a minute now,' said Melker. 'I've already rented this cottage, if I am not mistaken, and I was due to sign a new yearly contract today. Isn't that so, Mattsson?'

'Unfortunately, it can't be done,' said Mattsson. 'Mrs. Sjöblom wants to sell and no one can raise any objection to it. If you want to go on living here, buy the place—that is, if you can pay a better price than Mr. Karlberg has offered, of course.'

Melker began to tremble. He felt despair rising inside him, almost suffocating him. How could anyone come and wreck everything just with a few words, both for him and for his children? Only two minutes ago they had been sitting here, happy and gay, and then in one moment everything had been turned to dust and ashes. Buy the place—what a joke! Why, he couldn't buy so much as a dog's kennel with the income he had! A yearly rental was all that he could scrape together. But that he could do, at any rate, and so he had confidently looked forward to spending year after year at Carpenter's Cottage. At last he had found a place where his children could put down roots and where they could spend their childhood summers, as he himself had once done—something beautiful to remember all their lives. And then someone arrives and says a couple of words and everything is over! He did not dare look at his children, but he heard Pelle's trembling voice.

'Daddy, you *said* that we were always going to live here!'

Melker swallowed violently. What hadn't he said! He had said they would live here for always. And that all the weeping and wailing was to be at an end. At least he thought he had said that—and now here he was, unable to do anything but howl like a dog in helplessness and despair. In the meantime, Mattsson stood two yards away from him leaning against the whitebeam, looking as if it were just an ordinary day and all this just an ordinary bit of business.

'Do you mean,' said Melker bitterly, 'do you really mean that we have to leave here, me and my children?'

'Not at this moment, naturally,' said Mattsson. 'But if Mr. Karlberg buys—or someone else—then you will have to arrange with the new owner about how long you can stay on here.'

Mr. Karlberg did not look at Melker. He spoke to Mattsson as if no one else were present. 'Yes, I'll certainly consider buying if we can agree on the price. The house is nothing, of course, I can see that by looking at it, and it could easily be torn down. But you don't find a site like this every day.'

Melker could hear a dull murmur from his children and he ground his teeth.

Now Lotte Karlberg chimed into the conversation. 'You're right, Daddy. The house is really dreadful. But we could build a lovely little bungalow, couldn't we? One like Karl and Anna-Greta have.'

Her father nodded, but he looked a little worried. Perhaps he thought it was going a little too far to bring in Karl and Anna-Greta's bungalow at this stage.

Tjorven thought so too. She thought the whole thing had gone quite far enough. That Lotte, sitting there on the steps of Carpenter's Cottage as if the whole house belonged to her!

Tjorven went and stood in front of her. 'Lotte, do you know what?' she said. 'I think you're a bongalo yourself, you big fat thing!'

Lotte realized at once that she had made an enemy. And

not only one. All those children who were standing staring at her were her enemies. But she didn't care. On the contrary, she enjoyed it, for she was confident of her superiority. It was her father who could decide whether these children should be allowed to live here or not, so they had better behave. They needn't glare at her like that as if she had no right to be there.

'I suppose people have the right to buy places if they want,' she said to no one in particular, looking straight ahead of her.

'Of course,' said Teddy. 'And build bungalows like Karl and Anna-Greta's. Go ahead by all means!'

'This old rubbish dump can easily be torn down,' said Freddy. 'Just you try!'

Teddy and Freddy had arrived as soon as they heard what was happening. In the shop they knew in some supernatural way all that happened on the island almost before it had happened, and Teddy and Freddy wanted to be with their friends in their hour of need. What were friends for otherwise? Never had they seen Johan and Niklas so depressed and gloomy. And Pelle—he was still sitting at the breakfast table, his face white as chalk, and beside him sat Malin. Her arm was around Pelle and she looked quite pale too. It was all quite unbearable and then that snobby girl had to start shouting about building bungalows. Was it any wonder Teddy and Freddy were furious?

'What is a bongalo?' asked Tjorven of her older and wiser sisters.

'A crazy person, obviously,' said Freddy.

'Someone absolutely completely crazy, just like her!' said

Teddy, jerking her thumb towards Lotte. It was terrible to think that perhaps they would have her as a neighbour instead of Johan and Niklas and Pelle and Malin and Uncle Melker.

'It might be a good idea to take a look inside,' said Mr. Karlberg, and for the first time he turned towards Melker. 'Oh, with your permission of course, Mr. Melkerson,' he said, managing to sound both pleasant and superior.

'Yes, of course,' Mr. Melkerson consented. How could he do otherwise? He was a beaten man and he knew it, but he went in with them and so did Malin. Her father must not be left alone with these two men who wanted to take his Carpenter's Cottage away from him. And anyhow she would not dream of allowing anyone to wander around their home and criticize everything they had loved so much. It was a home for people to live in and enjoy, and it was theirs, Malin knew that. Carpenter's Cottage and the Melkersons belonged to each other. But now other people had arrived, who only noticed that the floors shook and the windows were a little crooked and there were patches of damp on the ceiling in one or two places. Poor old Carpenter's Cottage! Malin felt that she had to protect it, and so she stood holding the door open for the unbidden guests and for her father. She gave him a secret, comforting nudge and he looked at her with a grateful, apologetic, miserable smile.

Lotte did not go in with them. The house was to be pulled down if Daddy bought it and she wanted to stay out here with the children and enjoy her superiority. There were six of them, but it would be exciting to see if she could manage six enemies at once. She usually managed to deal with situations like this pretty well, for she was sure of herself. It had never been difficult for her to make enemies, so she had had plenty of practice. Besides, she had Missie, her poodle, so she was not quite alone, and Missie at any rate thought exactly as she did, that Lotte Karlberg was something very grand and important. It strengthened her to feel Missie's support.

She held the little poodle in her arms so that she would not go for Pelle's puppy, and then, humming, she walked around the house, as if to inspect it, although her real motive was to see how far she could go in annoying those children, who stood there staring at her in absolute silence. It took courage to walk up and down in front of their hostile eyes and she could never have done it if she had not felt so absolutely superior. She did not need to bother about six country children.

'Missie, darling,' she said, 'will you like living here in the summer . . . in a new house, of course, not in this rickety dump?'

She grabbed hold of a window to show Missie how rickety it was, but that window belonged to the larder and it was loose. The Melkerson children knew that, but Lotte did not and she was a little taken aback when she suddenly found herself standing with the window in her hand. She made totally useless efforts to put it back until Niklas came and took it from her. He fixed it up and said coldly, 'You could at least wait to begin tearing down the rickety old dump until you've bought it.'

Lotte stuck her nose in the air. She did not feel quite as

happy as before and to hide her embarrassment she tried to get into conversation with Pelle. He had a dog too, and dogs were something you could always talk about.

'I see you've got a cocker spaniel,' she said. Pelle did not answer. What he had was no business of hers and just now he was in such despair that it was hardly his business either.

'They're very sweet, of course, but not particularly intelligent,' said Lotte. 'Poodles are much more intelligent.'

Pelle remained silent, which made Lotte feel awkward. All this silence was making her feel unsure of herself so she turned to Tjorven instead.

'You would like to have a little dog too, I expect, wouldn't you?'

Tjorven had stared at Lotte with more hostility than anyone, but now she smiled broadly. 'I've got a little dog. Would you like to see him?'

Lotte shook her head. 'No, don't bring another dog. Missie will only get angry and go for him.'

'Then she's a bongalo too,' said Tjorven. 'But I bet you she wouldn't go for my dog.'

'That's what you think,' said Lotte. 'You don't know Missie.'

'Would you like to bet?' said Tjorven. 'Bet you a crown!' She held up one of the coins that Lotte's father had given her.

'All right,' said Lotte. 'But you'll only have yourself to blame.'

She noticed that a sort of sigh of expectation went through the crowd of children. Oh, well, if they were really so keen on dogfights, she would show them! Missie was certainly small but she was very quick-tempered and she often got herself into fights with dogs much bigger than herself—and smaller too, of course. The ladies in Norrtälje called her 'the terror of the town'. 'She goes around as if she thought she were a great Dane,' one of them had said only yesterday, when Missie had gone for her big boxer. So if these brats wanted to see a dogfight, they could. Missie always won.

'Keep your puppy out of the way,' said Lotte to Pelle. 'I'm letting Missie go!' And she did. She put Missie on the ground, and then all they had to do was wait for the dog to attack.

Bosun, back from his walk, was lying asleep behind the lilac hedge, but he got up willingly when Tjorven woke him. He rose to his feet and in all his towering hugeness he came around the corner.

There was a shriek. It came from Missie's owner. Missie herself stood stock-still for one dreadful moment, looking at the monster that was approaching. Then she gave a howl and raced out of the gate like a streak of white smoke.

Bosun looked after her in surprise. Why was she in such a hurry? She might at least have said how-do-you-do. Bosun himself, polite dog that he was, came forward to greet Lotte, but Lotte gave another shriek and ran behind the whitebeam.

'Take your dog away,' she shouted wildly. 'Take him away!'

'What are you screaming about?' said Tjorven. 'Bosun doesn't attack anyone. *He*'s not a bongalo!'

Johan was lying on his face in the grass, groaning with laughter. He might just as easily have been crying. In fact that would have been more understandable, but now he was laughing and he could not stop.

'Oh, Tjorven!' he moaned. 'Oh, Tjorven!'

Tjorven gave him a surprised glance, but then she turned to Lotte. 'I won! You owe me a crown!'

Lotte had emerged from behind the tree when she heard that Bosun was not dangerous, but now she was both shy and angry and did not want to stay with the children any more. Grudgingly, she fished out her purse and gave Tjorven her crown.

'Thank you,' said Tjorven. She stood with her head on one side, gazing at Lotte. 'People like you shouldn't make bets,' she said. 'That's only for people like me and Uncle Melker.'

Lotte looked impatiently towards the door of the Carpenter's Cottage. Wasn't her father ever coming so that they could go? She did not want to stay here any longer.

'Guess what Uncle Melker had a bet about once,' said Tjorven. 'Although it was years ago, of course.'

Lotte was not interested about what Uncle Melker had done years ago, but Tjorven did not worry about that. 'He bet with a friend that he wouldn't eat for fourteen days or sleep for fourteen nights. What do you think of that?'

'Crazy,' said Lotte. 'He couldn't.'

'Yes, he could,' said Tjorven dramatically. 'Because he slept in the day and ate at night! What do you say now?'

'Oh, Tjorven,' groaned Johan.

But then he stopped laughing for Mr. Karlberg had come out with Mattsson, and Johan had heard the awful thing he said. All of them had heard.

'The house is worthless, but I'll buy it nevertheless. I don't think one could go wrong with this site. I'll just talk it over with my wife,' he said. 'Shall we arrange that I come to your office tomorrow at four o'clock? Would that suit you?'

'Splendid,' said Mattsson.

They all sat in the kitchen of Carpenter's Cottage that evening, the Grankvists and the Melkersons.

They had sat there so many evenings but they had never been so depressed or subdued before. For what could they say? Melker was silent. He could not speak because of the awful ache in his chest. Nisse and Marta looked shyly at him. They had tried to convey to him how sorry they were about it all and how they would miss him and his family, but Melker looked so upset that they gave up. Now they sat in silence, while the summer dusk sank mercifully over the kitchen. In its darkness everyone could devote himself to his gloomy thoughts, quite undisturbed.

What a strange summer, thought Malin. She remembered the first one as calm, peaceful, and uneventful. But what had happened to this one? At one moment Petter, bringing complete and unbounded happiness; the next, tears and despair. First the business of Pelle and Yoka and now this last bitter, unendurable affair, which would be the end of everything. Yes, it was truly a bitter end!

Tjorven lay on the floor with Bosun beside her, and Pelle sat with his back against the woodbin and Yum-yum on his knee. As far as Pelle was concerned, life, even in the ordinary way, was something of a switchback ride, with enormous jerks between what was fun and what was sad, and just now, in spite of Yum-yum, he was as low as he could possibly be.

Worst of all was that Daddy was in such despair. He could endure anything but seeing Daddy so sad. Or Malin. Or Johan or Niklas. They must not be so miserable. Pelle could not bear it. He held Yum-yum against his cheek and sought a little comfort from his warmth and softness, but it did not help much.

Tjorven was crying quietly and furiously. This morning she had been brave because she had not really understood what it was all about. Now she knew and it was enough to make one burst! She was very sorry for herself too. Why should people make such a muddle of things? First it was Westerman, and now this old Karlberg and his stupid Lotte. To blazes with all of them. Poor Pelle, she wanted to give him something to make him happy. She had no seal to give this time. She had nothing.

Then she heard Freddy say, over in her corner, 'Money, money, money. It's not fair that it should mean so much. Blast Karlberg!'

And suddenly Tjorven remembered. Who didn't have money? She had a whole pocketful of it! Why, she had three crowns!

'Pelle, I'm going to give you something,' whispered Tjorven so that no one else would hear, and she smuggled the three crowns over to him. She was almost ashamed to give it, for even if it was a very large sum of money it would not go very far when anyone was as miserable as Pelle was.

'How nice you are, Tjorven,' said Pelle in a hoarse little voice. He did not think that three crowns were all that much help when one was as unhappy as this, but it helped that Tjorven wanted to give them to him.

The secret four sat together in a corner. They were not secret any more, only gloomy. They had planned so much for this summer. They were going to repair the hut on Knorken Island again. They were going to build a new and much bigger raft. They were going to go around the islands with tents and be away for a whole week. They were going to borrow the motor and go right out to Cat Point and look at the Great Cave there, and then Björn had promised to take them on a fishing trip. And they had thought they would make a headquarters for the secret club in the attic of Carpenter's Cottage. Of course, it was not too late even now, for Johan and Niklas were still at Carpenter's Cottage, so they could do a good deal of what they wanted to do. But it did not seem fun any more. The desire had gone.

'It's strange,' said Johan. 'I don't care about anything any more.'

'Neither do I,' said Niklas.

Teddy and Freddy sighed.

When the Grankvists had gone home and the boys were asleep, Melker and Malin still sat on in the kitchen. It was dark now. They could barely see anything more than the light square of the window in the wall and the glow from the fire, which shone behind the grating of the kitchen stove. They could hear the wood burning and crackling, but otherwise all was quiet. Malin remembered when Melker had lit the first fire in that stove. What a long time ago it was and what fun everything had been then!

Melker had been silent the whole evening, but now he began to speak. All the bitterness in his heart welled out of him. 'I'm a failure, I know. An absolute failure. Tjorven never spoke a truer word when she said I didn't have the right knack!'

'What nonsense,' said Malin. 'You do have the right knack. I know that very well.'

'No, I haven't,' Melker assured her. 'If I had, I wouldn't be sitting here this evening, unable to do a thing when something like this happens. A failure as an author! Why didn't I go into business instead—then perhaps I could have bought Carpenter's Cottage.'

'I don't want a businessman in the house,' said Malin. 'None of us does. We want you!'

Melker laughed bitterly. 'Malin, what good am I to you? I can't even give my children a summer holiday in peace. And I've always longed to give them so much. I've always wanted to give you all that is wonderful and happy in life.'

His voice broke and he could not continue.

'But that's exactly what you have done, Daddy,' said Malin gently. 'You have given us all that's fun and wonderful in life. It has all come from you, and no one but you. You've cared about us, and that's really the only thing that matters.'

Then Melker cried. It was just what Malin had said that morning. He was crying before the evening was out!

'Yes, I have,' he sobbed. 'I have cared about you, if that means anything . . .'

'It means everything,' said Malin. 'I don't want to sit here listening to any more of this nonsense about a father who's failed—whatever happens to Carpenter's Cottage.'

In the Uttermost Parts of the Sea

They all awoke next morning with one single thought in their minds: today at four o'clock Mr. Karlberg was going to Mattsson's office in Norrtälje to buy Carpenter's Cottage!

Nevertheless, they tried to behave normally and pretend that this was a perfectly ordinary day. An ordinary day which began with breakfast at the table in the garden in the usual way and with the usual wasps buzzing round the marmalade jar. Poor wasps. Pelle was sorry for them and said, 'When Mr. Karlberg tears down the cottage he'll tear down the wasps' nest too.'

'Yes, that's the only way of getting rid of them,' said Melker drily. 'You tear down the whole house. Why didn't we think of that?'

A long, thoughtful silence ensued, and in the middle of it Tjorven arrived.

'Uncle Melker, are you deaf? How many more times must I tell you that you're wanted on the telephone?'

The Melkersons had no telephone of their own but used the one in the shop. Melker put down his coffee cup and ran. Tjorven ran after him.

But she was soon back again, looking quite frightened. 'Malin, I think you had better come. I think something else awful has happened. Uncle Melker seems upset.'

Malin ran and so did Johan, Niklas and Pelle.

They found their poor father standing in the middle of the shop surrounded by Nisse, Marta, Teddy and Freddy in an anxious ring. He was obviously upset, and tears were running down his cheeks. 'It can't be true. No, it can't be true!'

'Daddy, what is it?' said Malin in despair. She felt she could not cope with any more upsets just now.

Melker sighed deeply. 'It's just that,' he said, and stopped. And then he pulled himself together. 'It's just that I have been given a State Grant for twenty-five thousand crowns.'

There was silence for a long time in the Grankvist shop. They all stood as if someone had hit them on the head. Tjorven was the only one who had any sense left. 'Why have you been given that—that thing you said?'

Melker looked at her and he smiled triumphantly. 'I'll tell you exactly why, young Tjorven. It's because I have got the right knack after all. See? What do you say to that?'

'Did they say that, those people who rang?'

'Yes, something of the sort.'

'What are you crying for then?' Tjorven wondered.

And then it was suddenly as if they all realized that something pleasant had happened.

'Daddy, are we rich now?' asked Pelle.

'Not exactly rich,' said Melker. 'But it means . . .' Then he stopped dead and his children looked anxiously at him. Surely he wasn't going to start crying again! Suddenly he shouted. 'Do you understand what it means? We may be able to buy Carpenter's Cottage—*if it's not too late!*'

He looked at his watch and at the same moment they heard the steamer *Seacrow I* hooting for departure down by the jetty.

'Run, Melker, run,' said Nisse.

And Melker ran, shouting, 'Come on, Johan and Niklas! Come on! Wait!'

This last word he shouted to the boat. The gangplank had already been drawn up as he arrived, but he looked so desperately imploring, with his hands stretched up to the heavens, that the captain relented. The gangplank was put down again and Melker rushed on board.

He shouted again, without turning around, 'Come on, Johan and Niklas! Hurry up!'

It was not until the boat was several yards out from the jetty that he discovered that not only Johan and Niklas were with him but Pelle and Tjorven, too.

'Why have you come?' said Melker reproachfully. 'This is no game for small children.'

'We wanted to come too,' said Tjorven. 'It's ages and ages since I was in Norrtälje.'

Melker realized that he could do nothing about it. He ld not throw the two of them into the sea, and after all just been given a State Grant, so it behoved him to be noble and kind. Besides, he was so breathless after his run that he could not utter any more reproaches.

'I can still run pretty fast,' he said breathlessly. 'Not like when I first went to school, of course. I could run one hundred yards in 12:4 seconds then.'

Johan and Niklas looked at each other and Johan shook his head. 'The strange thing with you, Daddy, is that the older you get, the faster you ran when you were at school.'

It was certainly a good thing for Melker that he could run pretty fast, because he had to do plenty of running that day.

It takes time to get to Norrtälje if one lives on Seacrow Island. First of all one takes a boat to a jetty on the mainland, and on that jetty one sits waiting for a bus for about an hour. And that bus takes one to Norrtälje, stopping at many places on the way. It does not hurry and it keeps to its timetable. At one o'clock it is supposed to arrive in Norrtälje and at one o'clock it gets there.

And by that time one has grown grey hairs, thought Melker, as he got out of the bus. He had sat in that bus, growing more and more nervous and saying to himself again and again, 'Now don't expect anything. You won't get Carpenter's Cottage, so don't expect it!'

But he would have a try, he certainly would! And so with the children in a row behind him he went as quickly as he could to Mattsson's office.

But Mattsson was not there. There was only a chubby little typist, who looked kind but knew nothing.

'Where is Mr. Mattsson?' asked Melker.

She looked at him primly. 'How do I know?'

'Well, when will he be in?'

'How do I know?'

Her eyes were large and innocent and it was quite obvious that she really didn't know anything. But suddenly she took out a mirror from her bag and began to put on lipstick, and that livened her up so much that she suddenly became quite talkative.

'He's always out and about. I believe he was going to buy rhubarb at the market. Or perhaps he's gone home. Sometimes he goes to the Grand Hotel for a drink.'

They got no more out of her and hurried out again as quickly as they had come in.

Melker looked at his watch. It was after two o'clock, and where was Mattsson? Where in this charming little town could they find him? They must get hold of him—and quickly.

Melker was so nervous that he was trembling and he did not like having Pelle and Tjorven hanging on behind him. It was a hindrance being so many in these narrow streets, so he decided to take action.

'Would you like some ice cream cones, children?' he said.

Yes, they would. So Melker bought them each an ice cream cone at a kiosk and manoeuvred them to a little green park, where there was a bench.

'You sit here,' said Melker, 'and eat your ice cream cones ᵈd wait until we come back.'

'ʰat about when we've finished our ice cream?' said

'You'll stay here.'

'For how long?' asked Tjorven.

'Until the moss begins to grow on you,' said Melker unkindly. And then he made off with Johan and Niklas behind him. Pelle and Tjorven stayed where they were, eating their ice cream cones.

In a dream you sometimes run and run after something that you feel you must find, and you are in a great hurry. It is a matter of life and death. You run and hunt and become more and more anxious, but you never find what you are looking for. It is all in vain. This is exactly what happened to Melker and his boys as they hunted for Mattsson.

He wasn't at the market. Yes, he had been there, one of the market women said, but a long time ago.

'What about his home then? Where is that?'

'On the other side of town.'

No Mattsson there either! Could he really be having a drink at the Grand Hotel?

No, that must have been a lie. There was no sign of Mattsson there and suddenly Melker realized what a fool he was. He clapped his forehead. 'I'm a fool,' he shouted. 'Why aren't we sitting in Mattsson's office waiting for him, instead of walking around and around and getting sore feet?'

At that moment, exactly that moment, he made a dreadful discovery. *His watch had stopped.* Suddenly he saw that the clock on the Grand Hotel showed five minutes past four. Not three-thirty as his own wrist watch said. It was a grim moment.

I warned you, Melker. You shouldn't expect anything.

You're too late, Mr. Melkerson! Those words will ring in my ears as long as I live, thought Melker, and in his despair he turned to Mr. Karlberg. 'For my children's sake, can't you give it up?'

Mr. Karlberg was offended. 'I have a child too, Mr. Melkerson. I have a child too.' Then he turned to Mattsson. 'Come now. Let's find Mrs. Sjöblom and sign the contract.'

Mrs. Sjöblom! The happy carpenter's widow. If that's who she was perhaps he could influence her with his prayers. Perhaps Mattsson did not have the last word. Melker gritted his teeth. He must try Mrs. Sjöblom. Not that he thought it would be any good, but he could not leave a stone unturned. Later, when his last hope had gone, would be time enough to think of those words, 'You're too late, Mr. Melkerson!'

He whispered to the boys, 'We'll go to see Mrs. Sjöblom, too, then.'

'Until the moss begins to grow on you.' Uncle Melker had said they were to sit on the bench until then. Tjorven did not agree to this. Nor did Pelle. An ice cream cone gets eaten so quickly and moss grows so slowly. By now they had been sitting for a long time and were very hungry and Pelle was so nervous that he could scarcely sit still. Why didn't Daddy come? He felt all on edge and he had a stomach-ache too.

Tjorven was upset. Norrtälje was fun. She had been here several times with Mummy and Daddy and she knew how many interesting things there were to look at. And they had to sit here, stuck to a park bench and feeling hungry at the same time!

'Have we got to sit here till we die of starvation?' she said miserably.

Then Pelle remembered something which cheered him up. He had three crowns in his trousers pocket. 'I think I'll go and buy us another ice cream cone,' he said.

So he did. He ran to the kiosk and bought ice cream cones, and then there were only two crowns left in his pocket. But an ice cream cone comes to an end so quickly and the time passed and still no one came. Pelle felt prickly all over. 'I think I'll buy us another ice cream cone each,' he said.

So he did. He ran to the kiosk again and then there was only one crown left in his pocket. And the time passed and no one came and the cones had been finished a long time ago.

'What about buying us another ice cream cone?' suggested Tjorven.

But Pelle shook his head. 'No, you shouldn't spend everything you have. You have to keep a little for unforeseen expenses.'

He had heard Malin say this to Daddy so often, but what 'unforeseen expenses' really meant he did not know. All he knew was that you shouldn't spend all you had.

Tjorven sighed. She became more and more restless with every minute that passed and Pelle became more and more nervous. What if Daddy could not find that horrible Mattsson? Who knew, perhaps everything had changed! Perhaps Mattsson had gone home with Mr. Karlberg and sold Carpenter's Cottage right away, instead of going to the market and buying rhubarb, instead of hurrying back to his office and selling it to Daddy. And here they had to sit. Just waiting and feeling what a stomach-ache he had. How he hated that Mr. Karlberg, and Mattsson too. What a pity that Mrs. Sjöblom had someone like that to look after her business. Why didn't she do it herself?

Mrs. Sjöblom. . . . She lived here in Norrtälje. Yes, she did. Imagine wanting to sell Carpenter's Cottage! She must be crazy! He'd like to ask her about it.

'Do you know Mrs. Sjöblom?' he asked Tjorven.

'Of course I do. I know everyone.'

'Do you know where she lives?'

'Yes!' said Tjorven. 'She lives in a yellow house, close to a candy shop and a toy shop which are exactly next door to each other.'

Pelle stood there silent and thinking. His stomach-ache was growing worse and worse. At last he jumped to his feet.

'Come on, Tjorven. Let's go and find Mrs. Sjöblom. There's something I want to talk to her about.'

Tjorven jumped up too, happily surprised. 'But what will Uncle Melker say?'

Pelle wondered that too. He did not want to think about it just then. He wanted to get in touch with Mrs. Sjöblom. Old ladies usually liked him. Surely there would be no harm in asking her—though he did not know exactly *what* he was going to ask her. He only knew that he could not possibly sit still any longer, doing nothing.

Tjorven had visited Mrs. Sjöblom several times with Mummy and Daddy. And yet she could not find the yellow house now. But she found a policeman and she asked him, 'Where is there a candy shop exactly next door to a toy shop?'

'Must you have everything all in one place?' said the policeman, laughing. But then he thought and suddenly realized where she meant and told them how to get there.

And they went on through narrow little streets and past rows of little houses and came at last to a toy shop next door to a candy shop. Tjorven looked around and then she pointed.

'There. Mrs. Sjöblom lives in that yellow house!' It was a two-storey house with a little garden behind it and a door onto the street.

'You ring,' said Pelle. He did not dare.

Tjorven put her finger on the bell and left it there for a long time. And then they waited. For a long, long time they waited, but no one came to open the door.

'She's not at home,' said Pelle, and he did not know whether he was disappointed or not. In fact, perhaps it was just as well to be able to get out of it, because it was difficult to talk to strange people. But still . . .

'Why has she got the radio on then?' said Tjorven and put her ear to the door. 'I can hear it playing.'

She rang once more and then she banged loudly on the door. But still no one came.

'She *must* be home. Come on, we'll look around the other side of the house.'

They walked around the house. There was a ladder leaning up against a window on the second floor. The window was open and the radio was on full blast inside. They could hear it very clearly now.

'Let's climb up and look in,' said Tjorven.

Pelle was frightened. You couldn't do things like that, just climb up and look in, it was crazy! But Tjorven was set on it. She pushed him towards the ladder from behind and, trembling, he began to climb. He regretted it before he had got halfway and wanted to turn back, but Tjorven was behind him on the ladder and she would not allow him past her.

'Hurry up, hurry up,' she said, and pushed him relentlessly upward. Terrified, he went on climbing. What in the world would he say if there was someone inside?

There *was* someone inside. She was sitting in a chair with her back to him and he was terrified. He stared at her neck for a long time. He coughed, first quietly and then quite loudly. Then the woman in the chair gave a shriek and she turned around and he saw that it was Mrs. Sjöblom. She was exactly as he had imagined her. She was very old and wrinkled and had grey hair, kind eyes and a funny little nose, but she stared at him as if she had seen a ghost.

'I'm not as dangerous as I look,' Pelle assured her in a trembling voice.

Mrs. Sjöblom laughed. 'Oh, really? You really aren't as dangerous as you look?'

'No,' said Tjorven, and popped her head over the window sill. 'Good morning, Aunt Sjöblom.'

Aunt Sjöblom clapped her hands together. 'Well, I never, if it isn't Tjorven!'

'Yes, of course it is,' said Tjorven. 'And this is Pelle, who wants to buy Carpenter's Cottage. I suppose that's all right?'

Mrs. Sjöblom laughed merrily, something which came quite naturally to her, and then she said, 'I don't usually do business with people hanging outside my window. You had better come in!'

It was not at all as difficult as Pelle had thought it would be to talk to Mrs. Sjöblom.

'Are you hungry?' was the first thing she said, and that was a fine beginning! Then she took them down to the kitchen and gave them sandwiches and milk. Ham sandwiches and cheese sandwiches and veal sandwiches too. It was a regular party. And while the party was going on she heard everything. About Mattsson and Karlberg and Lotte, and about Westerman and Yoka and Tottie and Yum-yum and Moses and Bosun. About everything that had happened on Seacrow Island. Tjorven talked a great deal about Lotte Karlberg.

'Bongalo!' she said. 'Don't you think that's absolutely crazy, Aunt Sjöblom?'

Yes, Aunt Sjöblom thought it was absurd, at any rate, on Seacrow Island. And, as for tearing down Carpenter's Cottage, she had never heard of anything so stupid!

A State Grant, sore feet, and I don't know what else, all in a single day! It was too much, thought Melker, but he strode on resolutely with Johan and Niklas at his heels, for they must not let Mattsson out of their sight. His ugly suit went on in front of them through the streets like a beacon and it led them to a little yellow house smothered in forsythia and jasmine.

As Mattsson rang the bell a pale-faced Melker came forward. No one was going to stop him from having a word in the discussion. Mr. Karlberg grew angry. 'Come, come, Mr. Melkerson. You really must give up. What in the world do you think you are doing here?'

'I suppose I have a right to speak to Mrs. Sjöblom if I wish!' said Melker bitterly.

Mattsson gave him a cold look. 'I thought, Mr. Melkerson, that I had made it clear to you that I am Mrs. Sjöblom's agent. What good do you think it will do if you speak to her?'

Melker knew only too well that it would do no good, but he *had* to make one last attempt and he was not going to allow anyone to stop him.

Then the door opened and there stood Mrs. Sjöblom.

Mattsson made his introduction. 'This is Mr. Karlberg, who is about to buy Carpenter's Cottage.'

He paid no attention to Melker and Mrs. Sjöblom nodded to Mr. Karlberg and looked him up and down. Melker gave a little cough. If only she would look at him, perhaps he could catch her eye so that she might understand that it was a question of life and death for him.

But Mrs. Sjöblom did not look at Melker. She looked at Karlberg and then she said quietly, 'Carpenter's Cottage is already sold.'

It was as if she had let a bomb drop. Mattsson stared sheepishly at her. 'Sold!'

'Sold?' said Mr. Karlberg. 'What do you mean by that?'

Melker felt himself turn pale, for now all hope was gone. It did not matter to him who had bought Carpenter's Cottage because it was lost forever to him and his children. And he had known it all the time. But it was strange that it should hurt so much when he finally heard it confirmed.

Johan and Niklas began to cry. Silent, bitter crying, which they tried in vain to control. The excitement was over and they were so tired. Who could help crying?

'What do you mean, Mrs. Sjöblom?' said Mattsson, when his powers of speech returned to him. 'Who have you sold it to?'

'Come in and you'll see,' said Mrs. Sjöblom and opened the door wide.

'You too,' she said to Melker and his two weeping sons. Melker shook his head. He did not want to see who had bought Carpenter's Cottage. It was better not to know who it was.

But then he heard from within a voice that he knew only too well. 'Uncle Melker has got the right knack, I can promise you that, Aunt Sjöblom!'

All was mild confusion in the yellow house for the next hour. Mr. Karlberg was very angry and shouted and made a fuss and scolded Mattsson, who was red in the face.

'I can't understand all this. You'll have to clear it up, Mattsson, and then you'll have to act as you think fit.'

Poor Mattsson, he seemed to shrink in his ugly check suit and was suddenly small and meek. 'There's nothing to be done,' he said in a low voice. 'She's as stubborn as an old goat.'

Mrs. Sjöblom had been standing with her back to them, but now she turned around. 'Yes, she is! And she's got sharp ears too.'

'Though not when the radio's playing,' said Tjorven.

But Pelle was being hugged by his father, pressed hard to his heart. 'Pelle, my little boy, what have you been doing? What have you been up to?'

'I paid a little in advance to Aunt Sjöblom,' said Pelle, 'so as to make it sure. And she's given me a receipt too.'

'Yes, indeed,' said Mrs. Sjöblom. 'Look!' And she held up a shining crown.

Mr. Karlberg turned and went. He slipped out of the door without looking behind him, and after him went Mattsson.

'That's a good thing,' said Tjorven, and they all agreed.

Johan patted Pelle on the head. 'And Daddy said this wasn't a game for little children! You were great, Pelle!'

'There's one thing I must ask you, Mrs. Sjöblom, before we leave,' said Melker. They were sitting in her kitchen and she had made some more sandwiches. They were the most delicious sandwiches they had ever tasted in their lives. Perhaps it was because they had eaten nothing since that morning. Or was it because everything was suddenly part of one great happiness, so that even the sandwiches had a heavenly taste?

'What do you want to ask?' said Mrs. Sjöblom.

Melker looked at her curiously. 'Carpenter's Cottage—why was it called that?'

'My husband was a carpenter. Didn't you know?'

Yes, of course he was, thought Melker. I must ask something I don't know. Aloud he said, 'Carpenter's Cottage, yes, of course. And you moved there in 1908?'

'1907,' said Mrs. Sjöblom.

Melker looked surprised. 'Are you sure it wasn't 1908?'

Then Mrs. Sjöblom laughed. 'I suppose you'll allow me to know the year I got married!'

Oh, well, one year more or less doesn't matter, thought Melker. And then he said, 'May I ask you one more question? What was your husband like? Was he a happy, gay soul?'

'Yes, he was,' said Mrs. Sjöblom. 'He was the gayest person I've ever known, though he lost his temper sometimes.'

Malin wrote in her diary, *Sometimes it seems as if life had picked out one day and said, 'I will give you everything. It shall be one of those rose-red days which shimmer in the memory when all others are forgotten.' This is just such a day. Not for everybody, of course. There are many who are crying now and will remember this day with despair; but for us, the Melkersons of Carpenter's Cottage on Seacrow Island, this day has been so full of joy that I scarcely know how to bear it.*

Melker did not know either. He sat on a rock with his feet in the water to soothe their aching. He was fishing. Pelle and Tjorven sat on each side of him, looking on, Pelle with Yum-yum on his knee and Tjorven with Bosun close beside her.

'You haven't got the right knack, Uncle Melker,' said Tjorven. 'If you carry on like that, you'll never catch a fish.'

'I don't want a fish,' said Melker dreamily.

'Why are you sitting here with a rod then?' asked Tjorven. And Melker recited to her in the same dreamy voice,

> *The sun was dipping near the sea.*
> *He wished to see its glow . . .*

Yes, that's what he wished—to see everything: the sun reflected in the still water, the white seagulls, the grey rocks, the boathouses on the far side of the channel which mirrored themselves so clearly in the water below them, all that was most dear to him, he wanted to see. He would have liked to stretch out his hand and touch them all.

'I think I'll stay here tonight and watch the sun rise and see the first flush of dawn . . .'

'Malin won't let you,' Tjorven assured him.

The wings of the morning, thought Pelle. I'd like to see that too!

'If I take the wings of the morning, and dwell in the uttermost parts of the sea . . .' Just think, they had such a place now, one that was absolutely theirs. A dwelling in the uttermost parts of the sea.

About the author

Astrid Lindgren (1907-2002) is one of the most widely-read children's authors in the world. In the course of her life she wrote over 80 books for children, and has sold over 160 million copies worldwide. She once commented, 'I write to amuse the child within me, and can only hope that other children may have some fun that way too'.

Many of Astrid Lindgren's stories are based upon her memories of childhood and they are filled with lively and unconventional characters. Perhaps the best known is Pippi Longstocking, first published in Sweden in 1945. It was an immediate success, and was published in England in 1954.

Awards for Astrid Lindgren's writing include the prestigious Hans Christian Andersen Award and the International Book Award. In 1989 a theme park dedicated to her—Astrid Lindgren Varld—was opened in her home town of Vimmerby. When she passed away in 2002, the Swedish Government founded The Astrid Lindgren Memorial Award (ALMA) in her honour. It is the world's largest prize for children's and young adult literature.

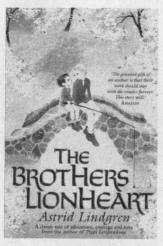

'In Nangiyala you have adventures from morning till evening . . .'

That's what brave Jonathan Lionheart tells his sick younger brother, Karl. So when both boys tragically die and are united in the 'land beyond the stars', they know their adventure is just beginning . . .

'The greatest gift of an author is that their work should stay with the reader forever. This story will.'

Amazon

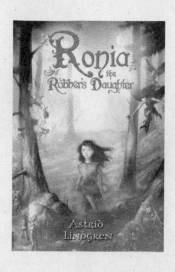

Ronia, the daughter of the robber chieftain, roams the forest but she must beware the grey dwarfs and wild harpies. When she befriends Birk, the son of her father's greatest enemy, it causes uproar. Ronia and Birk can no longer be friends—unless they do something drastic. Like running away . . .

Suddenly they are fending for themselves in the woods, but how will they survive when winter comes? And will Ronia's father ever accept her friendship with Birk, so they can go home?

Did you hear the news about a boy who disappeared?
No one knows what happened to him ... except me.

Young Karl leaves behind his unhappy life as an unwanted
foster child to escape to Farawayland. There, he learns that
his true name is Mio, and that he is the son of the King.

But the kingdom is under threat. The evil Sir Kato
terrorizes the land, and it has been foretold that Mio is the
only one who can defeat him ...

Ready for more great stories?
Try one of these . . .